Deception's
Pawn

DECEPTION'S PAWN

ESTHER FRIESNER

Random House 🏠 New York

Text copyright © 2015 by Esther Friesner
Jacket art copyright © 2015 by Larry Rostant

Visit us on the Web! randomhouseteens.com

Educators and librarians, for a variety of teaching tools,
visit us at RHTeachersLibrarians.com

Library of Congress Cataloging-in-Publication Data
Friesner, Esther M.
Deception's pawn / Esther Friesner.—First edition.
pages cm.
Summary: Maeve begins her royal fosterage but her new companions are full of secrets and jealousy, her only friends are an elderly lady-in-waiting and Kian, the prince who rescued her kestrel, Ea, and her future promises only household management and childbearing until someone from her past brings a message about her true love.
ISBN 978-0-449-81867-1 (trade) — ISBN 978-0-449-81869-5 (ebook)
1. Medb (Legendary character)—Juvenile fiction. [1. Medb (Legendary character)—Fiction. 2. Courts and courtiers—Fiction. 3. Princesses—Fiction. 4. Kings, queens, rulers, etc.—Fiction. 5. Sex role—Fiction. 6. Ireland—History—To 1172—Fiction.] I. Title.
PZ7.F91662Deb 2015 [Fic]—dc23 2014010448

Printed in the United States of America
10 9 8 7 6 5 4 3 2 1
First Edition

For Liz Williams

A great friend, a brilliant writer,
and a lot of fun to know!

Contents

Èriu

IRELAND IN
THE IRON AGE

ULSTER

DÚN BEITHE

EMAIN MACHA

FIR
DOMNANN

CRUACHAN

CONNACHT

TAILTEANN

TARA

ISLE OF
AVALLACH

LEINSTER

MUNSTER

N

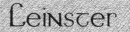

TECH DUINN

THIS WAY TO
TÍR NA NÓG

miles
0 10 20 30 40 50 60

Deception's Pawn

CHAPTER ONE

Women's Chatter

I WOKE WITH a gasp in a strange bed, my heart beating rapidly. *Where was I?* Midnight surrounded me. I'd been dreaming of unfettered flight, of joy, of soaring fearlessly across open skies. Now all that wild, glorious liberty was abruptly gone. A frightening thought shook me: *Was this harsh waking an omen?* I had worked hard to remake my life, to be more than the High King's daughter, the prize he'd once used to tempt and tame lesser kings. Could all my hard-won freedom be torn away from me so easily? I shivered at the possibility.

Thank all the gods, my good sense finally woke up as well. I took a deep breath and let it out slowly. *Enough,* I thought. *I left the safety of Father's home because I'm not a coward, and I won't act like an infant now, making monsters out of every nighttime shadow.* Yawning, I turned onto my side. *It will all be better by sunrise.*

"Ugh, is it morning?" I grumped like an old badger who'd been dug out of his burrow and brushed aside the tangled curls that had fallen across my face while I slept. All of yesterday's excitement and fuss surrounding my arrival at Dún Beithe left me too exhausted to braid my hair before bedtime. I'd pay for it this morning. I winced, imagining the pain of unsnarling so many knots.

My eyes blinked in the faint wash of daylight in the chamber I shared with three other girls. I stared up at the rafters and listened to the sound of unfamiliar breathing coming from their beds. One of my new companions snored so badly, it was as if she were breathing mud. Another muttered in her sleep. I thought I heard her say a boy's name, but then she giggled and rolled onto her stomach. At least she had pleasant dreams.

I wasn't used to this. When my older sisters still lived within the protective walls of Cruachan ringfort, the six of us slept in a single room. But year by year, by ones and twos, I watched them leave until I had a room of my own. I grieved most bitterly when my favorite, Derbriu, went off to fosterage. I hadn't seen any of them since, except for our eldest sister, Clothru. She was a girl when she left us, but she returned as a married woman with her first baby on the way.

How changed would *I* be when—and if—I went home again?

I turned onto my side but didn't go back to sleep. The bed coverings made my bare skin itch. They smelled . . . not *bad*, exactly, but different. Too different. They'd been washed in water that didn't come from *our* streams, water that never raced over the stones of *our* land, Connacht's land, my family's realm, my birthplace and my home. I wished I hadn't been so tired last night that I simply stripped off my clothes and threw myself into bed. At least the thin shift I sometimes wore to sleep would have carried a comforting, familiar scent.

The alien smell of my bedding was only the beginning. From this moment on my world would be nothing but unfamiliar names, places, customs, and expectations. From the food I ate to the people I met, everything would be strange. I'd come to Dún Beithe to find my Ea, the wild kestrel who'd bonded to me, but I'd come here to claim a new life as well. I'd fought to get free of being Father's little girl and I'd tasted the thrill of strength and self-reliance when I rescued our bard, Devnet, from Lord Morann's arrogant plotting. Why did I feel so vulnerable now, and so uncertain and weak?

A tear trickled down the side of my nose, shaming me. *Why am I crying?* I thought, angry at myself. *Ridiculous. This is what I wanted. I asked to leave home!*

I'd cast away the dust and shadows of my father's house to seek a fresh life of my own making. I would not let the lies and broken promises and deaths of the past touch it. Like a newly forged sword, I would draw it from the smith's fire and brandish it so that all the world could see how bright it shined.

Bold words, pretty words, and not one speck of a notion *how* to turn them into reality. I was free to be myself, but . . . what did that mean? My fingers clutched the bedclothes like a kestrel's talons, as if holding the cloth in a tight grip would also hold back more tears.

It didn't work. I buried my head and wept without a sound until my eyes were dry and I could take a deep breath that wouldn't come out as a sob.

"Lady Maeve?" A girl's voice sounded tentatively behind

me. "Lady Maeve, are you all right?" I felt the bed give a bit and heard the dried grass in the mattress crunch under her weight as she rested her hand gently on my shoulder. "Did you have a bad dream?"

"I'm fine." I wiped away the last of my tears and sat up, tucking the blanket under my arms. "Thank you, um . . ."

What was her name? We'd been introduced last night, during my welcome feast. What an uproar that had been! In the midst of the festive din, Lord Artegal and his wife, Lady Lassaire, took turns introducing me to every person present. So many! I smiled, nodded, and said how happy I was to meet them, but the noise that filled the great room swallowed all their names before they reached my ears. By the time I was allowed to stumble sleepily off to bed, I was still surrounded by total strangers.

The plump girl who perched on the edge of my bed was one of my fellow fosterlings. Why couldn't I recall *her* name, at least? I blushed with embarrassment. She'd believe I was too haughty, that I didn't think her name was worth remembering. Oh, what a bad start to a new life!

To my great relief, the girl gave me a shy smile and said, "I'm Gormlaith." She showed no sign that I'd insulted her by failing to recall who she was.

"Thank you, Gormlaith." I took her hand. It was a simple gesture of friendship, but it made her round, ruddy face dimple with pleasure. "I'm sorry. I'm still so tired from traveling that I can barely remember my *own* name."

"I hope you rested well, then, Lady Maeve."

"I'm not *Lady* Maeve to you."

"But you're the High King's daughter!" She had the most

astonishing blue eyes, bright as a summer sky. "Lady Lassaire hasn't stopped talking about what an honor it is to have you as one of Dún Beithe's fosterlings. She said we have to remember that always, and make sure you feel at home and happy here."

"I was just Maeve at home," I replied with a smile.

"But Lady—"

"Please?"

Gormlaith nodded and her dull blond hair fell forward like a faded curtain, dozens of small, untidy plaits hiding her face. Though we sat close together, I had to strain my ears to hear her say, "All right."

"I'd also be grateful if you'll be my guide," I added.

She raised her chin and looked puzzled. "Your guide? Dún Beithe's not that big. I don't think you'll get lost unless you go outside the ringfort walls."

"That's not what I mean. How long have you lived here, Gormlaith?"

"Eleven years, I think. I was five or six when I arrived."

"So you've grown up here. You know where things are but you also know *how* things are done. All the people I met last night are only names and faces to me." *And sometimes only faces,* I thought ruefully. "*You* know what they're like. I don't want to tread on anyone's toes by saying the wrong thing to the wrong person. And what should I expect day to day? Is Lady Lassaire our only teacher or do some of her ladies help? Who's strict and who's kind? Who'll help me if I need something I forgot to bring with me? And what if I—?"

Gormlaith laughed softly, as if she had no right to be heard. "So many questions, Lady—I mean, Maeve. I'll do my best to answer them, but you'll know as much as I do in a day or two."

"That's for sure." A second voice came from the dimmest corner of our room. It sounded sweet, but there was a definite sting to the words, like the speaker had gulped a spoonful of honey and discovered it concealed a thorn. A shadowy form rose and glided across the floor to join us. I'd never seen such a tall girl, or such a pretty one. She loomed over me like one of the towering, graceful birch trees that gave Dún Beithe its name. Her gleaming flame-colored hair fell unbound down her back, all the way to her hips. Like me, she hadn't braided it before bedtime, but hers remained smooth and free of tangles, as if by magic. I envied her wildly. The only sour note to her beauty was the iciness of her storm-gray eyes and the slightly mocking twist of her mouth.

"Good morning, Maeve," she said. "I see Gormlaith hasn't wasted any time in trying to lay claim to you. Don't pay too much attention to her. She clings like a burr if you let her." She was quick to give the other girl a small, brittle smile and added, "You know I'm only joking, Gormlaith, but you must admit I'm right. We all want to share Maeve's friendship, so don't keep her to yourself."

"I wasn't going to do that," Gormlaith muttered.

"Really?" One perfect eyebrow went up. "Well, maybe so. You might have learned your lesson after what happened with Aifric, but—"

"That wasn't my fault, Ula. Stop talking about it." Gormlaith hunched her shoulders and drew in her head, as though protecting herself from a beating. "I thought I heard Maeve crying and I only came to see if I could help her."

Her words made both of Ula's brows rise sharply. "Were you crying, Maeve?" The chill distance vanished from her voice. She sounded sincerely concerned. "You're not sick, are you?" I shook my head and she let out a sigh of relief. "That's good. I still remember how much my stomach ached after my welcome feast. I was nine years old and I'd never seen so much food set in front of me in my life! I gobbled it up like a starving dog."

"And then she was *sick* as a dog the next day." My third roommate spoke up drowsily from her bed. "Bryg and I laughed and laughed until Lady Lassaire scolded us and said that since we were so amused by the show, we could do all of the cleaning up after it." A loud yawn and a rustle of bedclothes ended her words.

"No one asked you to tell *my* story, Dairine." Ula strode straight for the girl's bed, grabbed the short end of the mattress, and then jerked it up and gave it a violent twist. There was a shriek and a thud followed by an outraged "Ula, you *sow*!" from the floor. Gormlaith smothered her giggles with a fist pressed tightly to her mouth, but I laughed out loud. I couldn't help it.

"Very funny, Lady Maeve." Dairine scrambled to her feet, scowling, and wriggled into her clothes as fast as she could. "You're next. Let's see how *you* like being dumped on the ground." She tried to sound threatening, but the playfulness in her voice betrayed her. "Just wait until I'm dressed and—"

"Not if I'm up first," I replied lightly. I peered over one side of the bed and then the other, looking for the garments I'd dropped there last night.

I found nothing. "Gormlaith, do you know where the servants put my—?" I began.

"Don't blame the servants, Maeve," Ula said. The green

gown I'd worn to the feast dangled from her grip. She exchanged a wicked grin with Dairine, who flaunted the blue dress I'd worn when I arrived at Dún Beithe. The two girls used my garments for partners in a merry dance, threading their way between the beds, always staying just beyond my reach.

"Oh dear, *this* again." Gormlaith sighed.

"Tsk. Don't feel left out, dear." Dairine ducked for a moment and rummaged briefly under her bed frame. "Here's something for you to play with too!" She yanked out my third gown and tossed it to Gormlaith, who stopped disapproving of the game the moment she became part of it.

"Give those back," I called out, trying to sound angry. It was no use; I laughed instead. This mischief was too harmless to take seriously. In fact, it was a welcome distraction from my waking doubts and worries. "Do you want me to start my first day at Dún Beithe naked?"

"If you dare," Ula replied cheerfully.

"Don't listen to her, Lady Maeve," Dairine said. "The less our lads see of you, the happier she'll be. The men are already talking about how beautiful you are. The poor thing's dying of envy! Isn't that right, Ula dear?"

The tall girl shrugged. "Men pay no attention to women's chatter and I pay no attention to men's jabbering. They're nothing but overgrown boys."

"So you *don't* want to marry one of them?" Dairine looked sly. "No, you'd rather stay here as a fosterling forever, or until one of your brothers takes pity on you, brings you home, and lets you raise his brats."

"At least I'm not *frantic* to get married. At least my brothers *want* to bring me—" Ula cut herself short and laughed a bit too loudly. "Why don't we put it to the test? Toss Maeve out the door right now, just as she is. If you're right, every one of Dún Beithe's warriors will fall in love on the spot. None will be left to woo us and we can *all* die unmarried."

"Speak for yourself," Dairine replied a bit testily. "I might not have your high-and-mighty family, but someday I'll get a husband even you will envy."

I thought Dairine was only pretending to be cross as part of the game, so I decided to join in. "If you want to get married, you'd better give me back my clothes. Otherwise I'll walk out of this room bare as an egg and reap a *harvest* of husbands. I won't even leave you a stableboy."

"Do as she says, Dairine," Ula urged. "Give her back that gown and she might let you have one of her men in exchange. You'd like that bargain, wouldn't you? Trading a dress for a highborn husband? Maybe even Lord Kian!"

Dairine's pale face flushed. "Don't give away what you want for yourself, Ula," she said in wintry tones. "Or what's not yours to give."

Ula's back straightened. She glared at Dairine with narrowed eyes. My green gown dropped from her hands and puddled on the floor between her feet. I wasn't sure what was going on between those two, and I didn't care; I saw my chance. I cast aside the bedcover and sprang, swooping down on the green dress right under Ula's nose.

"I've got it!" I cried, holding it close and twirling on the balls of my feet in a dance of triumph.

"What's all this racket? What are you girls up to in there? Are you slaughtering each other?" A deep voice broke like a thunderclap over our heads.

The bull-hide curtain in the doorway whipped aside. A tall, brawny young man stood grinning in the wooden arch, fists on hips. His short blond hair was spiked like a hedgehog's back and he wore such a thick gold torque around his neck that the weight would have brought a weaker lad to his knees.

His gaze focused on me where I poised in shock, holding my crumpled dress to my bare skin with trembling hands. His grin changed to a look of alarm. A bright blush came out in scarlet patches on his beardless cheeks. His jaw dropped, but soon began moving rapidly as a stream of stammered apologies rushed from his lips.

"Get out!" I cried, clutching my gown to my chest with one hand while fumbling to hold the flapping cloth closed behind me. "Get out, get out, get *out*!" My voice rose to a wail.

"I . . . you . . . didn't mean to . . . everyone's usually all awake and dressed by . . . ," he went on, frozen in place.

"Hey, Kian, what are you doing over there?" Another male voice sounded from the main area of the great house. "You know what Lady Lassaire told us about bothering her girls. If she catches you spying on them she'll box your ears, even if you are her *precious* little boy."

A burst of mocking laughter from Kian's unseen comrade shattered the petrifying spell on him. He whispered one final "Sorry, milady" and bolted. The bull hide swung back into place and I collapsed on the nearest bed with a groan, burying my face in the bedclothes.

The other girls gathered around me in silence. No one knew what to say. Finally, Ula spoke up. "We'd better go to breakfast. Lady Lassaire will be wondering why we're so late."

"I don't want breakfast," I said. "I want to die."

"I don't care what you want to do; *I'm* hungry. Breakfast first, dying later." Ula's mild joke made me giggle in spite of myself. She tugged gently at a strand of my hair. "Dairine, bring me my comb; you know where I keep it. While I unsnarl these tangles, you and Gormlaith can pick out something for Maeve to wear." She got no arguments. Any quarrels that had sparked among them were extinguished. I let myself be dressed and groomed as if I were a toddler. My mind was too overrun by humiliating memories for me to object.

When they were done, Dairine smiled and asked, "Ready for your first day at Dún Beithe, Lady Maeve?"

"I'd better be," I replied with a grimace. "It's off to a *wonderful* start."

CHAPTER TWO

Seeds

I SCARCELY TASTED my first breakfast at Dún Beithe. I was too filled with embarrassment to take more than a bite of bread. My mind refused to let go of the mortifying scene with Kian no matter how much I tried to think of something else. To make matters worse, when the girls and I dutifully presented ourselves to Lady Lassaire and wished her a good morning, she hurried forward to take my hands and drag me to sit beside her. It was a hospitable gesture and she meant no harm by it. The trouble was, sitting next to her also put me next to Kian.

Kian! Kian, who'd just seen me less than half-clothed. Kian, the young man Devnet believed now held my beloved kestrel, Ea. The single person I *needed* to speak with was now the one I couldn't even look in the eye.

I nibbled my lower lip nervously, keeping my gaze firmly fixed on the uneaten food before me. *What if Devnet's wrong about the bird?* I thought. *He told me he'd seen Lord Artegal's son with a kestrel that wore a red braid around one foot. I wove that token for Ea from a lock of my own hair—but am I the only person who'd do such a thing for a favorite creature?*

I remembered Odran, the dark-haired, gentle son of Master Íobar the druid. He had a passion for healing animals, a gift that must have come to him from Flidais, goddess of all wild things. Odran understood why I placed that plaited bracelet around Ea's leg. It wasn't a sign of ownership, master to slave. It was a mark of affection, friend to friend. Couldn't Kian feel the same, do the same for a cherished animal?

Odran . . . My mouth went dry and my lips grew warm with the memory of how we'd kissed. The abandoned crannog where we'd met to care for the ailing animals became our refuge, a place where our first hesitant attraction turned to the sweet pleasure of tender kisses. I'd wished it could last forever.

But Odran's father had other plans. He wanted his son to follow him on the druid's path. If that failed, he wanted to force us into marriage so that he could enjoy borrowed power as the High King's kinsman. I refused to let him have his way, and the innocent animals paid for it. Now they were gone. The ones that failed to flee were slaughtered by Master Íobar's sling-stones as he avenged his wounded pride. I saw my Ea soar away, only to be struck down in midflight. I thought she was dead until Devnet brought news that she might be the wounded kestrel Kian had found and healed.

Master Íobar hauled his son away to Avallach, the island where he'd be taught the druid's path. I would never see Odran again.

I *needed* to see Ea. I needed to know that Master Íobar's

cruelty wasn't powerful enough to destroy something so beautiful and free. I needed the memories of Odran that rode on her strong and graceful wings. I needed—

"Lady Maeve?" Lord Artegal leaned forward in his place on Lady Lassaire's other side and craned his neck to look at me. "You're not eating. Are you well?"

Before I could answer, Devnet intervened. "I fear Lady Maeve is glum because she's thinking about the farewells to come later this morning." He gazed at me fondly and added, "Lift your spirit, Princess. There are no final partings between friends as long as we hold each other's hearts. That's the truth I know; do you accept it?"

I lowered my eyelashes and smiled. "I must believe what you say, Devnet. I'm not foolish enough to call a bard a liar." My reply drew laughter and cries of good-humored approval from the household. I even thought I heard Kian murmur "Well said" from his place beside me, but when I dared to glance at him, he twitched his head away.

We had our goodbyes after breakfast. I'd been brought to Dún Beithe by Father's trusted charioteer, Fechin. Now he was driving back laden with gifts from Lord Artegal to the High King. His body bore the scars of countless battles at Father's side, but his courage crumpled when it was time to leave me.

"Fechin, are you going to carry on like this all the way home?" I hugged him tightly, then held him at arm's length. "Look at you! Your face is soaked with tears and your nose is— ugh. You'd better clean that stuff out of your mustache before you go." I kissed him repeatedly anyhow.

"This is how I am, Lady Maeve," he mumbled. "I'm too old to change my heart. I've known you since you were a baby. . . ."

"Well, I've known you since I was a baby, too, but you don't hear *me* carrying on about it," I said, trying to jolly him out of his sorrow. "If you don't stop crying, you'll use up every drop of moisture in your body, turn to dust, and blow away. Then what will I have to live for?" I linked my arms around his neck and pressed my cheek to his. "Don't do that to me, dear Fechin. You know I'd die without you."

A wobbly smile lifted the corners of his mouth. "Not so. Not while there are good-looking young men in this world—warriors, nobles, kings who'll want you for their bride. You can't break all those hearts if you die young, may the gods avert it!"

"Oh, where's the challenge in that?" I joked. "Men's hearts break too easily, and then they cry, and then their mustaches get all covered with—" I made such a revolted face that Fechin had to laugh his tears away.

One of our men came to fetch him with word of a horse that was acting strangely. When Fechin went off to look at the beast, Devnet approached me. "Time for our farewell, Princess." He spoke as if announcing a great festival.

"Why do you sound so happy about it?" I asked, hurt.

He lifted my chin with a fingertip calloused from years of weaving music on the harp's strings. "Would you rather I took up where Fechin left off and flooded the earth with my tears? No bard likes to be the shadow of another man's song. Besides, I fear that once we're on the road back to Cruachan, you'll have tears enough of your own."

I couldn't manage more than the most pitiful of smiles. "I wept plenty this morning. I hope I'm done."

"Done with weeping? In this world? That's up to you,

Princess. You're free to choose your battles, your triumphs, and your tears."

"Is that how it works?" I asked, leaning my head against him. His clothing smelled like home.

I heard him sigh. "Only in my songs."

Lord Artegal, his wife, his son, and the most important members of his household stood with me at Dún Beithe's gates as my people rode away. I didn't shed a single tear, but smiled sincerely as I waved and called out good wishes for a safe journey. The crowd with me echoed my shouts, but the clamor faded as men and women trailed off to resume their work. I held my place, outlasting even Lord Artegal. The smile never left my lips and my eyes never left the dwindling procession until they were completely out of sight. I was still smiling when I went back into the ringfort.

Gormlaith and the others were waiting to greet me on my return. She studied my face closely. "You didn't cry." She made it sound like an accusation.

I shrugged. "That would have been bad luck. Better to send them on their way with a smile, to ward off mischance on the road."

"I never heard that before." Ula sounded suspicious.

"Do any of the women here cry when their men ride out to risk their lives in battle or on a cattle raid?" I asked.

"No, but—"

"Oh, Ula, let it go," Dairine said, linking arms with me. "Just because *you* cried whole floods of tears when you were left here doesn't mean everyone's such a baby."

"I was nine years old," Ula said stiffly. "And besides, Bryg told me that when you came here, you wept louder than Aifric ever did, and she yowled over *everything*."

"Who's Aifric?" I asked. It was the second time I'd heard her name.

An uneasy silence fell over the three girls. Gormlaith looked ready to have the earth swallow her whole. Ula, cool and proud, was the one to answer me at last.

"Aifric was a fosterling here for longer than any of us. She was only three when her parents gave her to Lady Lassaire to raise. They were noble, but ranked almost as low as Dairine's father."

"My father *earned* his rank!" Dairine exclaimed, furious. "He's one of Èriu's foremost warriors. He wasn't born into a soft bed like yours."

Ula took the gibe as if it carried no more weight than a falling flower petal. "Aifric's mother died the year she came here, and her father the year after that. All she had left were some cousins, and they saw no reason to take her away from Dún Beithe."

"She was happy here," Gormlaith said quietly. "We were friends." She fidgeted with the end of one of her tiny braids. "Like sisters." Those words came out barely above a whisper.

I was confused. "Where is she now? Did she marry and leave?"

Again, no one answered my question until I raised a new one: "Did she fall sick and die?"

Dairine tossed her head, sending her three black braids flying. "We're all going to die if we don't hurry up and join Lady Lassaire," she said, artfully brushing my words aside. "Come on, Lady Maeve." She tightened her hold on my arm and broke into a run.

As I stumbled along beside her, I managed to say, "I'm not *Lady* Maeve to any of you, Dairine."

"Oh? Is that why Ula and Gormlaith haven't been using your proper title? I thought they were just being their usual bad-mannered selves." She seemed disinterested.

"I asked Gormlaith to call me Maeve when we first spoke early this morning and Ula must have overheard. You were still sleeping."

"Well, that's as good a reason as any for letting me be the last to know." She laughed, short and sharp as a fox's bark.

I pulled back, forcing her to slow down. "I didn't mean to slight you, Dairine," I said. "I want all of us to be friends. It was an oversight."

"Who said it wasn't?" Dairine was all smiles. Despite this, I wasn't reassured.

We found Lady Lassaire in the great house, seated by the hearth. Two of her women attended her, and a little girl dressed in yellow stood by with a basket of raw wool almost as big as she was. The distinguishing color of her dress marked her for a slave, the first one I'd noticed at Dún Beithe.

"There you are, my darling girls!" Lady Lassaire exclaimed, hurrying forward to meet us. Her thick, silver-blond hair was neatly braided into a single plait that hung down to her hips. If she'd worn it loose, I think it would have reached her knees. Her small, slender body moved with the grace of an elfin woman from the Otherworld, and when she spoke it was like hearing a little songbird chirping pleasantly in the sun. She drew me away from Dairine and embraced me, her cheek soft against mine.

"Welcome, my dearest Maeve," she said. "I hope you don't mind my calling you by your name alone? I think of all my fosterlings as the daughters I was never fortunate enough to have. Don't worry: Everyone else at Dún Beithe knows that you're to be called *Lady* Maeve."

"It's not that important," I murmured. "I like being just Maeve."

Her pale-blue eyes opened wide in surprise. "Oh, but it *is* important, dearest! It's a mark of respect. You're too young to understand how vital it is to maintain such things, but trust me, it's something we must *all* defend."

I understood more than Lady Lassaire suspected, though I doubted my view of the matter was the same as hers. "It's like the hero's portion," I said.

"Yes, exactly!" She was delighted. "When Lord Artegal gives the best serving of meat to his bravest warrior, it's not just a great honor, it inspires the other men."

Inspires them to do what? I thought. *To pick fights? To avenge insults that were never given? To shed each other's blood?*

Dark memories came back to me: My dear friend Kelan who'd agreed to my request and taught me to use men's weapons; the feast at which the warrior Caílte was awarded the hero's portion but claimed he heard Kelan say it was undeserved; the challenge to a duel between men so unfairly matched that it was just another name for Kelan's execution. And behind it all, Father's grudge against my friend for giving me those lessons, for helping me grow bold enough to face danger, to stand

and protect another person's life instead of running away and saving my own. He knew I'd hate him if he killed my friend himself, so he forced Caílte to put his hand into the fire.

He didn't know that I would learn the truth.

I swallowed the bitterness of the past and smiled at Lady Lassaire. "I understand. Thank you."

The little slave girl gave us handfuls of wool and carding combs. We set our hands to the task of turning the tangled fleece into long, soft fibers, ready to be spun into yarn. I thought that doing such a basic chore would be the same here as at home, but the longer I sat in the company of my three fellow fosterlings, the more I realized the great but subtle difference between Cruachan and Dún Beithe: The girls in Mother's care were older than I and were always gossiping about things I thought were trivial. Those who didn't shut me out only befriended me because they saw the chance to profit from being friends with the High King's daughter.

Now here I was after less than a day at Dún Beithe, but already I felt included. The other girls knew my rank, knew Lady Lassaire's attitude toward how important such things were, yet how had they treated me? As Maeve, only Maeve. If they saw me as the High King's daughter, they never would have dared to play hide-and-keep-away with my dresses. I was still smarting from that morning's deathly embarrassment, but the sting was soothed away when I recalled how all of them had rallied around to take care of me after their prank got out of hand.

Was this what it was like to have friends at last?

When we were done carding wool, it was time for the midday meal. It was entirely informal, just how Cruachan did such things. At that time of day, Dún Beithe's cook and her helpers had food ready for anyone who wanted it. People drifted in and out of the great house, either sitting down by the hearth to fill their bellies or carrying off bread and meat and cheese to eat elsewhere.

My friends and I took our food outside. Ula led the way, declaring we'd climb the ringfort walls so that I could have my first view of the country around Dún Beithe. Poor Gormlaith had a clumsy time of scaling the sloping earthwork walls and trailed the rest of us. She seemed to have difficulty keeping her balance while holding on to her meal.

"Give me your bowl," I offered, hoping to help her. "It'll be easier if you've got your hands free."

Dairine cut in before Gormlaith could reply: "Don't do that, Maeve! The last person who tried taking *her* food lost three fingers." She snapped her teeth together for emphasis and tittered.

"Ignore her, Gormlaith," Ula drawled. "She's just envious."

"Why—" Gormlaith panted, trudging onward. "Why would she—ever—envy—me?" The last word brought her to the top of the wall, where she sank to the ground.

"Because some of the lads like you," Ula replied in her cool, distant way.

"For warmth in winter and shade in summer." Dairine smirked. But I saw the poisonous look she shot at Ula.

"You don't have to tell me I'm fat," Gormlaith said glumly. "I know."

"So what?" I spoke up. "You heard Ula: You've got admirers who like what they see when they look at you."

"You wouldn't need me telling you that if you ever lifted

your eyes and looked *back*," Ula added. "But whenever we're near any man of Dún Beithe, from Lord Kian down to the stableboys, you stare at your feet or your hands or— You're doing it again!" She pointed an accusing finger at Gormlaith, who had her gaze steadfastly fixed on the rapidly vanishing food in her bowl.

"She probably caught sight of one of the sentries," Dairine said. She lifted her head and darted searching looks all around, like a hound avid for the hunt.

"That one?" I waved to the far side of the ringfort, where a lone man stood scanning the countryside. Even at that distance we could all see that his hair was heavily streaked with gray.

Ula made a scornful sound. "I recognize that one. He's got grandchildren. If he catches any of us staring at him, he'll come over and start boring us to death with battle stories." She popped one last piece of bread into her mouth and announced: "I'm done. Let's go."

I was still eating, but when the other girls hurried to follow Ula from the top of the wall, I felt compelled to join them. All the way down it was take a step, take a bite, take a step, chew, take a step, gulp, take a step, and nearly choke on a half-chewed scrap of meat until I reached the bottom.

We gave our empty bowls to the servants and hurried to find Lady Lassaire, who was waiting to guide us through an embroidery lesson. She took one look at me and her delicate lips stretched into a quizzical expression. "Why Maeve, my dear, what's happened to your lovely dress?"

Everyone stared at me. I looked down and saw that my bodice was covered in crumbs and smeared here and there with grease. That was what came of my attempt to eat while making a rushed, awkward descent from the ringfort wall. For the second time that day, I felt mortified.

One of the women attending Lady Lassaire chuckled and leaned toward her neighbor. "All decked out in a coat of breadcrumbs, ha! Didn't I tell you that they do things differently in Connacht?"

"Moriath, shame on you!" Lady Lassaire turned on the outspoken lady so fiercely that we all jumped as though we shared guilt for her rudeness.

"My—my lady, what did I . . . ?" she faltered. Could she truly believe that there was no harm in uttering such an insult?

Suddenly I understood what had happened: Lady Moriath looked to be the eldest of Lady Lassaire's attendants, with white hair, a wrinkled face whose lines showed a history of much laughter, and gray eyes that had lost their sparkle to the fog that sometimes came with age. If her eyes were failing, perhaps her ears were too. *She meant to whisper a jest to her friend,* I thought. *She didn't intend to offend me or my people. No matter how embarrassed I am, I can't let her suffer for that.*

"Well said, Lady Moriath!" I exclaimed gaily. "Well and kindly said, trying to make excuses for me, and for *this*." I casually brushed away the crumbs as if it meant nothing to me to be caught in such a messy state. "It is true that we do some things differently in Connacht, but I'm afraid this isn't one of them; it's just my carelessness. I'll try to do better in the future. Thank you for being so gracious to me. I hope I can repay you for it."

"Repay me?" The older woman was momentarily flustered,

but her confusion swiftly gave way to a look of relief. "Don't speak as though you owe *me* anything, my dear." She rose from her place and gave me a soft kiss on the cheek.

Lady Lassaire didn't know quite what to make of the way things had turned out between Lady Moriath and me. She was left with an interrupted scolding on her lips and for a moment looked almost as though she'd been cheated out of a treat. Then she shrugged it off and the embroidery lesson began.

I was never very clever with my needle. My frustration must have showed on my face because Ula noticed it and whispered, "Why are you scowling? Did the thread insult your family too?"

"Very funny," I hissed back, fighting a fresh knot that had magically tied itself. "Look at your work! You've filled that cloth with a whole legion of fantastic animals. And there"— I nodded toward the dress Gormlaith was adorning with mazes of intertwining vines—"I can't even manage a simple triquetra pattern." I spread my needlework across my knees to show Ula the full measure of my failure. I'd been given a clean new piece of fabric because this was my first day of lessons, but I'd already turned it into a rumpled rag. Lady Lassaire glanced my way and frowned. Gormlaith flicked her eyes at the drunken parade of too-big, too-small, too-loose, too-tight threads disgracing my cloth and offered me a pitying look.

"May I see that, Lady Maeve?" Lady Moriath's wrinkled hands took the fabric from my grasp and held it close to her eyes. "Ah, there's the problem." She began undoing the mess I'd made as if she dealt with such catastrophes every day. "You want a stronger thread to begin with, and a sharper needle."

"Maeve has been given everything she needs for her lesson," Lady Lassaire responded crisply. "The *best* of everything."

"Of course, of course." Lady Moriath hastened to ease away her mistress's ruffled feelings. "I'd have seen that if not for my poor old eyesight. Well, if it isn't Lady Maeve's tools, the fault lies in her confidence. She should practice making designs on something more easily corrected than cloth, don't you agree?"

Lady Lassaire's pride was soothed. "Just what I was going to suggest myself."

"Then permit me to carry out your wonderful suggestion. Let Lady Maeve take her needlework lessons privately with me until her work improves."

A fresh frown creased Lady Lassaire's high white forehead. "How will you see her work when you failed to see the quality of the supplies I gave her? I can't give charge of something as important as needlework to someone too blind to see stitches."

I gasped to hear such casual meanness. Why remind the poor woman of her failing body? But Lady Moriath remained as serene as if she'd been paid a compliment.

"I can still see my own handwork if I hold the cloth close to my eyes, but I won't need to do that for Lady Maeve," she said calmly. "My plan is to have her gain self-assurance by making embroidery designs with a bit of charcoal or even with a stick in the dirt. She can make them as large as necessary for me to see them. Once she knows her hand is capable of creating intricate, beautiful patterns, it won't be hard for her to reduce their size when she re-creates them on cloth."

"I want Maeve to feel like she's a part of this household, and the sooner, the better. How will singling her out and separating her from the other girls help accomplish that?"

"It wouldn't be for long, my lady. I used to be the best needlewoman in Dún Beithe from the time Lord Artegal's father ruled these lands. I can teach as quickly as she's willing to learn. She'll be back with the others in less than fourteen days, if she applies herself. But if she continues to produce work like this"—she gestured at my dreadful attempt at embroidery—"she'll be singled out from the other girls forever, and badly."

Lady Lassaire pressed her lips together. "I'll think about it."

The older woman lowered her eyelids. "I know you'll make the wisest decision."

It didn't take Lady Lassaire long to reach her decision. That night at dinner she told me to meet Lady Moriath on the east side of the great house after breakfast the next day. "There's a bench there that catches the morning sun. She says it's very kind to her old bones."

I rose early and dressed quickly, rushing out of the sleeping chamber before any of the others were awake. Helping myself to a piece of thickly buttered bread and a hefty wedge of cheese, I raced out of the house. I wanted to show Lady Moriath how grateful I was for her willingness to teach me, and that meant being ready to greet her when she arrived at our meeting place.

"Oh!" I stopped short as I rounded the curve of the wall. "You're here already?"

The old woman looked up from the basket of food in her lap and smiled. "At my age, sleep doesn't come easily and seldom stays long. Luckily, my appetite is still as good as ever. Come share." She indicated the basket, which provided a much larger meal than what I'd grabbed. "I want to talk with you before we begin our lessons. Tell me this, my lady: if one of the

Fair Folk came to you with a magical needle and thread, gifts with the power to give life to whatever you embroidered, what would you make?"

I took a big bite of bread and chewed it slowly while I considered my answer. "Birds," I said.

"Why birds?"

I thought about my dreams, and the way my heart leaped whenever I watched my Ea claim the sky. "When they fly, it's as if they can stay up there forever. Nothing ties them down."

"Mmm. So you're not talking about chickens."

"Chick—?" I caught the twinkle in her eye and we both laughed. "No, not chickens," I said. "Hunting birds are my favorites, especially—especially kestrels."

"Birds of prey?" The old woman gave me a searching look. "Even small ones like kestrels are a rather bloodthirsty choice for a young girl. I was expecting you to say swans. They're lovely birds, but what ugly tempers!"

"Why are you asking this, Lady Moriath?" I was done eating, and very happy to see that there wasn't a crumb or a smear marking my dress.

"I need to know what you *want* to create. You'll be more willing to concentrate on our lessons. If I order you to make a line of triquetras, your mind will wander and your stitches will show it. That is, unless you *like* triquetras?" My expression of distaste answered her. "I'm not surprised. Follow me." She stood up and walked away.

"What about my lesson?" I called after her.

"It's begun, if you want it." She didn't bother looking back.

I caught up to her easily and walked beside her as we passed through the morning bustle of Dún Beithe. "Where are we going? I thought you wanted me to draw patterns in the dirt with a stick."

"Do you think we'll have trouble finding sticks and dirt?" she teased, spreading her hands to include the ringfort's many buildings, sheds, and storage places. "Tsk. Young people have so much time and so little patience, even the lucky ones like you."

"Lucky?" Would a lucky girl have been surprised half-dressed by Kian on her first morning here? "Why do you say that?"

She stopped in front of a large shed, rested one hand on the door, and turned to face me. "Because I'm too old to go chasing swans for my student."

She pushed the door open, but stood aside to let me go in first. Mystified, I crossed the threshold.

Kee-kee-kee!

I knew that cry. Oh, how well I knew it! It came from the shadows of the shed and I rushed forward to meet the well-beloved sound. She sat on a perch made from the unfinished branch of an oak tree. A few dead leaves still clung to it. She was hooded, so I couldn't see her face, but I knew her. I knew her with all my heart.

I looked at her strong, taloned feet. There it was: the thin red braid I'd woven for her from my own hair with my own hands.

"Oh, Ea," I whispered, and began to cry with joy.

CHAPTER THREE

Rekindling the Flame

LADY MORIATH HAD to call my name at least three times before I could tear myself away from Ea. I must have been a sight, all tears and smiles at the same time. Judging by the look on her face, she didn't know what to make of my reaction.

"You—you really do like birds," she muttered.

I burst into laughter. "You have no idea, Lady Moriath. This one—this one is special to me. I know her. See this?" I lifted the braided loop around Ea's foot with my fingertip. "I made it."

The old woman squinted hard, then shook her head. "See what? I'm lucky I can still see the bird. I don't know what you're trying to show me, dear, so you'll have to tell me about it instead."

The story poured from my lips and my heart, but not the whole truth. I talked about healing Ea's broken wing, bonding with her, having her fly away and yet return to me with the loyalty of a well-trained hunting hound. I explained why I'd made a braid of my own hair to mark the kestrel as a token of how special she was to me. I told her how my precious bird had been struck down by a slingstone, leaving me heartbroken, believing she was dead.

I didn't mention Odran. Speaking about him now that I'd never see him again would only fill me with sorrow and longing. I kept his image securely locked away in my heart, mine alone. I didn't utter Master Íobar's name. I couldn't face the memory of how the druid had slaughtered the small creatures that Odran and I had cared for so tenderly together.

Lady Moriath listened attentively to my tale. "Amazing," she said. "Marvelous. The gods have brought you and this bird back together for a reason. I wonder what it is. You must tell this to Master Cairpre, Lord Artegal's chief druid. He'll know."

I shook my head. "Please don't tell anyone," I said. "The gods have nothing to do with this, unless it's to show that sometimes they take pity on us. It's enough for me to know that she's here, alive and well, and that I can be with her again."

"Well, at least you have to tell Lord Kian about it. He's the one who brought her here, badly wounded as she was. I never knew the lad had a gift for healing until he nursed that bird back to health."

I stroked my Ea's soft breast feathers affectionately. "He did very well."

"He did more than that: he taught her to hunt for him. Did you ever hear of such a thing? A bird of prey willing to make a kill and surrender it?" Lady Moriath was as proud of his feat as if she'd performed it herself. "Our young Lord Kian must be the son of the Horned One, god of the hunt, to have such power!"

"Whose son am I?" Kian's jovial voice boomed through the storehouse. He came striding in like a conqueror. "Shame on you, Lady Moriath, if you say I'm anyone's child but Lord Artega—"

Then he saw me. His smile vanished and his face turned pale. It was like our first ill-omened encounter all over again, except this time I wasn't half-naked.

I forced down my own embarrassment at seeing him and stood tall. "Good morning, Lord Kian," I said with as much dignity as I could summon. "Lady Moriath was just showing me this beautiful kestrel. She says you found it, healed it, and trained it. How remarkable!" I caressed Ea's wings.

"Careful!" he exclaimed, hastily shouldering his way between Ea and me. "It'll bite you."

"It won't." I put one hand on his arm and tried to move him aside, but he resisted. My brows came together. "And if it does, it does. I'll take all the blame. You don't need to shield me from it."

"Lady Maeve, please." He sounded pained. "This bird is my prize, my treasure. If it hurts you, the High King's daughter, my father will tell me to release it forever."

"I'm sure it would hate that."

The irony in my words sailed right over his head. "Yes, so you see why I can't risk having you stay so close to it. What are you doing in here anyway? This is where we store weapons and supplies to repair them. There's nothing here to interest a girl."

Lady Moriath spoke up before I could reply. "I brought her here, Lord Kian. It's part of our embroidery lesson."

He stared at her as though either she had lost her mind or

he had and he wasn't sure which one. "Weapons and—and embroidery? Uh . . ."

The old woman rolled her eyes. "Lady Maeve wants to do better needlework and your mother graciously gave me permission to help. I say the best path to improving anything is to find a project that sparks your passion and begin there. This young woman loves wild hunting birds, as you can plainly see." She waved to where I still stood my ground within arm's reach of Ea. "I wanted her to see one at close range, to inspire her design."

"Oh." Kian rubbed the back of his head, still ill at ease. "Well, I guess that's all right, as long as I'm here to make sure nothing goes wrong." He turned to me. "But you can't get too close to her, understand?"

We'll see about that, I thought.

"You spent *how* long with Lord Kian yesterday?" Ula's voice rose to shrill heights. Her normally detached demeanor was gone. It was raining outside, a shower that had blown in out of nowhere, so we four were seated on benches, having our midday meal by the great house's central fireplace.

"Shhh, shhh, not so loud. People will hear you." Gormlaith made frantic shushing motions with her hands. The weather had driven many other folk indoors and the hearthside was crowded.

"Don't you tell *me* to be quiet, you bowl of bog mud," Ula shot back. But she did speak more softly.

"Shouted or whispered, what a stupid question." Dairine calmly munched an apple. "What's *interesting* is that she got to share his company so . . . cozily."

"I'm sorry I told any of you one word about it," I grumbled. That just provoked Dairine into making kissing sounds. "Stop that! And stop talking as if Lord Kian and I are sweethearts. I've only known him two days."

Ula put on an arch face. "Didn't I tell you they do things *differently* in Connacht?" she said in a perfect mockery of Lady Moriath. The others laughed, though Gormlaith tried to pretend she was coughing.

"Ugh! I wish Lord Kian were on the moon and the rest of you were with him," I exclaimed, exasperated. "The only reason he and I were thrown together was Lady Moriath. She wanted me to study that hunting bird of his and when he discovered us with her, he wanted me to do it from seven spear lengths away!"

"I don't think . . . I don't think he wanted you to stay *that* far from the bird," Gormlaith offered. "Seven spear lengths would . . . would leave you outside of the—"

I raised my hands in surrender. "All right, I'm exaggerating, but—"

"*That* was your special needlework lesson?" Dairine cut in. "Staring at some stupid bird while a handsome prince gazes at *you*?" She laughed raucously. "Remind me to botch *my* embroidery tomorrow!"

"Do what you want," I said sharply. "It's over. Your precious prince got nervous seeing me so close to the bird. He must have run tattling to his mother as soon as we left, because this morning Lady Moriath told me that Lady Lassaire's taken back her permission for our lessons."

"That's a bit extreme," Dairine remarked. "Couldn't she just forbid you to go near the bird?"

"That's a silly question, coming from you." Ula had the superior expression of someone who knew it all. "You've lived here for years. Have you ever seen our *dear* Lady Lightning act reasonably when she wants to assert her authority? Nothing by halves, not for her! You never know what's going to make her strike, but when she does, it's total devastation."

"I'm sorry, Maeve," Gormlaith said. "Maybe I can help you improve your needlework instead."

"We'll *all* help," Ula decreed. "It will be much more fun for you than spending time with a half-deaf, half-blind husk like Moriath."

"That's mean, Ula," I said. "None of that's her fault. Do you think you'll be any different when you get old?"

The tall girl tossed her head in disdain. "Aren't *you* her champion! Why don't you go persuade Kian to draw his sword against me and avenge the insult to your *dear* friend Moriath? You could do it. Just show him your bare backside again. He'll be your slave."

My mouth fell open. I was so stunned by Ula's attack that I fought my way through half a dozen failed replies before I stammered, "How—how can you say—?"

Ula laughed in my face. She shrieked with so much glee that she doubled over and dropped the remains of her midday meal on the floor. Dairine joined in, clutching the tall girl's shoulders and burying her face in her back as the two of them rocked back and forth. Even Gormlaith shared their hilarity, though she didn't look like she was enjoying it. All the other members of Lord Artegal's household who'd gathered at the hearthside stopped their own conversations to stare at us.

"What's going on out here?" Lady Lassaire stormed out of

her chamber, her long, silver-blond braid flying behind her like a comet's tail.

"No-no-nothing, my lady." Ula gasped for breath. "It's only that Maeve was—that I said—that we— Oh, Maeve, if only you could see your face right now!" She howled and collapsed backward against Dairine, nearly carrying both of them off the bench.

"Ula was . . . We were all just joking, Lady Lassaire," Gormlaith said, twisting two of her tiny braids together into a terrible snarl. "And Maeve thought we were serious."

"Joking?" Lady Lassaire was doubtful.

Ula stood up, once again the picture of cool dignity. "I was teasing her a little, that's all. You know that Dairine and Gormlaith and I do that sort of thing to each other all the time. Was it any different years back when you were a foster-ling, my lady?"

Lady Lassaire's frown softened into a smile. "Oh, Ula, you make it sound as if ages and *ages* have passed since I was young. Yes, I do remember how we teased and jested and even played tricks on each other. Some of the girls never did understand that it was all in fun, but I suppose there are some people who'd bite into a honeycomb and say it tasted sour."

"Maybe we should give Maeve a mouthful of something sweet and see if she goes like *this*." Dairine puckered her lips and made a grotesque face. Everyone laughed at her comical expression, including Lady Lassaire and me.

"I'll take any test you dare to give me, Dairine," I said lightly, trying to get into the spirit of things. If jests were part of a fosterling's life at Dún Beithe, I'd share in it. I didn't want them thinking I was as humorless as Master Íobar. "Just make sure you bring me a *big* chunk of honeycomb, in case the first bite's got a bee in it."

"Not *too* big," Gormlaith said in her meek way. "You don't want to end up as fat as me, do you?" Her halfhearted chuckle lasted no longer than a hiccup.

Lady Lassaire took my hands. "I'm so happy to see that my girls are treating you like one of their own already, darling Maeve. I remember my time in fosterage with so much joy. I was my parents' only child, and then to suddenly have a whole *flock* of sisters—! We behaved toward each other just like you dear girls. It was wonderful."

I beamed at her. "I'm glad you have such good memories. I hope I'll have the same someday."

"As good or better," Dairine said, linking arms with me. "We'll see to it that you do."

The rain clouds sailed away by sunset and the following morning was a beautiful gift from the gods. I woke before the other girls, my whole body thrilling with the strangest feeling, as though an invisible presence were whispering in my ear, *Run, Maeve! Run and see the glorious treasures that are waiting for you out there. Chase them, catch them, or lose them forever!*

I was in my clothes and out of the great house in an instant. A brilliant sky welcomed me, and a breeze sweet with the scent of nearby woodland drew me to the ringfort gate, already open. I'd never had the opportunity to go beyond the walls of Dún Beithe on my own; I took it with both hands.

"Milady, wait! Where are you going?" The guard at the gateway called out as I dashed past him. I was in such high spirits that I kept on running without a single sign I'd heard him. His pursuing footsteps pounded at my back, but before he could overtake me, the sound of hoofbeats brought us both to a standstill. We turned together to see Lord Artegal and Kian come riding toward us down the sloping path. Father and son were armed with bows and arrows, ready for an early morning hunt. Their horses' black flanks were glossy as ravens' wings. Midnight-colored manes and tails streamed in their wake. How Fechin would have longed to lay hands on them!

Then I saw my Ea and nothing else mattered. She rode Kian's wrist with regal ease, talons clutching the protective leather sheath on his forearm. I couldn't see her eyes because he had her hooded, but I knew they were blazing with anticipation. Soon she would be flying!

As the horses raced past, I waved my arms and shouted, "Good luck! Good hunting!" as loud as I could. Lord Artegal rode on, but Kian pulled back on the reins with one hand and brought his mount back up the path to face me.

"Thank you, Lady Maeve," he said. "I'm glad you're wishing me well."

For a moment I considered saying *I wasn't talking to* you, *tattle-tongue,* but I thought better of it. A plan had sparked to life in my mind. It would take skill and patience to nurse it into a fully blossomed flame.

"I'm not, Lord Kian," I replied with a half-smile. "It only proves I'm a fool, repaying your insults with kindness."

"Insults?" Kian was so startled he tightened his hand on the reins, making his horse take a few steps backward. "When did I insult you? If you're talking about what happened on your first morning here—"

I raised one hand sharply. "I will *never* speak of that again, and I hope you'll do the same. I mean the insults you heaped on me when Lady Moriath brought me to see her." I nodded at Ea. The kestrel's head turned sharply toward the sound of my voice. "I appreciate your concern for my safety—that's a wild bird, after all—but did you need to take it to such extremes?"

"I'm—I'm not sure what you're saying, milady." A look of confusion came over Kian's handsome face.

Just as I intended. If you want to knock your opponent off his feet, first put him off-balance.

"Why did you tell your mother to end my needlework lessons with Lady Moriath?"

The bluntness of my question hit him hard. He began babbling a host of reasons and excuses stitched together with denials and dodges. He'd done nothing wrong, someone else had done it, he'd only done it for my own good, he never got mixed up in women's business, he hadn't said one word to his mother, she ignored every word he said to her, and so on and so on until I thought he'd gag on his own tangled tongue.

Since I was choking back the overwhelming urge to laugh, that made us even.

By this time, Lord Artegal had doubled back to see what was keeping his son from their hunting foray. He arrived in time to hear me say, "The worst thing about what you did, Lord Kian, isn't how you offended me, but how you insulted yourself. Your cousin Lady Íde is my mother's dearest friend, and it breaks my heart to imagine how she'd take this news if it reached her."

"What news does she mean, Kian?" Lord Artegal demanded.

"Er . . . I'm not sure, Father." Kian's horse caught his rider's uneasiness and danced nervously in place. Ea reacted too, mantling her wings and snapping her beak before settling down once more.

"Lord Artegal, your son's an able fighter, isn't he?" I asked innocently. "He knows how to handle the spear, the sword, and the bow? If I had to travel from one end of Ériu to the other, could he keep me safe from the dangers of the road?"

The answer came without hesitation: "Of course!"

"Then why can't he protect me from one small bird?"

I explained myself swiftly and artfully. If Devnet had been there, he'd have been proud of me. I used a bard's skill for weaving words and fashioned a tether that let me lead both men down the path I wanted them to follow. Make no mistake, when I spoke about why I'd lost my embroidery lessons, I never said anything *against* Kian. If I'd done that, Lord Artegal would have taken his son's side at once, and I needed him as my ally. Instead I heaped the young lord of Dún Beithe with praise for his courtesy, his concern about my well-being, and his loyalty to the High King.

"Have you never heard that the greatest heroes have the greatest hearts?" I asked Lord Artegal. "That's what made Lord Kian go a bit too far, trying to protect me from that bird's keen beak and talons. His good intentions blinded him to my good sense. I'd never approach any beast that would hurt me, although"—I smiled playfully—"there *is* that story about how I caught a black bull by the tail when I was five."

Lord Artegal threw back his head and roared with mirth. "I remember that tale, Princess! It traveled here on the lips of many bards, and my cousin Íde confirmed that it was true." He turned to his son. "It's decided—when you and I return from our hunt, we'll find your mother and have her set things right. A girl with the courage to stand face to face against a bull can take care of herself with the fiercest bird of prey."

"We weren't exactly face to *face,* Lord Artegal," I said demurely, and was rewarded with more laughter.

Laughter can sometimes be more valuable than a fistful of gold. I know that Lord Artegal's mirth bought me my heart's desire: he swore that Lady Moriath and I could have access to Ea's refuge for as long as necessary and I swore I'd take no risks while I was with her. I'm sure what he heard in my vow was: *I'll stay well away from the bird.* What I meant when I spoke it was: *The only danger I face when I'm with Ea is holding her too close to my heart.*

That night there was great buzz over Lord Artegal's decision. The entire household learned about it well before it was time to gather for the evening meal. When the lord of Dún Beithe returned from the hunt, he went straight to his wife to present her with a small deer, half a dozen rabbits, the bag of birds Ea brought down for Kian, and his decision. The servant who witnessed the results couldn't run fast enough to spread the word.

Lady Lightning was true to her nickname: When her husband said he was overruling her orders, she tried to blast him off the face of the earth, then stomped away into her sleeping chamber and stayed there.

She did not stay quietly. Her angry voice gusted from behind the bull-hide curtain, making the great house ring with Lord Ategal's countless failures as a husband. When she exhausted her rage, she wept so loudly we all thought a bean sidhe had slipped into the house to bewail the coming death of a great warrior. She only fell silent when Kian dared to enter her room. He emerged looking pale but determined, like a hero who's braved the perils of the Otherworld and come back to tell the tale.

Meanwhile, rumors danced around the hearth. I tried to eat my dinner as though all the whispers and the darting glances had nothing to do with me. As if that were possible! Part of me wished I could hear what Lord Artegal's court was saying about me, and part of me was glad I couldn't.

The worst of it was the other fosterlings. I expected them to seize the news, shatter it into a thousand needles of mockery, and begin pricking me with them mercilessly. Instead they said nothing at all.

What are they waiting for? I wondered, steeling myself for the inevitable hail of jests. Instead they gathered around me after dinner in a ring of friendly smiles, congratulating me on my restored lessons with Lady Moriath. Before anyone else could approach, the girls carried me into our sleeping chamber, away from curious eyes.

I should have felt reassured, but their behavior pulled my nerves taut as a bowstring. My edginess must have showed because Gormlaith asked what was wrong.

"You're not going to tease me about this?" I asked. "No jabs about *why* I got my lessons back?"

Ula looked honestly startled. "We'd rather know *how* you did it. Lord Artegal doesn't usually interfere with his wife's household decisions."

"That's because he values his skin," Dairine murmured.

I shrugged. "All I did was ask." I wasn't trying to hide anything; I simply didn't know how to explain what I'd done any more than I could have explained how to walk. I sat down on my bed and added: "Thank you for not making this into more than it is."

"Why should we bother? There are plenty of other people out there dying to do that." Dairine nodded in the direction of our bull-hide door. "You're one of us now, Maeve. We stand with you."

CHAPTER FOUR

Luck and Skill

MY DAYS FELL into a soothing rhythm, like the rocking of a baby in her mother's arms. Having friends made it easy to find my special place in the life of the ringfort. Ula, Dairine, and Gormlaith helped me, teased me, defended me, braided my hair (and dipped a strand of it in pinesap while I slept), washed my soiled bed linens when my moon time surprised me by arriving early, and put a dead mouse in one of my shoes. I couldn't tell from one day to the next if we'd end up quarreling or giggling together, but I gave as good as I got and none of our disagreements lasted longer than a dewdrop in the sun.

I'd come to Lord Artegal's stronghold because I didn't want to stay under Father's roof. I'd have been happy to go anywhere, as long as it meant escaping Cruachan. The girls' friendship changed that. Now I was glad to be at Dún Beithe instead of being relieved *not* to be at home.

Even though I'd been welcomed as one of them, my friends and I didn't spend every moment in each other's company.

Dairine always seemed to have at least three flirtations going on at the same time. If one of these grew intense, she'd sneak away and make Gormlaith cover her tracks when Lady Lassaire questioned her absence. When she was in a mood, Ula took long walks alone, pacing around and around the top of the ringfort walls. I once tried asking her if anything was troubling her or if she'd want my silent company. She reacted so ferociously that if her tongue had been a sword, she'd have had my head for a trophy.

No one knew where Gormlaith went when she didn't want our company. Ula and Dairine didn't seem to care. When I questioned her, I was met with shrugs, silence, and sky-blue eyes that begged desperately, *Please, oh* please *let me keep my secrets!* I wanted to help her, but not if it brought her pain. Willingly or not, I respected her need for solitude.

I didn't understand everything about my new friends and how they chose to live their lives, but I needed them. They were my ringfort, forming a defensive wall around me against Lady Lassaire. Ever since Lord Artegal had overruled her decision about my special needlework lessons, her attitude toward me had soured. There were no direct attacks, but she had less obvious ways of showing her resentment. Instead of criticizing my handwork, she gave me compliments like ripe apples with wormy cores.

One afternoon at our weaving lesson, she said, "My goodness, Maeve, what a surprisingly fine piece of work from you! And just when I'd given up all hope of seeing you shine at any womanly art. Do you think Lady Moriath will ever be able to bring up the quality of your embroidery to this level? Or even get you to *finish* a design?"

Her words made me cringe. The longer I dawdled over completing an acceptable piece of embroidery, the longer Lady Moriath would need to teach me and the longer I'd be able to spend in Ea's company. "I'm sorry, my lady," I replied meekly. "It's taking more time than I thought. I'm using very small stitches."

She clicked her tongue. "Small or large, I'd love to see what you've accomplished after so many lessons, if anything. I don't want to have any misgivings about your handwork skills when I send you off to your husband."

My face blazed with embarrassment, but before Lady Lassaire could badger me more, Ula snorted. "Even if Maeve couldn't thread a needle, you won't have to worry about her future. When it comes to marriage, men look for riches, not stitches."

"Shame on you, Ula!" Lady Lassaire snapped. "You make our brave young warriors sound like common traders. That is dreadfully disrespectful."

"I apologize." The tall girl's gray eyes were frosty. She returned to her work, but I heard her mutter, "It's still true."

Is it? I wondered. Though my eyes were on the loom, my mind wandered. I was no longer the heir to all Connacht, the High King's bargaining token for making alliances, but did that mean my future held *absolute* freedom? How many choices would I really have?

What was the life of every woman I'd ever known? Marriage, children, the carding combs and the spindle, the loom and the needle . . . what else awaited me? I'd raise my sons to be warriors and my daughters to be wives, but what would *I* be? What else *could* there be for a girl?

I'd had a taste of something more. When Mother's difficult pregnancy kept her confined to bed, Father turned to me for companionship and advice. He took me with him when he made a king's decisions for his people, and he asked my opinion often. That ended once my brothers were born, but there were other times when I'd looked beyond the loom. Hadn't I helped free two slaves from a cruel master? Hadn't I rescued our bard, Devnet, from Lord Morann and saved myself from becoming part of his plot against my father?

I wasn't ready to leave all that behind, buried under a pile of prettily woven cloth. I wanted my life to make a difference, and not just for myself. But how? If I could possess a kestrel's wings and fly above the land of Èriu, would I be able to see the road that could lead me to my dreams?

My head began to spin. A vision of Ea rose in my mind, and I longed to go to her. Her company always comforted me. The silences we shared would help me think more clearly about where I was now and where I needed to be.

When Lady Lassaire told us that we'd spent enough time at the loom that day, I nearly knocked it over in my haste to be gone.

"Lady Maeve! What do you think you're doing?"

The shouted accusation sounded so loud inside the little storehouse that it seemed to make the wooden walls shake. I gasped and froze where I stood, confronted, caught, and guilty. The evidence against me perched on my wrist, her talons firmly closed on the leather sleeve I'd made in secret, her head unhooded, her golden eyes shining.

Kian bore down on us like a charging bull. His fierce

look made me think he was possessed by the battle frenzy, an awesome force that transforms men into terrifying warriors. Devnet sang about it so often, it was easy for me to imagine what wasn't there. Smoke seemed to rise from Kian's nostrils, his spiked hair bristled and quivered so rapidly that it sounded like a swarm of angry bees, and his eyes were filled with blood.

Stop this nonsense! I commanded myself. *Such things aren't real; they're a bard's magic.* I blinked and the illusion vanished, though—bad luck—Kian didn't.

"Are you *trying* to get your face torn off?" he bawled, waving his arms.

I spun around so that my back shielded Ea from seeing this madman and prevented her from flying away in a panic. "Be quiet," I said softly. "You're scaring her."

"How would you know what the bird's feeling? It's not a dog! Hand her over now." He thrust his arm in front of me.

That was a stupid move. It startled Ea from her place on my arm and made her jump onto his, but in his rage he forgot he wasn't wearing anything to protect his flesh from the kestrel's talons. They pierced the fabric of his tunic easily, turning his indignant scolding into a yowl of agony.

To his credit, he held still despite the pain. I don't know what I would have done if he'd flung his injured arm around wildly, trying to make Ea let go. She could have been injured, though not before fighting back. If she slashed at his face, Lord Artegal would see to it that she paid with her life.

Murmuring thanksgiving to the goddess Flidais, I coaxed the kestrel back onto my wrist and returned her to her wooden roost. She glowered at Kian, then settled down to preen her ruffled feathers. Meanwhile, her victim flooded the storehouse with curses. I had to admire how many he could rattle off without repetition, and I didn't even mind that I was the object of every one. When he began to tire of insulting me, my family, my ancestors, and all of Connacht for breeding such thoughtless, contrary, unnatural girls, I spoke.

"Call me whatever you like, but you don't have to bleed while you do it. Let me bind that for you."

For the first time since Ea sank her talons into his arm, Kian looked at his injury. The kestrel was a small bird, but she'd done him some damage. His right hand was streaked with scarlet. "This is nothing. I wouldn't want you getting blood on your dress."

"It's my dress and I don't care." I lifted my eyes to the storehouse rafters. As usual for such uninhabited buildings, the high spaces were the haunt of spiders. I moved a small wooden chest to a spot where the webs hung low, stepped up on it, and gathered a fat wad of them. When Odran and I shared our sweet, lost days together, secretly healing small creatures, he taught me to use those sticky threads to stop bleeding and seal wounds. Now I used that lore to help Kian.

The young lord of Dún Beithe didn't try to stop me. His bemused expression while I tended him made me feel as if I were some strange beast that had escaped from the Otherworld. He was observing my every move, waiting to see what I'd do next—laugh, weep, or grow antlers.

"Where did you learn to do this kind of thing?" he asked.

I wouldn't lie, and speaking of Odran made my heart ache, so I sidestepped the question: "Doesn't your mother take care of her people when they're sick or hurt?"

"She does what she can with herbs, but she hasn't got much

talent for healing. It's better for everyone that she leaves it to her attendants, Master Cairpre, or even one of the fosterling girls." He looked at the way I was dealing with Ea's work. "Not bad. I'd almost trust you to heal a *real* wound." He tugged aside the neckline of his tunic to display a scar proudly. "Got it on my first cattle raid three years ago." When I made no comment, he turned sulky and added: "It was a spear. I could have *died*."

"Are you trying to impress me?"

He grinned. "That's only fair—you've impressed me."

"So easily?" I raised one eyebrow and smiled. "Wait until I tell the other girls that all they need is a gob of spiderwebs to get your attention."

"They'd probably spin their own." Abruptly, he grabbed my right hand and stared at the leather sheath covering my forearm. "This isn't mine."

"I made it. Yours would be too loose for my arm," I said calmly, trying to pull out of his grasp without making a fuss. "Besides, taking it without your permission would make me a thief."

He acted reluctant to let go. "And yet you took my kestrel." It was hard to tell if he spoke seriously or in jest.

"I didn't *take* her anywhere," I said sharply. "All I did was hold her. I did remove her hood, but only because I wanted to see her better. She has the most beautiful eyes. Have you noticed how golden they are, and how they sometimes hold a flash of fire?"

"When I came in here, all I noticed was her beak and your face too close together. Where did you get the idea that you could manage to hood her again, here on your own?"

I indicated the leather sheath on my arm. "Shouldn't *this*

tell you that I know something about handling a falcon safely? I've done it before and my face doesn't have a single scar to show for it." I turned my head side to side to prove my words.

"So I see." He smiled. "You're either skilled or lucky."

"Both," I replied. "But mostly, I'm skilled."

"Skilled with birds, but not with your needle. Has Lady Moriath given up on teaching you? Is that why she's not here?" Now he was chuckling. I wondered how amused he'd be if I told him he sounded just like one of my friends when they teased me.

"Lady Moriath isn't feeling well. When I went to her for today's lesson, she sent me away."

"Shouldn't you have joined the other girls instead of coming here?"

"Shouldn't *you* go find Master Cairpre to have a look at that wound?" I said, lightly dancing away from giving him a direct answer.

Kian was easily distracted, thank the gods. He glanced at his arm. "What you did for it is good enough."

"Good, but temporary. It should be washed and bound with a cloth. See to it."

"And leave you here alone again?" He shook his head. "I'm the one who'll answer for it if your luck with the bird runs out."

I marched up to Ea's perch and slipped the hood over her head as easily as donning my own dress. "There," I said with a backward look at Kian. "Now will you go?"

"I'll leave when you do." How stubborn he was!

"Why? There's nowhere else I have to be, but you do need to have your druid take care of that." I pointed at his web-covered injury. "If I promise I won't unhood the kestrel again today, can't I stay here in peace?"

"What's the point, milady? The only things in here are this hunting bird and all these stores of weapons. I don't see any embroidery to keep you busy. What are you going to do? Practice swordplay?" He wore his most insufferable grin.

I lifted my chin. "Maybe I will."

That made him laugh so loud that I prayed no one was passing by outside the storehouse. They'd want to know what was going on in here and I'd have a hard time convincing them that Kian and I weren't in the midst of a lovers' tryst.

"What's so funny?" I challenged him. "The bards sing about women who are unbeatable fighters!"

"Women who live so far from Èriu that no one can prove they really live anywhere but on the bards' tongues," he countered.

"*I'm* here," I said. "Let me have a blade and I'll show you what I can do." Seeing the wry look on his face, I quickly added, "Don't you dare make fun of me! My dearest friend was a warrior of Connacht who taught me how to use a sword and shield and spear. If he hadn't died—" My throat tightened, a barricade against the tears that always came when I remembered Kelan. The passing years did nothing to numb my sorrow. Even something as trivial as the similarity between his name and Kian's could send a needle through my heart.

"A blade, eh?" The young lord of Dún Beithe looked around the storehouse, lifting the lid of one chest after another without finding what he wanted. "There are none being kept here just now. Use this." He drew his own sword and tossed it to me. I jumped back and let it hit the ground. He smirked. "I thought you'd try to catch that in midair, little warrior."

"I'm going to show you what I can do, not show off," I said, stooping to pick up the fallen blade. "I'm not stupid." I fell into the defensive stance I learned in one of my first lessons. I was pleasantly surprised by how well I remembered Kelan's teachings.

I wish you could see me now, Kelan, I thought. *Oh, I know what you'd say: "Maeve, is that a* real *sword in your hand? We only used wooden ones when I trained you, and you claimed you hated every moment of it!" Yes, I did, but this is different.*

And it was, I *knew* it was, though at that moment my mind couldn't say exactly why. It was still only an inescapable truth of the heart.

Kian studied my pose and rubbed his chin in thought. "You actually look like you know what you're doing," he said, not bothering to hide his amazement.

I let that rude comment slip past. "Is this all it takes to convince you that I can handle a weapon? You'd better give me more to do than just stand here."

"All right." He found a headless spear shaft in one of the piles. The wood was badly split and looked ready to splinter at the slightest impact. Some lazy servant must have dumped it with the rest, not noticing that it was beyond repair and should have gone for firewood. Kian held it out sideways at arm's length, using his unwounded hand. "Break this," he said.

"Too easy," I replied. "Don't baby me."

"I won't." He raised the wooden pole and spun it above his head one-handed, then tossed it just high enough that it missed hitting the storehouse rafters. Snatching it in midair, he offered it to my blade again. "If you're going to prove something to me, little girl, prove it."

"Little girl" am I? He can't be more than two or three years older than me, the arrogant lump! I felt anger rise in my chest. I was ready to throw myself at him, but before I could make that hotheaded mistake, I realized it was exactly what he wanted me to do. I breathed deeply and cleared my head.

"What will you give me?"

My question hit him like a splash of icy water. All he could do was echo: "Give you?"

"What are the stakes?" I went on calmly. "You don't think I can do this, I say I can, and so we've got a wager going. Fair enough, but what are you willing to bet"—I showed my teeth—"and lose?"

"Ha! You're confident."

"And you're stalling. If I don't pick your wager for you, we'll be here until it's time for dinner. If I break that staff, you have to admit it's safe for me to handle E—the kestrel and swear you'll never try to keep me away from her."

"Those aren't high stakes," Kian said. "Afraid to risk more, milady?"

"All right, if I show you I can use this sword well enough, you'll have to teach me to use it even *better*." I don't know why I said that. I'd had Kelan teach me how to fight only so I could become the son that Father wanted, but I'd never willingly pictured myself as a warrior. "*And* the shield, *and* the spear, *and* any other weapons you've mastered!" If those stakes weren't high enough to tweak the smirk off his lips, I'd eat nettles.

"What will you do with so much training, Lady Maeve?" Kian's eyes crinkled. "Planning to lead a cattle raid?"

"Are *you* planning to name your prize before Samhain comes?"

"Fine, I'll choose: a kiss. When I strike that blade out of your grip, I'll kiss you so hard it'll knock all this silliness out of your head. Agreed?"

"Agreed." I met his grin with a wider one. "Especially since that's the only way you could ever get a girl to kiss you, *little boy.*" I raised the sword, gave a warning shout, and lunged.

It was only a feint to get him off-balance. I didn't plan for this to be a true duel. Me against a seasoned warrior? I was confident, not crazy. His weapon gave him a longer reach than mine, but because our battle was indoors, he couldn't always swing the spear shaft freely. I moved as swiftly as my dress let me, darting into range, tempting him to strike, and then dashing back. When he came after me, I led him into tight spots where I could use my iron blade to hammer at the split in the wood without allowing him to corner me. I didn't have the strength to break the spear shaft with a single blow, but I persisted, hitting it again and again.

The noise of our scuffle upset Ea. She stamped her feet on the perch and spread her wings. The hood kept her from seeing what was going on around her, but she still raised a piercing *kee-kee-kee!* to challenge her unseen enemies. As I led Kian back and forth among the piles and boxes of stored goods, I took care never to bring the battle close to her. Despite my best efforts, I took a misstep and stumbled backward, bumping her perch with my shoulder as I fell. Ea screeched in distress, her wings flapping wildly.

I struggled up again, grabbing for her feet. I had to catch them and hold her to the perch. I didn't care if she mangled my hand; I *couldn't* let her fly blind—she'd hit a wall with bone-shattering force.

Another hand reached her before mine. Kian dropped his staff and dove between us. I watched in awe as he clasped his hands over Ea's small body, pinning her wings safely. He must have been in pain from his wound, but that didn't stop him. The moment he had her, he began murmuring soft words to soothe her. When she was calm enough, he placed her back on the perch and looked at me. We were both breathing hard.

"I didn't do that on purpose," I said.

"I know. You can't plan what happens in a fight."

"I'll be more careful." I nodded to where the headless spear lay. "Shall we finish this?"

He retrieved his weapon, but instead of grasping it around the middle, he picked it up by one end. The wood groaned, sagged, and fell into two splintered parts. He looked at it ruefully. "I'd say we're done."

Kian honored his part of our wager admirably. He never whined about the outcome of the match or tried to force me into giving up my prize. He could have turned my combat lessons into one long punishment, leaving me so beaten down that I'd quit. Instead he was a patient, encouraging teacher, much like Kelan. I came to believe that my lost friend's spirit had slipped away from Tech Duinn, the land of the dead, to share Kian's body while he taught me the ways of weaponry.

Kian only threw one obstacle at my feet: "We'll both be sorry if anyone finds out about this arrangement of ours. If my father catches us, he'll forbid it and my mother will cheer him on. Not even your clever way with words will make him change his mind a second time. When I send word that I'm free to teach you, you'll have come to me without anyone else knowing."

"If you're trying to discourage me, it's not working," I said boldly. I didn't add that I was well experienced at this sort of deception. Odran and I preserved the secret of our hideaway at the crannog for a long time before his father discovered and destroyed it. That was my fault, but I'd learned from it and I wouldn't be caught the same way again.

"I don't think you *can* be discouraged, Lady Maeve," he replied. I didn't bother correcting him.

We set up a simple system for him to let me know when it was time for my lessons. At breakfast I was to look his way casually. If his dagger lay on the ground by his feet, that was the signal. Days when he kept his dagger at his belt meant he had other duties. We agreed never to meet before noon.

As for *where* we'd go, Kian told me about a place in the woodland near Dún Beithe, a clearing marked only by the moss-shrouded stump of an ancient stone. No one knew if it was the work of nature or the remnant of some lost or hidden passage to the Otherworld. Who would dare scrape away its soft green cloak to see if it bore the carved symbols the Fair Folk sometimes left behind?

The first time Kian gave me our signal, it took me several false starts before I reached the clearing. Luck seemed to favor me initially, because we fosterlings had been given that day to use for our own purposes. My friends went off to follow their usual routines at such times—Dairine to her flirtations, Ula to her pacing on the battlements, Gormlaith to her secret place in the shadows.

"How will you spend today?" Dairine asked me as she pinched her cheeks to make them glow for her sweetheart.

"Don't worry, I've got plenty to do," I replied.

"What, washing and mending and that sort of drudgery? I gave one of the servant girls a bronze ring and she's been looking after my clothing ever since. You could do the same."

"I'd rather do this myself," I told her, and since I didn't say what "this" was, I spoke no lie.

It took very little to put my friends off the scent, mostly because they were too involved with their own plans to meddle with mine. I now know I should have taken more interest in why Gormlaith and Ula chose such joyless, solitary paths, or why there was always such an air of desperation to all of Dairine's romances. At the time all I could think of was how convenient it was that their choices left me free to follow my own.

Sidestepping the girls was easy. Leaving Dún Beithe was not. The guard minding the ringfort gate wanted to know where I was going.

"I'm picking berries," I told him.

"Early in the year for that," he said.

"I'd still like to look. You never know."

"I know you won't be bringing many back without a basket." He smiled.

I stared at my empty hands. How could I be so stupid? My cheeks burned with shame at my blunder. Fortunately for me, the guard misguessed the reason for my blushes.

"Never mind, milady, you go ahead. Don't keep the lucky boy waiting."

I ran so fast that he must have thought I was half-mad with love. *I hope he won't jabber to the other men about this,* I thought. *I don't want them putting their heads together, trying to figure out who my nonexistent sweetheart could be.* I was so lost in thought over what had just happened that I forgot some of Kian's directions for finding the clearing. I had to backtrack almost to the edge of the woodland before I put myself on the right path.

"You took your time," he said pleasantly when I emerged from the trees. "This will have to be a short lesson." He handed me one of the two wooden practice swords he'd brought, and we began.

CHAPTER FIVE

Swords and Slingstones

SHORT OR LONG, that first lesson tried my limits. Before I knew it, I'd collapsed in a heap on the grass, panting for breath and sweating heavily. Kian dropped down beside me, looking concerned.

"Are you all right, Lady Maeve?"

I pressed my lips together and inhaled deeply to recover. "You're not to blame, Lord Kian. I'd do better if I were wearing something besides this cumbersome thing." I grabbed the skirt of my gown with both fists and shook it. "I spend more than half my effort trying not to trip on it."

"How did you manage before, with your friend at Cruachan?"

"He gave me some of his old garments."

"I could do the same. You can change behind the trees when you come here."

It would have been churlish of me to ask *If I do, will you promise not to spy on me?* Something about Kian made me want to believe that he was honorable, no matter what his smaller failings. *He sacrificed the chance to win our bout to protect Ea, I thought. That shows his true nature better than a hundred promises.*

"You'd have to keep those clothes for me," I said. "Otherwise the girls will find them."

"Those three are like mice, into everything," he said. "I'm surprised you could shake them off your track to come here, especially Dairine."

"Don't you mean Gormlaith? The others say she likes to cling to people."

"Her? That could be. I say if she wants to get close to you, what's the harm? The poor thing's lonely."

"With all four of us in one room, at meals, and having lessons together?"

"True, but that's—" He waved his hand. "Well, it's *different* from what she used to have." He saw my puzzled expression and went on: "There are friends and *friends*. You know Connla, right? Taller than me, redheaded, ridiculous mustache?"

"I've seen him *and* that mustache." I giggled just thinking about it. The poor boy looked like he was carrying a flame-colored stoat under his nose. "But we've never spoken."

"That lad's been a brother to me since we were babies. If he wasn't such a good fighter, he'd have asked to serve as my charioteer. I'd mourn any of our warriors who fell in battle, but if the Morrígan sent her ravens after my comrade Connla— may it never happen!—I might go mad with grief. I'd fight the gods themselves to drag him back from Tech Duinn, and he'd do the same for me."

"Gormlaith had a friend like that?"

He nodded. "Aifric."

Aifric . . . How could I have forgotten? Once more I heard Gormlaith murmur, *"We were friends. Like sisters."* I also recalled how Ula and the others had avoided answering the questions I'd asked about Aifric's fate. Was that why Gormlaith sometimes hid herself away, to be alone with the ghosts of past happiness?

"Do *you* know what happened to her?" I asked Kian.

"I don't think anyone at Dún Beithe does. One day she was here and the next, gone. It happened in the late autumn, after Samhain. My father sent hunting parties after her, but the weather turned foul and they lost her trail early, too early to tell where she was headed. If she went into the boglands . . ."

His voice trailed off. I could tell he was imagining the worst but didn't want to say it and make it real. Bogs could be as treacherous as they were beautiful. There were pathways through some, but not all, often with planks laid down to keep the traveler safe. And yet one step off the known road, and the mire could gulp you down. Devnet sometimes sang of kings who tried to change their fortune by giving men and maidens to the soft, hungry earth as sacrifices. Such tales never failed to send chills through all who heard them.

I tried to distract him from those dark thoughts. "Wouldn't she have gone home?"

"Home? If you could call it that, with no living mother or father to welcome her return." He sighed. "I rode with the men who took that road, but we reached her kinfolks' house without finding her along the way." A pained look came into his eyes. "I thought it would be hard for them to hear she'd run off, but she'd been with us so long that she was no more than a name to them. When they said they were sorry, it was only because they had to say *something*."

"I wonder why she left," I mused.

Kian shook his head. "There were rumors at first—there are always rumors—but they died quickly. If anyone knows the real reason, they're not talking."

I recalled more of Gormlaith's words: *"She was happy here."* Happy hearts don't flee the place or the people they love.

"She never confided her plans?" I asked. Even though I'd never known her, I was unwilling to abandon Aifric to oblivion. "Not even to her best friend or any of the other girls? Didn't any of them have the slightest idea where you could have searched for her?"

"I've told you what I can. Whatever became of Aifric, it happened years ago." He stood and offered me his hand. I was still so worn out from wielding the wooden sword in an unmanageable dress that he had to haul me to my feet. "If you want to learn more weaponry today, we're running out of time. You know we'll have to go back to Dún Beithe separately, before dinner's ready. But if you'd rather chew on old stories, it's all the same to me."

He spoke as if he knew I'd take the easier choice, a comfortable chat instead of a strenuous session of exercise with the blade. Nothing was more likely to spark my temper and make me keen to prove him wrong. I flung myself back into our sparring and didn't rest for more than a few breaths between bouts until Kian declared it was time to go home.

I left the clearing first, head high. *I showed* him *what I can do with a sword!* I reveled in my triumph.

My smugness lasted up until the moment that my aches and pains began. My body wasn't accustomed to working so hard at such a long-neglected skill. I could barely stir an arm or a leg the next morning and went creeping around the great house like an age-twisted old woman, not moving more than I absolutely had to. When Kian kept his dagger at his waist, I gave silent thanks.

I did my best to conceal the pain as I sat carding wool with the others, but it was more than a false smile could cover. Lady Lassaire noticed and asked if I was suffering from my moon time.

"Not yet," I said truthfully.

My discomfort made her forget that she bore a grudge against me. "You poor child, I understand. I used to feel worse before my red days than when they came," she said with a sympathetic look in her eyes.

"It's the same with me," Dairine declared. "How did you cure it, my lady?"

"I had a baby." She smiled. "I don't think any of you girls are ready for *that* remedy yet." A chorus of horrified squeals agreed with her.

Lady Lassaire's renewed kindness to me went farther than words. "Would you like to lie down for a while, Maeve?" she asked gently. I accepted at once and felt a little better by dinnertime, but far from fully healed when the next day dawned. To make matters worse, as I sat down with my breakfast of bread and cheese, I saw Kian's dagger at his feet.

I didn't *have* to go to our meeting. I could have found an excuse—Lady Lassaire had some special task for us to do; the gateway guard refused to let me pass; I'd twisted my ankle and couldn't fight. Lies, every one. After my morning duties and the midday meal, I picked up a basket and went to the woods.

I might as well have gone empty-handed—the gateway guard that day was a lazy fellow who didn't even blink when I left the ringfort. I don't know why I felt compelled to tell him, "I'm going to pick some berries for Lady Moriath. She's still not feeling well and they'll cheer her."

"Huh? Oh," he said, then fell back into his waking doze.

When I reached the clearing, I was startled to find Kian there without any of the wooden weapons we'd been using. A faint uneasiness crept up my spine. I hadn't spent my life wrapped up in a fluffy little cocoon; I knew that not all warriors were honorable and that a girl who went alone to an isolated place to meet a young man ran certain risks. Kian hadn't attempted anything improper at our first meeting, but he'd also arrived equipped for our lesson. His empty-handed presence here looked suspicious.

I failed to hide my edginess. Kian took one look at me and his brows came together. "Lady Maeve, what's troubling you?"

I exhaled forcefully to calm myself and put on a pleasant face. "Nothing, Lord Kian. I'm simply puzzled: how can you teach me swordsmanship without a sword?" I made a sweeping gesture over the clearing. "Have you hidden the weapons? Do you expect me to prove myself by finding them?"

"Ha! I never thought of that," he said. "No, you're the one who's been hiding things."

"What are you talking about?"

His expression softened. "You worked yourself too hard at our first lesson and now you're hurting—it shows."

"Your mother told you." I lowered my eyes. I didn't want him to see my annoyance at having been discovered.

"Mother? She never said a word. I've got two good eyes. It's brave of you to act as if you're ready to fight again, but I won't allow it until you've had a few days to recover."

"Then why did you give me our signal this morning?" I said heatedly. "If you wanted to spare me, you could have left me—"

Kee-kee-kee! A keen, familiar, beloved cry came from the far side of the clearing. I froze in midspeech, all my anger transformed to surprise, disbelief, and delight. Grinning hugely, Kian bounded across the grass, ducked in among the trees, and returned bearing Ea on his arm. I uttered a wordless cry of joy and rushed to welcome her, though every step I took sent a twinge through my legs.

I was so caught up in the happiness of seeing the hooded kestrel that I only half-heard Kian say, "I didn't want to make you pick up any heavy weapons until your aches were healed, but I also didn't want you thinking I'd given up on your lessons. That's why I sent for you, to tell you that no matter how many days we have to wait between meetings, I'll keep on teaching you as long as you want to learn."

I didn't stop to think about what I did. I simply acted, throwing my arms around his neck and kissing him on the cheek. Ea flapped her wings and scolded what she couldn't see. When I stepped back I saw his free hand cup the spot I'd kissed as though shielding a newly struck spark from the wind. He had the most comical look on his face—astonishment and pleasure against a background of bright red.

"If that's my reward for such a small gift, what will you

give me when I say I'm taking you hunting now?" he wondered aloud.

"Hunting?"

"With this one." His fingertips smoothed Ea's wings. "I know you admire the bird, and it must like you or it would've had a chunk out of you. I thought you might enjoy seeing what it can do besides look pretty."

"She," I said quietly.

"What?"

"You keep calling that lovely kestrel 'it,' but see those broad dark bands across her tail feathers? That's how you can tell she's female, and you tell a male by his cap of blue feathers."

"Huh! I guess I learned something. How did you come to know that?"

I hesitated. The thin braid I'd made from my own hair was still tied to Ea's foot. For whatever reason, Kian hadn't removed it. Did I want to point it out and tell him the full story behind my bond with her?

Not yet, I thought. *I can't talk freely about Ea without naming Odran, and I won't—I can't speak of him to Kian. Kian's been kind to me—he might even become my friend someday—but Odran is my heart. I can't entrust anything so precious to Kian yet.*

I shrugged and gave him a hedging reply: "I've talked with people who know about wild birds. Isn't there anyone like that here, or are you the only person at Dún Beithe who knows their ways?"

"I'm no expert, or I wouldn't have needed you to tell me that my hunter's a huntress," Kian said amiably. "So, as long as we're out here, do you want to see it—I mean, do you want to see *her* work?"

"Yes. More than anything." My heart began to beat rapidly. I had to hold myself back or I'd give that young man another kiss. One was safe, but two? He might get ideas—ideas involving a third kiss, and a fourth, and then what? I would rather not have to waste time explaining why I'd kissed him twice and no more when we could be watching Ea fly.

Kian led me beyond the trees on the far side of the clearing to where the woodland ended and an open field awaited. It wasn't a short walk, but my aches became an afterthought as I looked forward to seeing my Ea take to the skies again. Part of the field was plowed farmland. I could see a small house in the distance and a thin trail of smoke from a cookfire lazily climbing its way into the clouds.

"This is a good place," Kian declared and removed Ea's hood. The kestrel uttered a fierce cry of impatience, spreading her wings and turning her head sharply, taking in her surroundings. "Go on then, pretty one." He jerked his arm up and she soared.

I held my breath in rapture. Nothing I'd ever seen was as beautiful as this, nothing had the power to enchant me so deeply. I followed Ea's flight with more than my eyes; my spirit soared with her. "How lovely," I whispered.

"I agree."

Something in Kian's tone made me tear my eyes from Ea to discover him staring at me in a vaguely disturbing way. I remembered such looks from the days before my brothers were born, when I was still the High King's prize, the hero's portion, the promise of wealth and power that he dangled before the lords of Èriu to earn or keep their allegiance. I didn't like it then and I liked it less now, here far from Dún Beithe and alone with Kian.

"Do you mean me, Lord Kian?" I imitated the flirtatious lilt I'd heard Dairine use when trying to catch the attention of a new man. "You're certainly not the first to tell me that, so I do hope you've got a new way of describing why I make all other girls look like rag-dressed sticks topped with handfuls of straw. Where do you want to start? My eyes?" I fluttered my lashes. "My hair?" I tossed it with both hands. "Will you start at my feet and work your way up or start at my head and work your way down? I don't care, as long as you're original. I've heard it all so many times before that if I listen to one more repetition—"

His smitten look faded into a very wobbly grin. The poor young man didn't know what to make of me, but he pushed ahead anyway. "Lady Maeve, I truly think that you're as beautiful as . . . as . . . as the sun that—"

"Not that! Not the whole dreary 'You outshine the sun and the moon and the stars' again! Didn't I warn you to say something *new*? Oh, the sameness, the fatal *sameness*! I'm done for!" I cried, clutched my heart, and keeled over in the worst imitation of sudden death you could ever hope to see.

I lay in the grass with my eyes closed, still as a block of wood, drawing shallow breaths, waiting. I waited no more than four heartbeats before I heard the sound I'd hoped for: Kian's rousing laughter.

"Get up, you foolish girl," he said, gently nudging me with his toe. "Get up before a field mouse crawls into your *beautiful* hair, or a crow pecks out your *beautiful* eyes, or a raven gobbles up your *beautiful* tongue."

I sprang to my feet willingly. "That's not a very big feast for a full-grown raven. What about my *beautiful* brain?"

"The brain that thought I was actually flattering you?" he scoffed. "There's not enough meat there to make a meal for my kestrel."

I breathed easier. My ploy had worked: Kian wouldn't be able to look at me without recalling my deliberately silly display. How could he ever court a girl he couldn't take seriously?

Relieved, I set my attention on Ea once more. She hovered over the field, searching the grass for signs of prey. Suddenly she dropped and struck, ending the life of some unlucky insect or rodent in the grass.

Kian cheered. "*That's* my beauty! She's too small to go after anything worth eating, but she sometimes flushes hares for my arrows. I'll bring along my bow next time and you'll see."

Next time . . . The promise of those words filled me with happy anticipation.

"What about tomorrow?" I blurted. "You could teach me how to shoot instead of how to use the sword. I wouldn't need to change my clothing for that and I'd be standing still, so my aches wouldn't bother me."

Kian regarded me with grudging admiration. "Taking charge of everything, are you? I'm not ready to swap my tunic for your dress just yet, milady. It's not a bad idea to teach you archery, but not tomorrow. You'll need a bow of your own and I'm the fool who'll have to find one for you."

"Can't I use yours?"

"You're not strong enough to pull it. Trust me on that. But

wait a moment—" He fished in the pouch at his belt and produced a piece of leather with two thongs attached. "I could teach you how to use the sling instead."

I felt a cold wind rush through me. I was at the crannog again, watching Master Íobar use just such a weapon to slaughter the animals Odran and I had nursed so carefully. Once again I saw a slingstone strike my Ea in midflight and send her plummeting to the earth.

"No, not that." I held my hands up, palms forward, pushing away the very idea of touching such an accursed thing. "Never."

"Why not?" Kian was honestly perplexed. "It's small, handy, and effective."

I know, I thought bitterly. "I'd rather learn how to use the bow," I said. My voice came out as hoarse as a raven's croak.

"Suit yourself. But if that's what you want, it'll take time for me to find or make one you can handle; maybe too much time. We're on the brink of losing many days from these meetings. Samhain will soon be here and I'll be called away to oversee the cattle. You girls will have more duties as well, working on our winter food supplies. If we lose more days while I get you a bow—" His lips twisted into a look of resignation. "Perhaps we should just admit we're done with this until next spring." He began to put the sling away.

I hadn't come so far from home to sink into being just another one of Dún Beithe's fosterlings. I had no clear vision of who I was going to become. I didn't know what I was going to do to make my life into something more than what everyone else presumed it had to be. I was only certain of where I *didn't* want to end up, and that wasn't good enough to carry me to the destination I *would* want to reach.

If I let the sorrows of my past rule me, they'd bind my wings. If I allowed cruel memories of Master Íobar's crime to limit my choices now, he'd always hold my future hostage.

I seized Kian's wrist with all my power. "Teach me."

Chapter Six

Samhain Shadows

I DID WELL that first day of sling lessons, so well that Kian wound up scratching his head as he asked, "Are you sure you've never done this before?"

"What are you talking about, Lord Kian?" I asked. "I haven't hit the mark even once." I waved across the field at the target he'd chosen, one of the oldest, broadest oaks at the woodland's edge.

"No, but you *have* launched your shot every time," he said. "When I was starting out, I'd cradle the stone in the strap, twirl it by the thongs, and hear the other lads laughing at me for spinning an empty sling. It took days before I 'improved.'" His wry face matched the sarcasm in his voice. "I managed to keep the stone spinning in the sling long enough for it to drop out and knock me on the head."

I couldn't help it: I snickered.

Kian pretended I'd devastated him. "That's right, make fun of the poor boy who lost his brains in a slingstone accident."

"Several times," I reminded him blithely.

"Hmph. And lucky for you. Only a man with a scrambled brain would've let the time slip away like this."

"What?" He was right: I'd been concentrating so hard on acquiring this new skill and he'd been so fascinated by my flair for using the sling that we hadn't noticed the dimming daylight.

He mistook my surprise for panic. "Don't worry, Lady Maeve, I'll make sure you get back to Dún Beithe safely." He fetched Ea from the tree where he'd tethered her.

I picked up my still-empty basket. "I was supposed to be picking berries but there's no time now. Tongues will wag over this when we're seen coming home together."

"I'll let you reach the gate alone once Dún Beithe's in view," Kian offered. "And if you'll carry the kestrel, I'll scare up enough berries and mushrooms and the like to give you a basket full of excuses for having been in the forest."

A chance to hold Ea! Once again the urge to thank him with a kiss overtook me and once again I pushed it away, though the effort made me blush. Why did I feel so compelled to offer him my gratitude with more than words alone?

A disturbing thought crossed my mind: *Do I want to kiss him because I'm grateful or . . . do I just want to give him a kiss?* I swept the question aside at once, furious with myself. *How can I want such a thing? What is Kian to me? He may be handsome and strong, a battle-proven warrior, but he's not Odran.*

No, he's not Odran. A small, insinuating whisper stirred dangerously within me. *But aren't you just a little curious to discover what he* could *be?*

Those words and the unwelcome heat they kindled in my

blood made me walk fast—too fast—and preoccupied me so much that I lost track of my surroundings. I broke from the forest and was well up the path to Dún Beithe, Ea on my arm and Kian in my wake, before I realized it. We were already within the gate guard's sight, and bad luck for us, this one was fully alert and paying close attention. We'd also stirred the interest of the sentry atop the wall.

Now there are two *tongues ready to wag about seeing us together,* I thought bitterly, only to spy my final fate: tall and elegant in the fine red cloak that was her pride, Ula stared down at us from her interrupted pacing around the ringfort ramparts.

Kian was by my side, the basket at his feet while he carefully took charge of Ea, sliding the leather sleeve from my arm to his, kestrel and all. "Lady Maeve, didn't we agree to split up before—?"

"I wasn't thinking," I replied wearily, when the truth was I'd been thinking too much. "I'm sorry, Lord Kian, but it looks like we're both doomed. And what a way to die: death by gossip." I tried to smile.

His jaw set and all of his dismay transformed itself into determination. "I won't allow it. If anyone speaks disrespectfully about you, my sword will teach them better manners."

"Poor Ula," I murmured. "She won't stand a chance. And after you've killed her, and Gormlaith, and Dairine, what then?"

"Who?"

"No one." Now I could truly smile at him, my bold defender. His grand, heroic desire to protect me gave me back my spine. I didn't need anyone else to fight my battles. I laid one hand on his shoulder. "I'm sorry if I've dragged you into an awkward situation, but I can weather it if you can. There'll be no need for challenges or duels."

"But if they claim that you and I—"

"I don't care. Dogs bark at anything. Besides, this gives me a fine excuse to do something I've wanted to do for a long time."

His eyes widened. Was that apprehension I saw in them or expectancy? "What's that?"

"To stop calling each other lord and lady when we should be only Kian and Maeve." I picked up the basket. "Above all, to ask that you call me your friend." I popped a ripe berry into my mouth and another between his lips before he could react. "Now let anyone who's watching chew on *that*," I declared, and entered Dún Beithe like a conqueror.

For days after that, I wore my confidence like the richest, heaviest gold torque a king could bestow. It was a heavy burden, but I forced myself to hold my head high, even if it cost me a snapped neck. Wherever I went in the great house, whispers followed—a rushing sound, a stream in full springtime flood that would have swept me off my feet if I took a single misstep. I stood firm and let it rush past me. I pretended that all the delighted, scandalized, speculating murmurs were the rustle of wind through the dying leaves.

To my surprise, the one refuge I had from all those rumbling rumors was behind the bull-hide curtain of my sleeping chamber in the company of Ula, Gormlaith, and Dairine. That first evening after I returned to the ringfort with Kian, Ula remarked, "You're quite the huntress, aren't you, Maeve? When I go into the woods, I only come back with mushrooms."

"I didn't go there for any sort of sweethearts' meeting," I replied calmly. "If you think that, stop hinting and say so straight out."

She spread her hands. "If that's how it was, I take your word for it. What I saw from up on the wall could mean many things, but you're the only one who knows the truth."

Dairine couldn't resist adding: "Kian knows a bit about it too." Her mischief earned her a slap from Ula.

"How would you like it if we didn't defend you when those magpies out there started twittering about *your* escapades?" she demanded, jerking her thumb at the doorway. "If Maeve says there's nothing between her and Kian, that's that."

"Thank you, Ula."

I hugged her and then Gormlaith, but when I came to Dairine, the dark-haired girl took advantage of our closeness to hiss in my ear: "You do know she's only on your side because she wants to believe you've got no claim? She's been after him for years."

"She can have him," I whispered back, though a small part of me countered with a beguiling vision of Kian and a whisper of its own: *Are you* sure *of that, Maeve?*

Autumn turned the birches' leaves to honey-gold and Dún Beithe buzzed with activity like a hive of bees. Everyone was caught up in preparations for the coming winter. Gossip grows stronger when people have nothing else to do, so that busy time of year killed the rumors about Kian and me the way frost kills flowers. Or so I thought.

Samhain and all its solemn rites came rushing toward us in a war chariot's headlong charge. It marked one of the great divisions of the year, a time of awe and dread. On that night the barrier between our mortal lives and the unknown realm of the Otherworld would grow thin enough to let the spirits of the dead slip through. Sometimes they didn't return alone, but traveled in the company of monstrous beasts, tusked, taloned, and fanged, with flaming eyes. Sometimes they rode on dark whirlwinds as they followed the Fair Folk's wild hunt through the night. When dawn came, they plunged back through their gateway mounds and took the earth's warmth and light away with them until spring.

As Kian foretold, we had far too few opportunities to steal off so that I could continue my practice with the sling and share his forays with Ea. Lady Moriath recovered her health, so I was still able to visit my sweet kestrel on her perch when we renewed our embroidery lessons, but it wasn't the same as seeing those wings slice effortlessly through the sky.

Kian did find one chance to meet with me before his own duties claimed him completely. The night before he left Dún Beithe to help his father thin the herds, he sat beside me at dinner and murmured, "It's dark out, but can you find your way to the place where I keep the kestrel?"

"Tonight?" I whispered, taken aback by such a strange request. "Yes, easily; the moon's full. But why? There'll be more talk if anyone sees—"

"Where's the brave girl who didn't care how loudly those dogs bark?" he replied smoothly, then moved on to join his friend Connla, leaving it for me to decide whether I'd accept or refuse his dare.

I took it, of course, and I made it a point of honor to find my way to the storehouse without being seen. He was waiting by Ea's perch, holding a small oil lamp. "I knew you'd come, Maeve. Here, this is for you."

I stared at the gift he dropped into my cupped hands. "Why are you giving me your sling and shot pouch, Kian?"

"Look again. Those are new and they're yours. I don't know when I'll be able to continue our lessons, but why can't you practice what I've already taught you?"

I loosened the thong sealing the small leather pouch and poured the contents into my hand. "These are real slingstones!" I exclaimed. I recognized the specially formed round missiles that Kian used when he showed me how to use his weapon. He always tried to recover them after a cast, and he gave me only ordinary pebbles and rocks when it was my turn.

"Yes, so don't be careless with them. When I come back I'll want to hear that you never miss your mark."

"You will, I promise! Thank you, Kian." I turned my eyes to Ea. "Who'll take care of her while you're away?"

"She comes with me."

"Oh." I tried not to sound downcast.

Kian chuckled. "Sorry, Maeve. You know I'd trust her to you in a heartbeat, but you're going to have enough to do without the added responsibility of looking after this pretty lady." Before I could argue, he put on a soppy face and added in the most ridiculous lovesick tones: "My beloved princess, I'll die of loneliness without her, and every time I gaze into her eyes, I'll think of you."

I laughed so much that he had to beg me to stop before the noise drew unwelcome ears to the storehouse. Biting my knuckles to keep silent, I slipped back through the night to the great house.

Kian was right: it would have been difficult for me to care for Ea in his absence, exhausting if not impossible. Too soon the demands of the harvest season took over every aspect of my life in Lord Artegal's stronghold. Lady Lassaire became a war leader, commanding every girl and woman in her household as we all fought against the threatening spirits of oncoming hunger and cold.

We fosterlings had to master all ways of readying a settlement for winter. The day would come when we'd have households of our own to manage. I relished the work. I was in no hurry to have a husband, but the idea of being responsible for the comfort and security of others appealed to me. I wanted to learn all the skills I'd use for my people's benefit when the time came.

My friends didn't share my enthusiasm. Dairine dragged herself from task to task, muttering and doing work that was just barely good enough. Ula was silent and competent, but she went about her duties with such a look of disdain and cold fury that no one dared to correct her mistakes except Lady Lassaire.

And Gormlaith? The nearer we came to Samhain, the less we saw of her. She'd disappear before breakfast and not show herself again until sundown. Her strange absence bothered me, but I was the only one who seemed to care about her whereabouts.

"Does she always do this?" I asked Dairine quietly while the two of us toted a barrel filled with butter to the cold storage shed.

"Just for the past few years. Ugh, this is heavy! Is it filled with butter or rocks?"

"Have you got any idea where she goes?"

"What do you care, as long as she comes back?" Dairine snapped. "Are you carrying your share of the load, or are you tilting it so that I'm stuck with the whole weight?"

I could see I wasn't going to get any answers the direct way, so I changed tactics. "Poor Dairine, I know how you feel. It's not fair that Gormlaith vanishes and leaves you stuck with her work and your own. If I had even a hint of where to find her, I'd put a stop to that."

Dairine's scowl softened and her voice dripped honey. "That's so sweet, Maeve. You're my best friend, and you must know that I'm yours."

"What, not Ula?" I teased gently.

"*That* envious thing?" Dairine made a rude sound. "Until you came here, she was our Lady Most: *most* highborn, *most* graceful, *most* beautiful, and *most* important. Oh, and did I forget *most* courted by all the best young men? Not that she lowered her precious self to encourage any one of them. She'd like to snare no one less than Lord Kian."

"Who's stopping her?"

"Lord Kian himself." Dairine snickered. "She found *that* out once the field was cleared and it was safe for her to go after him. I wish you could've seen her face when all she won was the kind of smile you'd get from a big brother."

"What do you mean, 'once the field was cleared'?" I asked.

"Oh, just that if you want to steal a prime cut of beef, it's smarter to try taking it from a puppy than from a wolf. Ula expects to get things, not fight for them, especially if it's a messy fight she's bound to lose."

"I don't understand."

"You don't need to." And no matter how many additional

questions I asked, Dairine brushed them aside like a cloud of mayflies.

I did want to find out where Gormlaith went when she vanished day after day. I believed her disappearance had nothing to do with avoiding work, and I was growing more and more concerned about what unhappy shadow might lie at the root of it. All I desired was to speak with her about it privately.

I never got the chance. One morning I woke up to hear her mewling in distress. Ula and Dairine stood over her bed with their backs to me, so I couldn't tell what was going on. I put on the nearest garment I could find and rushed up behind them.

"Gormlaith, what is it? Are you sick?" I cried, peering over Ula's shoulder.

No light was kindled, but enough seeped in from the great hall to let me see the rope binding the girl's ankle to one leg of her bed.

"Sick of doing her fair share," Dairine said, without bothering to look at me. "We should have thought of this days ago."

"Here she is and here she stays until she swears that she'll stop running off, leaving us to do all her work," Ula decreed. "*Swears* it!"

In three strides I was on the far side of Gormlaith's bed, facing her captors, so indignant that my skin prickled as though a thunderstorm were rising through my bones. "Let her go."

"Not until she gives her word—No, not until she swears a *blood oath*." Dairine grinned. "Something strong enough to bring the gods' wrath on her if she breaks it."

"I'm sorry . . . I couldn't help it . . . I've been so upset, so scared," Gormlaith moaned. "You know how bad it is at this time of year; I can't help thinking of her, remembering—don't you feel it too? Don't you worry if this will be the Samhain that she . . . that she comes back?" She was trembling.

"Be quiet," Ula snarled, but her face turned pale and so did Dairine's.

"Who'll come back?" I asked. When they ignored my question, I shrugged, dropped onto Gormlaith's mattress, and began untying the rope on her ankle.

Ula made a grab for my wrists, trying to stop me. I swatted her hands aside, but she persisted, striking back. What could I do but defend myself? Gormlaith lay like a log and Dairine stood bouncing in place, richly enjoying every moment of our fight.

It ended when Ula drove her fingernails into my flesh and I reacted with a violent shove, toppling her backward. Her head struck the corner of a wooden chest and she let out such a yowl that our sleeping chamber flooded with all manner of people, from Lady Lassaire's noble attendants to the cook's soot-smudged assistant. I took advantage of the confusion to set Gormlaith free.

Later that morning, the four of us got a harsh lecture about how horseplay was for boys and *not* young ladies. Ula didn't speak to me for the rest of the day, though by evening her mood had softened.

"You were right, Maeve," she said reluctantly as we sat at dinner. "Snaring Gormlaith that way solved nothing."

"And I'm sorry you were hurt," I replied.

Ula touched the back of her head gingerly. "No lump, no blood, no harm done." But though she smiled at me, I thought I saw an iron-hard speck glinting in her eyes.

Gormlaith no longer ran away from our chores. She did her share quickly and without complaint, but also without volunteering a word beyond *yes* and *no*, *please* and *thank you*. She shrugged off my attempts to bring her into conversation, and if I tried to break through to her with a joke, all I got was a brief, wobbly smile.

"You might as well give up," Dairine whispered to me. We fosterlings were elbow to elbow at a long board, salting the newly butchered beef to preserve it. "It's painful watching you waste your time on that tongue-tied lump."

"That 'tongue-tied lump' is my friend," I muttered hotly. "I thought she was yours as well."

Dairine rolled her eyes. "We're *all* friends here. Who else have we got? But that doesn't change who she is. Listen, if you're fretting about her, let it go: she's always like this when Samhain comes, but she's her old, dull self as soon as it's over."

"Why?"

"Why what?"

"Why does she act this way?"

Dairine made an impatient sound, as if she were trying to explain things to a doorpost. "I *told* you, it's because of Samhain. It's a bad time of year to be a coward."

I rubbed more salt into the bloody flank in front of me and frowned. "We're all afraid of what happens on that night, Dairine, but that doesn't make all of us cowards. Or is that what you think I am too?"

Immediately she changed her tone, showering me with apologies and excuses, swearing that she'd never question my courage. "Amn't I your best friend, dear Maeve?" she wheedled. "Oh, I know I'm nowhere near your equal—my father wasn't highborn and he's only chief of a petty kingdom—but you're not a snob like Ula. You never act like you're too good for me or the rest of us, even if you think it."

"I never thought—"

"Tsk, there I go again, tripping over my own stupid tongue. *You* know what I mean." She threw herself back into our chore, humming merrily.

Lady Lassaire's war against a hungry winter ended in victory. All of Dún Beithe celebrated Samhain knowing that our supplies of meat and drink were more than enough to see us through the cold, dark days. We stood together, massed around the great bonfires, clinging to their light. Mead flowed, songs soared from the earth to the stars, and we feasted until we fell into our beds to welcome the first sliver of sunlight at dawn.

That first morning after Samhain, Gormlaith drew me aside. "Thank you for trying to help me, Maeve," she said shyly. "I'm sorry I was a bother."

"Don't thank me; I haven't done anything for you yet," I replied. "But if you want to start talking, I'll listen. Maybe together we can make things better for you."

Her laughter shivered and fell short. "There's no need. I'm all right now. I just wanted to say how grateful I am to count you as my friend."

That was the last she'd say about her haunted days.

I'm glad she's herself again, I thought. *But shouldn't friends share more than happiness?* That troubling question set its teeth in me and refused to let go.

CHAPTER SEVEN

The Most Annoying Boy
in Ériu

"WELL DONE, MAEVE!" Kian shouted, his breath making little clouds in the chilly air. "Oh, *well* done! That's your best score yet." He strode across the stubbled field to examine my newest target, a slender aspen. "One, two, three—" He peered at the trunk closely. "Is that all? I could have sworn . . . No, wait, here's another." He pointed at the small scar my fourth slingstone had made in the bark, then stooped to gather the fallen missiles.

"Do you see the one that missed?" I called out to him, agitated. Ever since Kian's return home for Samhain, I'd been desperately eager to show him how much my skill with the sling had improved. I drove myself to find ways to practice even at the height of the Samhain preparations, but for those times I used ordinary rocks. Now I used the specially formed slingstones Kian had given me, and I dreaded the thought of losing one.

"I don't think so." He rubbed the back of his head, surveying the space between the tree and the spot where I stood. "Too bad you couldn't demonstrate your progress with mice instead of slingstones. I know *someone* who'd find them fast enough!"

We both turned our faces to the sky. A small, familiar shape flew gorgeously against the watery winter light.

"Thank you for bringing her, Kian," I said softly. "I've missed this."

"'This'?" He pounced on my words like a lad scooping up a ball, ready to play. "Why 'this' and not *me*? You're a cruel girl, Maeve, tearing out a man's heart for no good reason."

"But I do have one," I countered, getting into the game. "You gave me our signal at breakfast and I was so thrilled that I couldn't eat a bite. Now I'm hungry and your heart is *soooo* tender, soft as a woman's, that I can't resist."

"Don't devour it just yet, lass. I want to give it to at least one girl before I die."

"You mean you haven't done that yet?" I pretended to be shocked. "*I* heard there isn't a serving girl in Dún Beithe without a chunk of your heart as a keepsake."

"Who'd you hear that from? One of our household gossips? They always get their stories wrong. It's not my heart that I've been giving so generously." He burst into rough laughter.

"Oh look, there's my missing slingstone. I see it; wait here, I'll be right back." I dashed from his side before he could catch sight of my blushes.

A trick of the light befriended me: I did spy the errant stone in the dead grass and stowed it lovingly in my belt pouch along with its mates and my sling. By the time I returned to him, Kian was done enjoying his own crude joke.

"Putting your toys away so soon?" he teased. "I was hoping you'd keep at it until all fives stones strike the target."

"Next time," I said.

"All right, and next time I'll bring the rest of our practice gear. It's been too long since you put your hand to the sword and the spear. I won't push you too hard. Better to have you go slow than lose days because you're in pain. Ah, and I'll bring you a short tunic to wear. I'll bet you thought I forgot about that." He was very proud of himself. "You'll be cold at first, but once you get going, you'll warm up fast enough, and if your feet can move freely, you'll find that—"

"I'm not going to take up the sword again, Kian," I said.

"What's this? After how fiercely you argued to make me give you these lessons?" He was outraged and insulted. "Are you one of those girls who only wants what she can't have? Is it all about *winning* for you, and not keeping?"

I bit my lower lip and bowed my head. "I value what you've given me."

"Value it enough to cast it aside."

"That's not how it is!" My eyes flashed up into his. "Will you listen? Will you promise not to make fun of me when I tell you the truth? While you were gone and left me to practice using the sling on my own, I had time to think about our other lessons. The sword, the shield, the spear—they're not for me. I first wanted to master them so I could become someone I was never born to be. I wish I'd never done it: it cost my friend Kelan his life."

"How did that—?"

"Please don't ask." I fought against tears. "Let me choose my own time to tell you, if I ever do."

Kian rested a comforting hand on my shoulder. Its strength felt good and I leaned closer to the shielding warmth of his body. "Go on, then."

"The second time, I wanted to prove something to myself, to you, and maybe even to Kelan's spirit."

"I remember," he said. "You argued that there are women who wield swords as ably as any man. The bards say so."

"And I still say it might *be* so," I replied. "But I can never be one. My training didn't start early enough, it's been interrupted, and . . . and what I really desire to do with my life has nothing to do with weapons."

"What's that?"

I shook my head, unwilling to confide in him just yet. What could I tell him? *I want to be more than a wife and mother of kings. I want to rule in my own right, in my own name, but not for the sake of wealth or pride. If I want power, it's only so that I can help the people I rule. I want them to come to me for justice. I want to protect them from hardship. I want them to know that if this world's unfair, I will still treat them fairly.*

How could I say such things until I felt secure enough to face the incredulous laughter that might follow, even from a friend? No matter what else I might share with Kian, I wasn't ready to share my dreams. The one person with whom I could share them was far from me now, walking the unknown shores of Avallach. Once again the pain of missing Odran tore my heart.

Kian accepted my silence, and I was thankful for that. "If that's what you want, Maeve, let it be so." He looked up to where Ea hovered over the cold land. "We should go home." He turned to call back the kestrel.

"Wait, Kian," I cried, grabbing his arm. "I don't want you to teach me more swordsmanship, but I still need you to help me master this." I touched the pouch holding my sling. "Didn't you hear me say that next time I'll hit the target with all five of my stones? I can't do that without your training."

"You did well enough without me before Samhain," he said gruffly.

"Well enough isn't good enough for me. Please, Kian, *think:* suppose you taught me everything you know about spears and swords. What could I do with that knowledge? Do you honestly see me carrying those weapons, riding off on a cattle raid? But this—!" I pulled out the sling. "I can *use* this. It'll be my hidden strength, my independence. With your help, I'll never need to rely on anyone else to protect me. I'll be free to take care of myself!"

He looked at me wistfully. "I think you can do that now, Maeve. Fine, I'll do what you ask. Did I ever have another choice? You've picked your weapon. I only hope you'll be able to pick your battles as wisely."

I grinned. "What battles, Kian? All I want is to be able to hit one tree with five stones."

"Next time. We're losing light. Let's go."

As always, I watched in fascination as Kian called Ea back to him. First he got her attention with a shrill whistle, then tied a bit of meat to a long string and whirled it over his head. The kestrel came flying to claim it, landing prettily on his leather-sheathed forearm. After she'd swallowed her treat, he hooded her and we headed back to the ringfort.

"I wish you'd teach me how to do that," I said. Every time I'd let Ea fly from the crannog, she'd returned when it suited her, not on my command. "You let me send her flying, so why won't you let me bring her back? It looks easy enough."

"I don't know if she'd return to you," Kian replied.

Oh, is that so? Just give me the chance and you'll see! I kept my defiant thought to myself and instead spoke as calmly and reasonably as I could: "*I* can spin a loaded sling overhead without braining myself, unlike *some* people. I think I can spin that lure too."

"Yes, but I'm as much a part of what brings her back as the lure is," he countered.

"Hmm, so she comes back for *two* pieces of meat instead of one." I said it so that he'd know I was only joking.

He laughed without taking offense. "You're not going to give me any peace until I let you have your way, Maeve. I might as well surrender now. Come this way."

We turned off from our accustomed homeward path and came to a place where the trees ended abruptly and a wide expanse of well-trampled earth lay before us.

"This looks like the road I traveled when I first came to Dún Beithe," I said.

Kian nodded. "You'll have room to swing the lure and I'll be able to watch her flight in case I need to step in."

"And rescue me if I fail?" I arched one brow at him.

"Rescue *her*," he corrected me with good humor. "Are you ready?"

He wrapped his cloak over his free arm and coaxed Ea onto it so I could claim first the leather sleeve and then the falcon. I removed her hood with care. "There you are, my love," I cooed. "You're a lucky bird: you'll have one more flight today and then you'll come back to *me*, understand?"

Kian chuckled. "If all I had to do to make her return to me was talk to her, I could've trained her in a morning."

I sent Ea flying. The kestrel was still avid to spread her wings. She circled over the unfamiliar landscape, then turned her fiery eyes to the southwest, where the road led to Connacht, our former home.

"I wonder what's drawing her attention," Kian mused. "Maybe you should try summoning her now, before she gets any unlucky ideas." He handed me the string and took a leaf-wrapped piece of raw meat from his pouch. "Good thing I packed a few extra tidbits for her. Do you want me to tie that on for you, or can you manage?"

I ignored the gentle jab and deftly attached the bait. My summoning whistle was so loud and piercing that it made Kian gape. Ea must have heard it too, for she turned in her flight just as I stepped into the middle of the pathway, twirling the lure above my head. Her wings dipped, then rose as she came flying toward me. She was so beautiful that my eyes stung with tears of joy to see her, and my heart raced so wildly I thought I heard it pounding ever louder in my ears.

"That's the way, my darling," I whispered. "That's right, you know me, you're going to fly right to my—"

"Get out of the way! A hundred curses, you stupid girl, stand aside!"

I wheeled in place. Why hadn't I heard the hoofbeats coming up fast behind me? I'd been too rapt in Ea's flight. The lone rider sped down the road straight at me, yet I still stood where I was, looping the sky with the lure.

"Maeve!" Kian bellowed, and swept me out of the horse's headlong course so violently that I dropped the string and ended up sprawled in the yellow-flowered gorse and dead bracken by the roadside.

The rider pulled his steed to a halt and came back toward us. "Is she all right?" He didn't look much older than I. His long red-gold hair fell in tangles to his waist and his pale-green eyes fixed on Kian. I might as well have been a mushroom.

"You fool, why didn't you stop before you overran us?" Kian shouted, closing in on the young stranger. "Why didn't you turn your horse? You had plenty of room!" He threw his arms open as wide as they could go.

"Watch what you're saying." The green eyes narrowed dangerously. "I *couldn't* stop. My mount's one of the finest and fastest in all Èriu. When I give him his head in a gallop, I'd sooner be able to rein in the lightning! If I'd pulled him one way, the girl might've panicked and dashed into our path, and if I turned him away from her then, she could've played the squirrel and scurried right back under his hooves. Now do you understand?"

"*I* do." I stood up, pulling bits of dead leaves and flowers out of my hair. "Whoever you are, you're the worst horseman I've ever met and the rudest man as well. A capable rider wouldn't try to cover his mistakes with excuses, and a gallant man would ask *me* if I'm all right, not him." I pointed at Kian. "I don't need anyone to answer for me. I've got a tongue of my own."

"Only one? It sounds like you've got two at least, and both dipped in hemlock." The stranger had a wolfish grin that was much too charming for such an unmannerly man. "Your little tumble doesn't seem to have done you any harm, but why were you standing in the middle of the road whipping a string around your head?" He leaned in Kian's direction and in a false whisper asked, "She's not crazy, is she?"

My friend was not amused. "You will apologize to Lady Maeve here and now or I swear I'll show you the color of your guts."

The rider raised both hands. "I was only joking. *Lady* Maeve?" He peered at me. I held my head high so that he could see the thickness and brilliance of my gold torque. It confirmed my high birth and noble status more eloquently than words.

So did the gleaming collar around his own neck.

He dropped from his horse's back and came within a hand span of me. "I'm very sorry for any insult or offense I've given you, Lady Maeve." The corners of his eyes crinkled with hidden mirth.

Before I could accept or reject his apology, Kian made himself into a wedge between us. "Well said. Now go on your way. I'm sure *someone* wants you elsewhere. We haven't any more time to waste in your company."

"And you called *me* rude?" the stranger murmured for my ears only.

I took a long step back, away from him. "Lord Kian and I do have an important task at hand; one that you interrupted. I wish you a safe journey and farewell." I showed him my back as I went to retrieve Ea's lure.

I heard his retreating footsteps behind me, followed by the sound of his horse trotting away. "*Yes,* I called you rude," I muttered as I searched for the baited string. "You proved it, didn't you? Not even polite enough to tell me your name."

"What did you say, Maeve?" Kian asked. He stood scanning the sky for Ea, the lure already in his hand.

"Nothing."

I failed to call Ea back to me. She was used to returning on command to Kian's hand, not mine, and the hubbub the stranger caused upset her. She was in no mood to try anything new. I conceded temporary defeat and let Kian bring her down and hood her.

We no longer bothered splitting up before returning to Dún Beithe. It was an inconvenience and did nothing to stifle gossip. I'd learned that when malicious folk wanted to wag their tongues about something, they'd do so despite all the opposing evidence. As long as Kian understood that we were nothing more than friends, I'd put up with the irritating buzz of rumors.

As we entered the gateway, I saw a big commotion outside the door of the great house. Lord Artegal and Lady Lassaire stood in the midst of their most nobly born warriors and attendants while servants hovered nearby with food and drink. My fellow fosterlings waited among the other women. They wore demure expressions, but any time someone tried to edge in front of them, they deftly moved to hold their places. Then the crowd shifted and I got a good view of the reason for all this fuss.

"No," I said, shaking my head. "Tell me it's not him I'm seeing, Kian. Please."

But Kian couldn't lie about what we both saw: the wild, insolent young man—no, the rude *boy* who'd nearly trampled me on the road—was being welcomed to Dún Beithe with the citadel's most elaborate show of hospitality.

"Kian!" Lady Lassaire caught sight of her son and waved happily. "Come here and greet our guest."

My friend gritted his teeth into the stiff semblance of a smile. "See to the kestrel," he told me in an undertone as he took my hand and managed to slide Ea from his arm to mine, along with the leather guard.

I gave Ea only a moment to adjust to the abrupt shift, then hurried away to restore her to her perch before anyone decided I should welcome that unbearable boy too.

It was a moment too long.

"Maeve! Maeve, dear, is that you?" Lady Lassaire's voice trilled with pleasure. "Where have you been roving? And—oh my, what happened to you? Your dress and your hair look like . . . like—" She paused and darted a sideways look at her son.

Oh, wonderful, now she's blushing, I thought bitterly as I approached the lady of Dún Beithe. *There's no doubt about what she thinks Kian and I have been up to, and I can't say one word to deny it. It'd only reinforce her silly fantasy.* I sighed deeply. *At least she's smiling.*

"I'm sorry for my appearance, Lady Lassaire," I said, stroking Ea's feathers. "I've always been curious about this beautiful bird, and today Lord Kian was kind enough to let me watch him fly her. She's a graceful creature, but I'm not." I indicated my rumpled appearance. "I fell on the way home."

A few snickers and some muttered jests came from the crowd, but one glare from Lord Artegal silenced them. "Are you hurt, Lady Maeve?" he asked solicitously. When I shook my head, he turned a frowning face to his son. "Why is she holding that bird of yours? It's too dangerous for a girl!"

The stranger's hearty laugh broke over us. "For some girls, perhaps, but for Lady Maeve?" he declared. "That birdie knows better than to take a nip out of her fair skin. She could snap its tiny neck with two fingers!"

"Is that how they treat animals where you come from?" I shot back. "Make *their* necks pay for *your* failure to guide them wisely? I'm surprised your horse is still alive!"

My words scandalized Lady Lassaire. "Maeve, that's no way to speak to our honored guest! You must apologize. And Kian, *do* take that bird away from her."

My friend obeyed his mother, this time using his cloak to shield his arm.

"Careful, Lord Kian," the stranger said smoothly. "You wouldn't want to get a scratch."

Kian sent spears flying from his eyes. With his gaze locked on the stranger, he deliberately let Ea grip his bare flesh, though her talons drew blood. Head high and proud, he left us.

"Well, Maeve?" Lady Lassaire said impatiently. "What do you have to say to Lord Conchobar?"

She was expecting an apology. What she got was a wide-eyed, gape-mouthed stare. "Conchobar?" I echoed. "Conchobar of the Ulaidh, Fachtna Fáthach's son?"

"*Lord* Conchobar and *king* of the Ulaidh, thank you." He grinned. "That's me. So you're *that* Lady Maeve? Old Lord Eochu's littlest girl?"

"Yes, I *am* the High King's daughter." How haughty I sounded! But I couldn't allow that puppy of a king to belittle me or my family.

Lady Lassaire cleared her throat. "Maeve, we are still waiting for your apology."

Conchobar had his arm around her waist and planted a kiss on her cheek with such a loud smack that it made her jump and squeal like a startled child. "May the gods bless you, my lovely woman, but why should the girl apologize? I couldn't be insulted by anything she'd ever have to say. Is that beef I smell cooking? And—let me guess—venison too? I'm famished."

"We don't let our guests go hungry here," Lord Artegal said jovially. He looked relieved. "Come in and see how well we fill your belly, my lord." He and his wife linked arms with the young chieftain and escorted him into the great house between them.

Though Conchobar had come to us without warning, Dún Beithe's cook set out a feast worthy of the noblest guest. While the roast meat was served up, more food was seething in the huge cauldron on the central hearth. Mead filled every cup, and by Lord Artegal's orders there was wine as well, brought from the eastern coast and the lands beyond the sea. Conchobar's arrogance set my teeth on edge, but at least his presence also gave them something tasty to sink into. I could enjoy the meal even if I didn't care for the company.

After so much food, all I wanted to do was drop into my bed and sleep, but my friends had other ideas. All they could talk about was Conchobar.

"Isn't he *handsome*?" Dairine gushed. "What wonderful eyes, and such *strong* arms." She sat on the edge of her bed and hugged herself in rapture.

"I like his hair," Gormlaith said in her timid way. "It shines and it feels like silk."

"Liar! When would he let *you* touch it?" Ula snapped.

"By accident. Lady Lassaire told me to fill his cup and when he leaned forward it brushed over my—"

"Ugh, enough! I don't want to hear about it." Ula sounded

as though Gormlaith had described some unspeakably disgusting crime.

"Oh my, who's jealous?" Dairine couldn't resist the opportunity to taunt. "If you're going to envy anyone, shouldn't it be Maeve? She *talked* to him."

"I'll trade you *that* privilege for a worm-eaten apple core," I grumbled. "If I'm lucky, I won't have to trade words with him for the rest of his stay. Why did he have to come here anyway? Who goes riding around the country after Samhain? He's king of the Ulaidh! He belongs back home looking after his people."

"Maybe he came here looking for a wife," Gormlaith ventured.

"He could do worse," Dairine said with a distant, thoughtful smile.

"I'm sure he could," Ula said, looking straight at Dairine.

Her meaning was clear and Dairine wasn't slow-witted. The next thing I knew, they were embroiled in a quarrel that didn't confine itself to words. Gormlaith squeaked with dismay and dithered until I told her, "You take Dairine, I'll take Ula, and let's end this before Lady Lightning strikes or we'll all be confined to this room for the rest of Lord Conchobar's visit." No matter how little I cared for that bothersome boy, I was thankful for the magic peacemaking power of his name. By the time one of Lady Lassaire's drowsy attendants came to investigate the uproar in the fosterlings' chamber, we were all in our beds, pretending to be sound asleep.

The next day Dairine wore her hair unbraided, black waves concealing the scratches on her face. Ula didn't bother with such ploys, carrying herself even taller than usual, daring anyone to remark on her bruises. Mousy Gormlaith slunk through the morning, acting as if everything was her fault. When Lady Moriath came to fetch me for my embroidery lesson, I almost rushed into her arms, grateful to escape the storm cloud still looming over those three.

By this time I'd stopped making drawings in the dirt of the storehouse floor and was well on my way to completing a needlework image of Ea. Lady Moriath checked my efforts and grew happier each time she saw how much progress I had made. I'd begun these lessons as a ruse to spend more time with my kestrel, but I was surprised to find I was enjoying the task itself.

I studied the embellished cloth as Lady Moriath and I made our way to the storehouse. *Have I really made something so beautiful?* I marveled.

"I don't know why you insist on working in that dim place," Lady Moriath said as we walked.

"The weather's not warm or sunny, so we can't have this lesson outside," I said reasonably. "If I have to stitch indoors, it might as well be where I can have another look at the bird that inspired my design. I'm going to sew this into a belt pouch for Lord Kian and I want the last details to be perfect."

"Is that so?" Her eyebrows rose and dimples stole years from her wrinkled face. "My, my, the rumors about you two were right after all. Now I feel bad for having told Lady Lassaire she was mistaken. Won't *she* be pleased!"

"What? Oh no, this isn't a sweetheart's gift, Lady Moriath," I protested. "It's just to thank him for all the ways he's befriended me." To ensure there'd be no confusion, I added: "Like a *brother*. Nothing more."

"Of course, my dear." She spoke in an innocent-sounding

way that as good as said *You are a very bad liar, child, but I think it's sweet.* "Now do take care to keep your cloth out of sight when we enter the storehouse, just in case Lord Kian's there tending the bird. You wouldn't want to spoil the surprise."

He was there. So was Conchobar. I could have sworn that I heard the gods laughing.

CHAPTER EIGHT

An Unexpected Messenger

"WHAT ARE *YOU* doing here?" I blurted out the words without thinking.

Conchobar and Kian turned at the same time, startled by my outburst. Kian waved weakly at Ea. Conchobar recovered his infuriating grin much too quickly and pointed at Kian.

"After you and the other delicate flowers of Dún Beithe went to bed, my friend here and I fell to talking," Conchobar drawled.

"You're friends now," I stated drily. "That's news." False news, if Kian's guarded expression was any indication of the actual state of things.

Lady Moriath didn't know what to make of how bristly I was when speaking to the young lord of the Ulaidh. "Really, Lady Maeve, why shouldn't they be friends? There are no grudges between Dún Beithe and Emain Macha." She looked at Conchobar. "That *is* what you call your chief stronghold, isn't it? I tend to forget so much these days."

"Your memory's good, milady, and if you ever have reason to travel there, I promise you'll experience the most generous hospitality in all Èriu." He offered Kian a conciliatory smile. "Though after all I've enjoyed here during this visit, I'll have to work hard to be more openhanded to my guests than Lord Artegal."

"That's very gracious of you to say, since you've only been here one day," Kian said.

"How many more will you stay?" I asked, then scrambled to soften my blunt words by adding: "It would be such a shame if we had to say goodbye to you too soon."

"Yes, I can see that the very thought of it is breaking your heart, Lady Maeve." Was that a *wink* he gave me? "I'm sorry to say that I'll be going home within a day or two, as soon as I've taken care of the business that brings me here. On the other hand, I look forward to telling my men about the wondrous thing I've discovered here, a hawk that hunts like a hound!" He made a grand gesture at Ea with both hands.

She's a falcon, *you . . . you turnip head!* I thought, insulted on Ea's behalf.

"That's what we spoke about last night," Kian said. He didn't look as if he'd relished that conversation. "Father told Lord Conchobar about my bird and insisted I show her to our guest."

"Well, Lady Maeve and I will leave you two to that," Lady Moriath said. "We can have our embroidery lesson elsewhere today."

"No, no, please stay with us!" Conchobar grabbed the elderly woman's hands and gazed at her with all the charm he could muster. "Lord Kian was just about to tell me how he came to train this lovely hawk."

Hawk again? I couldn't stand it.

"She's not a hawk, she's a falcon," I said. "Don't you know the difference?"

"Apparently not." Conchobar sounded amused. "But I'm sure you'll tell me now, and why it matters."

"Ignorance always matters, especially when you act like it's something to be proud of," I said fiercely. "Falcons are smaller and faster. They use their beaks more than their talons to make their kills, and . . . and . . ." As I spoke, I remembered Odran teaching me the very facts I now repeated. I saw his gentle face so vividly before my eyes that all of my resentment of Conchobar's provoking ways faded into memories of how sweet it was to kiss him and hear him—and hear him—

To my horror, I realized that I couldn't hear him anymore. I could see his lips moving, whispering endearments, but I could no longer recapture his voice. I fell silent.

Conchobar didn't notice. "If you say so, milady, but hawk, falcon, owl, or eagle, I never heard of any man able to command a bird to come willingly to his hand. How did you do it, Lord Kian?"

"Food. There's nothing simpler," Kian replied. "I fed her while she was healing. After her wing mended, I tied a leash to her leg and let her fly short distances, but always brought her back to my wrist with more food. Now she looks at me and thinks, 'What's for dinner?' It's not like a dog's loyalty, but as long as it works, who cares?"

"Why did she need to be healed?" Conchobar's interest

became fascination. "Did you shoot her out of the sky and change your mind once she struck the ground?" He laughed as if he'd made a wonderful joke.

Kian scowled murderously. He cared about Ea and plainly didn't like being accused of harming her, even if that accusation came from Conchobar's clumsy attempt at humor. With his fists clenched, he told his unwelcome guest the tale I already knew: "I was hunting far from Dún Beithe when I found this fine bird wounded on the road, her wing broken. I could have ridden on, but she had such a courageous gaze and so much fire in her eyes that I couldn't bring myself to leave her there to die. I had to try helping her. Someone like you would call me foolish for that."

"Not foolish, Lord Kian; admirable," I spoke up again, giving Conchobar a look that defied him to say otherwise.

My support drew off some of the tension thrumming through Kian's body. He relaxed enough to chuckle and remark, "That's not what Father said at first, but he came around."

"To heal a hawk—! I mean, a falcon." Conchobar's lame bid to ingratiate himself with me missed the mark. "Lady Maeve is right: that *is* admirable. Where did you learn that skill?" He addressed Kian with admiration so sincere that my friend couldn't help but be charmed and flattered.

"I can't claim credit for what's not mine," Kian said modestly. "This bird owes her life to Bryg."

Lady Moriath's hand flew to her mouth, stifling a small cry of pity. "That poor, lost child."

"Why?" I asked. "What happened to her?" Lady Moriath's reaction sent an irrational chill skittering across my skin.

"Never mind." The older woman turned brisk with me. "I

am supposed to be teaching you needlework, not letting you waste time in idle chatter. Lord Kian, Lord Conchobar, I look forward to seeing you at dinner." She walked out and I had to follow.

I finished embroidering my falcon that day and turned the cloth into a belt pouch the following morning, but I didn't give it to Kian.

"For me?" Lady Moriath held my gift gingerly, as if afraid the stitched bird's beak would bite her. I'd presented it to her after breakfast. Her expression wavered between pleasure and confusion. "You said you were making this for Lord Kian."

"Wasn't that the best way to surprise you?" I smiled. "With your help and patience, I've mastered the needle. This is my thanks." I unpinned a silver brooch from my gown and pinned it to hers. "This too."

She grew teary. "Now you have no more need of me."

I embraced her, pressing my cheek to hers. "We both know that's not true."

"What's not true, Lady Maeve?" Conchobar appeared out of nowhere. It amazed me how such a tall, brawny young man could move so stealthily. I didn't like it.

"If it were any of your business, my lord, I'd tell you," I said.

Lady Moriath sucked in her breath sharply. "Oh! Lady Maeve, that is *not* the way to speak to a guest."

"You're right, milady, it's not." Conchobar's fiery brows met and he glared at me darkly. "I think I've been insulted. If you were a man, I'd fight you for that, as your father once fought mine. But you're no warrior; you're only a loose-tongued girl, so perhaps I'd better have a word with the one who failed to teach you courtesy." He turned to Lady Moriath. "Where can I find Lady Lassaire at this time of day?"

"She . . . she . . . I think she's gone ahead to the dye vat to . . . to see that the fire's been kindled. She wants the girls to learn how to color wool before . . . before—"

The older woman was thrown into a terrified flutter by Conchobar's temper. I wanted to step between them and shield her, but before I could say or do anything, he seized my wrist. "This one's going to get a different lesson," he decreed, and tried hauling me out of the great house.

I pulled back, struggling to free myself from his grip. "How dare you?" I cried, digging my heels into the dirt. "Let me go! If you want me to come with you, *ask*. I'm not a beast to be pulled along!"

"No, you're a sweet little barrel of honey," he said, and scooped me off my feet, slung me over his shoulder, and carried me away.

His audacity left me too breathless to protest. I wasn't the only one stunned by Conchobar's daring and insolence. Not a single one of Lord Artegal's household who saw that horrible boy making off with me said a word, though I had no doubt they'd find their tongues soon enough to send rumors flying.

Conchobar's long legs swiftly took us from the great house to a quiet part of the fortress, the woodpile that fed Dún Beithe's hearth. By the time I'd recovered myself enough to try fighting my captor, he'd set me back on my feet.

"Let's make this quick," he said.

The sling was out of my belt pouch almost before he finished speaking. "Yes, let's," I said, swinging it slowly back and forth, poised to whirl it and strike.

Conchobar goggled at me and stepped back, hands raised. "Where did a girl like you get that?"

"Again, my lord, if that were something that *truly* concerned you—"

"Is this the way you always greet a messenger?"

"Messenger?" What was he talking about? I wanted to know more but refused to let down my guard. The loaded sling stayed ready and my unblinking eyes remained locked on his.

"Yes, and the sooner I'm done with this thankless role, the sooner I can go back to Emain Macha and girls who know the *right* way to behave. I used to hate your father for killing mine, but after meeting you, I've got nothing but pity for poor old Eochu Feidlech. At least he has *one* decently raised daughter! Tell me, do the rest of your sisters take after you or Lady Derbriu?"

The sling dropped to my side. "What do you know about Derbriu?" I demanded.

"She's the reason I'm here. That sweet lady married one of my best men and filled his household with so many fine sons that I'm afraid he's raising a war band against me!"

He was laughing; I was not. Out of my five sisters, Derbriu was the one closest to my age and my heart. She'd been sent into fosterage among Conchobar's people, the Ulaidh, though it broke both our hearts to be separated. I still missed her and often pined for some word from her, but none ever came.

Now this, a message sent in the mouth of Emain Macha's brash young king? I couldn't tell whether to dread or hope for what it might be.

Conchobar noticed my troubled look. His aggravating grin shriveled like a feather held in a flame. "Don't worry,

Lady Maeve, I bring good news for you. Your sister is alive and well, thriving and happy. She has yet another baby on the way and asked me to tell you she longs for a girl this time, since she's always wanted to give you a namesake. She misses you and wishes she could have gone back to Cruachan at least once in all these years, but leaving fosterage might've insulted the household that took her in. She might've done it after she married, but the children—! One after the other, like hiccups. The first one arrived before her husband finished asking, 'Will you be my wife?' and I swear the infant looked up at him and answered, 'She will!'"

"And of *course* you were there to see it." I had to smile.

"Who'd be a better witness than one who never exaggerates?" Conchobar said, doing a fine job of looking innocent. "You should give me that nasty thing as a gift for your sister." He indicated the sling now dangling from my hand. "She needs *some* way to hold off that husband of hers, if only for a year."

"Lord Conchobar, I'm grateful to hear about Derbriu, but why didn't you tell me this sooner, and without so much"—I gestured at our isolated surroundings—"fuss?"

"If I'd known you were Lady Derbriu's sister when we first met on the road here, I'd have told you then," he said. "That is, if your watchdog Kian would've let me. I've met more than one girl named Maeve, you know. By the time I knew you were the one I was after, we were inside the ringfort walls with all of Lord Artegal's household. I thought you might want to receive her message without needing to share it with the eyes, ears, and tongues of Dún Beithe."

"Yes, but the news you've brought me about her isn't

shameful and it's only brought me joy. Why would I want to conceal it?"

His shoulders rose and fell slightly. "Not conceal, savor! Keep it to yourself for a little while before you have to share it. That's what *I* like to do."

I was so elated by what he'd told me that I didn't bother replying, *"Yes, but* I *am not* you." He'd meant well. Perhaps Conchobar wasn't the most irritating boy I'd ever met after all. I regretted having judged him too harshly and put away my sling.

"Maybe next time you have a message for me, you could find a subtler way to take me aside and deliver it," I said with a warm smile.

"Next time?"

"I want to send word back to Derbriu and I hope she'll have more to say to me. When her baby's born—"

"What do I look like, a *sliotar* ball to be knocked back and forth between you?" he protested. "I'm lord of the Ulaidh! I have more important things to do. Find your own messenger, Lady Maeve." A slow, insinuating grin crept across his lips. "Or find a way to reward this one. Make it worth my while to ride between Emain Macha and Dún Beithe as often as you command."

So much for having misjudged Conchobar.

"I wouldn't dream of doing anything to take the great lord of Emain Macha away from his responsibilities," I said demurely. "I'll do as you suggest and find someone else to carry my words to my sister and hers to me."

"Oh." Conchobar's whole body sagged. "You know, I

might've spoken too quickly. I wouldn't mind doing that for you if I ever happen to ride here some other—"

"No, thank you. I'd hate to be in your debt, especially since I'd never repay it to your satisfaction." I spoke as sweetly as I knew how, on purpose.

"Lady Maeve, forget what I said about making it worth my while," he pleaded. "I don't want to leave you thinking ill of me when I leave Dún Beithe. I can't promise to come here as often as I'd like, but once the winter's gone, after the great Beltane gathering at Tara, I'll be free to keep your ties with Lady Derbriu as tight as you please!"

I considered turning him down again, even though I had every intention of accepting his offer. Then I thought, *Why would I do such a mean-spirited thing, teasing him just to see him squirm? Even if I've got the power to keep him dancing to my tune, I don't need to prove it.*

"Thank you, Lord Conchobar," I said. "I'd appreciate that."

"Milady, leave *Lord* Conchobar at Emain Macha to rule the Ulaidh." His high spirits were back as fully as though he'd never known a moment's disappointment. "When I come here, I'm only Conchobar the willing messenger."

I laughed. "And I'm Maeve to you from now on, though Lady Lassaire might not like it. She's very strict about respecting status."

"I know someone else who won't like it." The rascal flashed his teeth. "But Lord Kian can console himself by teaching that bird of his some new tricks."

"Kian's my friend. Nothing between you and me will change that," I told him.

"Maybe not yet," he murmured, but when I asked him to

repeat it, he pretended he hadn't spoken at all. I chose to let it pass.

"I should join the other girls," I said. "I'm sure the rumors about you and me are already kindled, but I don't want to give them any more fuel."

Conchobar pulled himself up to his full, imposing height. "I will swear that I dropped you as soon as we were out of the great house and that I went straight to look after my horse. We were never together and for all I know, you scampered away to avoid your lessons. If anyone dares to contradict that, I'll strip off his skin and weave it into a belt!"

I shook my head. "I won't let you tell lies for my sake. A king's word must be trustworthy." *Unlike yours, Father,* I thought sadly. "If I can't depend on you to tell the truth, I don't want you for my messenger."

"I only want to protect you, Maeve." I'd never seen such deep sincerity in those wondrously green eyes. I felt drawn closer to him, and I didn't know whether to fall or flee.

Why do I feel like this? It isn't right. He's not Odran! I sprang back from the perilous brink by throwing a jest as if it were a slingstone.

"Who says I need anyone's protection? I can skin my own enemies, though I'd rather wear their finger bones strung together for a bracelet." I twirled the forefinger of one hand around my other wrist and laughed to break the spell he'd cast over me. "But I do need you to keep me in touch with my sister. I wish one of us had thought to do this long ago. I've lost too many years with no word from her at all."

"What are you talking about?" Conchobar asked. "From the first year of their marriage, Lady Derbriu's husband always told the High King how she was faring whenever the lords of Èriu met at Tara. I was there often enough to see it for myself, and to hear old Eochu send back his own news."

"Is that . . . is that true?" I felt a sour burning in my stomach. "He never said a word about her at home."

"Are you certain? I overheard him give her husband special messages from Lady Cloithfinn, mother to daughter, about raising her little ones."

"They never told me." I spoke like someone newly wakened in a strange, disturbing world. "She was my favorite sister and they left me with no news of her. I knew she wasn't dead—they'd have to tell me that—but for all I knew, she'd been stolen away by the Fair Folk to the Otherworld. Not one word. . . . Why?"

Conchobar fell silent, but it wasn't for lack of something to say. He had the guilty, guarded look of someone holding on to a secret.

"What is it, Conchobar?" I asked quietly.

"I don't know what you mean." He faced me boldly, but failed to hold my gaze for more than two breaths together. "You should go. Lady Lassaire will be asking questions. You don't want to be found here with me."

"If it happens, I'll take the consequences, but I won't move from this spot until you tell me everything. Why didn't my parents share the news they had about Derbriu, not even once?"

"I don't know."

"Is that another lie to protect me?" I clutched his forearm. "Or are you protecting yourself?"

He jerked out of my grasp. "How can I tell you anything I know about this? You won't believe me. You'll say I'm making up stories to turn you against your father because I hate him for killing mine, and then . . . and then you'll hate me."

I reached for him again, taking both of his hands in my own. "You wouldn't do that, Conchobar; you couldn't. You're a king and a warrior. You don't fight a coward's battle, twisting the truth until it breaks. Now tell me." I squeezed his hands gently. "Please."

He surrendered. "It was your father's will. I was there the first time Lady Derbriu's husband came before the High King, and I heard one of his attendants—his chariot driver, I think it was—say, 'Our sweet princess Derbriu, a mother! I can't wait to see how happy this will make Lady Cloithfinn and Maeve.'" Conchobar's normally smiling mouth was a thin, hard line. "Your father turned on him and thundered that no one was to speak of Derbriu when they returned to Cruachan. He said that she was still his daughter and it was his news to share or keep. If he caught the slightest hint that he'd been disobeyed, there'd be one less tongue to drink his mead and eat his bread."

He said that to Fechin? *The man he trusts with his life when they go into battle?* I was incredulous, though I kept my disbelief to myself. I didn't want Conchobar thinking I doubted his words.

"And . . . and no one challenged. . . ." Who'd dare to challenge Father? "I mean, no one questioned his command?"

"That fellow, his chariot driver, stood up to him," Conchobar said. "He told the High King that after his years of loyalty, he at least deserved to hear a reason. I won't forget how bravely he spoke, saying, 'You can take my head for this if you like, but that's the only way you'll take my right to speak freely.'"

"His name is Fechin," I said. "He's fearless enough to defy

Father, but he came home with his head still attached to his neck, so what could have happened?"

Conchobar finally withdrew his hands from mine. "I'm not the only one who wants to protect you, Maeve," he said. "The High King told Fechin that if you heard any news of Derbriu, you'd break your heart wanting to see her again, and if he allowed you to visit her, you'd never agree to come home again. He said, 'If I forbid her to go to Derbriu, she's too brave and headstrong to accept that. Will you be responsible for what happens to her if she runs away to seek her sister on her own? You know how much I need my girl, my beloved spark. I can't let her out of my sight. She'll be Connacht's lady someday, if I ever find a hero worthy enough to have her for his wife. If you love her and you're truly loyal to me, let her go on believing that Derbriu's too wrapped up in her new life to spare a thought for her little sister.'"

I stared into the past, hearing Father's voice as clearly as if I'd been standing beside Fechin, or in Conchobar's shadow. "So that's what he did," I said under my breath. "That must have been how he kept Mother silent too. Wherever his threats wouldn't work, he used love."

"You don't seem surprised," said Conchobar, who did.

"I know my father."

Conchobar left Dún Beithe two days later, on a morning so bright and cloudless that every golden leaf of the birch trees stood out as sharply edged as a knife. He rode away bearing my message for Derbriu, words that held nothing but love and my hopes that her coming childbirth would go well.

I didn't say anything about all the years her messages to

Cruachan had been kept from me. What good would it do to pain her with the knowledge of Father's selfish manipulation, done in the name of "protecting" me?

It was only after Conchobar was gone that I realized I was doing the same thing, protecting Derbriu by not telling her the whole truth. I was my father's daughter after all.

CHAPTER NINE

Children of Bards and Kings

"I'M GLAD HE'S gone." Kian stood by Ea's perch, whipping bits of meat into the falcon's eager beak as if flinging rocks at an enemy. "If I never have to see that conceited, pushy, obnoxious lump of dung again, I'll give half my cattle to the first person who asks!"

"Lucky for you that you'll have to see him at Tara, when Beltane comes," I said with a wry smile. "If your father heard you make such a stupid oath, he'd take the entire herd away from you. Fools and cattle don't stay together long."

Kian didn't care for my jest. "If you think I'm a fool for despising your sweetheart, I'll live with that."

I rolled my eyes. "How many times must I say it? He is *not* my sweetheart." I saw Kian's mouth open, ready to repeat the words he'd already voiced far too many times since Conchobar's departure. My hand flashed up, preventing him. "And don't you *dare* say, 'Does that mean you two are betrothed now?' It wasn't funny the first time."

"It wasn't supposed to be," he grouched.

"It also isn't true."

"That's what my mother said. She doesn't like Conchobar either."

"Then she's the only other female under your father's roof who feels that way."

It was too true. Just that morning I'd had to dampen a fiery quarrel that sparked among my friends as we all sat carding wool by the hearthside. Since the task was simple, Lady Lassaire left us to do it alone. Though the moon had showed all her faces twice since Conchobar's departure, he was still my friends' favorite topic of conversation. Even Ula, distant and elegant, giggled worse than Dairine when she recounted how the young king of the Ulaidh had lavished her with compliments.

"Don't think you're special. He said gallant things to *every* girl," Dairine sniped.

"Yes, even to you," Ula replied with smooth malice.

Gormlaith made the mistake of tittering, which turned her into Dairine's new target. "Even to *her*," she said, stabbing a finger at the blond girl. "Isn't it wonderful to find a warrior who knows how to feel pity?"

For once Gormlaith didn't shrink from the duel. "Just as wonderful as finding one who doesn't mind getting on the same tired horse every man's been riding," she said.

"Can we *please* talk about something else?" I protested, seeing Dairine's hands tighten on her carding combs. I didn't think she was going to throw them at Gormlaith, but I couldn't be sure.

"Oh, all right, Maeve," Ula said wearily. "If we're upsetting you that much, we'll stop, but I wish you wouldn't take these things so seriously. It's childish."

"Don't say that about Maeve." Dairine set aside her combs and put one arm around me. "I think it's sweet, how much she cares about us. We're lucky to have her."

"Yes, we are." Gormlaith followed Dairine's lead and moved in to hug me from the other side. "I hope we'll always be together."

"Even after she becomes Lord Conchobar's bride?" Ula remarked, slipping a needle into her words.

"Oh, I doubt one woman would be enough for *that* boy," I said casually. "He'll have to take all four of us or none." The idea of such a marriage made my friends laugh until they gasped for breath and took our conversation elsewhere.

It was too bad that I couldn't distract Kian so easily. I did try. Unfortunately, he had an awful talent for bringing every topic back to how deeply he loathed Conchobar.

There are times when the only way to put out a fire is to set a bigger blaze.

"Why do you envy Conchobar so much?" I asked. "Do you think he's that much better than you?"

"What? Better than—?" Kian sputtered with confusion. "When did I—?"

"You wouldn't try tearing him down so thoroughly and so constantly if you didn't see him as a threat. Do you think he's going to lead a cattle raid against your father when the summer comes? Are you afraid you won't be able to fight to keep him from taking what's yours? I hope you're not jealous of him because he's your age and already a king in his own right. Remember the price he had to pay for that."

"Maeve, you don't understand." Kian looked miserable. "I don't fear or envy him, except for how you—"

I was so intent on cooling Kian's anger against Conchobar that I wasn't really listening to him. "Well, you shouldn't." I sweetened my tone. "If anything, he should envy you. You're his equal by birth, by the battle scar you bear, and someday—may my words not ill-wish your father—you'll be as great a king as he. But there is one way you outdo him." I touched Ea's perch. "Any man can kill, but you can heal."

"Oh. Is that all?" Kian was downcast. "That's the only reason he should envy me?"

"It's not enough?"

"I was hoping—" He took a breath and sighed. "Never mind. I know you want me to feel better, but you've picked the wrong cure. If Conchobar ever *would* envy someone for saving this pretty bird, it should be Bryg."

"Did she really do that much?" I asked, struggling to salvage my mistake. "You're the one who brought this kestrel here safely."

He gave me a wistful look. "It's all right, Maeve; you don't have to scrape up ways to flatter me. If you'd been here at Dún Beithe when it happened, you'd agree that I did next to nothing. It happened back before Bryg went mad with grief and had to leave us."

"Mad?" The word crept over me with dread and pity.

"It was a great tragedy. She was a sweet girl, a bard's daughter, but she had a druid's gift for healing. I'm just glad she believed in what I wanted to do, otherwise I'd have bungled the luckless bird to death. That girl knew what was needed, and when she didn't know, she asked Master Cairpre or the man who tends our hunting hounds when they're sick or hurt. I wish she were here to see how well this fine lady's thriving now, thanks to her." He gave Ea an affectionate glance.

"I wish she were here too," I said. "Couldn't Master Cairpre help her when she . . . when she fell ill?" I didn't know how to speak of Bryg's affliction. I didn't want to say anything that would make it seem I was shunning her for it. I was in a strange land and had no idea of how to go on.

I'd heard of people who'd become possessed by the spirits of madness, how they shrieked or shut themselves up in a ring-fort of their own silence forever. Some had suffered the mind-shattering loss of a lover, a child, or a friend so dear it was like tearing away a piece of your own flesh. Some were cursed by the Fair Folk and some were possessed by the spirits of wild beasts. Still, all of these were only stories brought to Cruachan by our wandering bard. Even Devnet admitted he'd never met a mad-man face to face, though a friend of a brother of the fellow bard who told him one of the tales swore it was true.

Kian frowned. "Master Cairpre never had the chance to try healing her. It happened close to Samhain, about two years ago. Bryg's father, Fintan, came to visit."

"He did?" I was surprised. Once you were placed in fos-terage, you seldom saw your birth family until after you left to establish a home of your own. "Did some accident happen while he was here? Is that why she grieved herself sick?"

"Not because of him, Lady Maeve, but because of what he told her: her brother was dead. Bryg loved that lad, even though he was older and they'd been separated so long. He'd died some years before, but Fintan wouldn't let her hear such tragic news from the mouth of a messenger." Kian sighed. "I think he stayed away from Dún Beithe longer than he honestly had to, because he wanted to put off such a horrible duty."

"But he did tell her," I said in a low voice, picturing the awful moment: Fintan saying, *I have to tell you about your brother;* Bryg beaming, expecting his next words to be, *He has a wife, he has a child, his courage has earned him rich rewards and honor from the lord he serves, and he sends you his love;* but instead of that, hearing her father say, *He's dead.*

Kian nodded. "I was away from home when it happened, helping thin our herds for the coming winter. By the time I returned, days later, she was gone. Master Cairpre told me that she'd wailed like a wild creature of the Otherworld and fought off his attempts to give her a sleeping potion. It took two strong men to hold her and a third to make her swallow it. When it took effect, Master Cairpre counseled Fintan to bring his daughter to Avallach. It's home to druids, but to healers too. Their only study is how to restore health to a person's body, so I don't know if they've helped Bryg. She may still be there, but no word's reached us since she left."

Avallach. My pulse became stronger at the name. That eastern isle was a place of great learning, a training ground for those who chose the druids' hard road, but for Odran it was a place of exile. *I wonder if they've taught him more healing skills than he already knows,* I thought. *How marvelous if he were the one to restore Bryg's health, after everything she did for Ea!*

"No news doesn't mean there's no hope," I said. "Perhaps you're not meant to hear anything about Bryg's health until she's fully cured."

"That's comforting to believe." Kian managed a faint smile.

"I'll make an offering to Airmid and ask for her help," I

said, speaking of the goddess whose tears caused every healing herb in existence to sprout from her brother's grave. "She'll guide the healers of Avallach to the right remedy. Bryg will be well again; you'll see!"

"And when that prediction comes true, I'll make an offering to whichever god gave you the gift of happy prophecy." It was good to hear my friend's laughter.

Winter seemed to make Dún Beithe a smaller place. The cold and dreary days wove a spell that turned the ringfort walls into a giant's hands that cupped themselves for warmth ever tighter around a tiny flame. Lord Artegal's men didn't have enough to occupy their time, so quarrels and outright fights were frequent, especially among the younger warriors.

Dairine loved that. A fresh squabble meant fresh entertainment for her, and she wasn't above provoking clashes where there'd been none. She wasn't the only one to blame: boredom changed our fighters into would-be lovers. They flirted with anything in a dress. We fosterlings and the other highborn women who lacked husbands could allow their advances or refuse them with a single word. Maidservants weren't so lucky. If they had no interest in the men pursuing them, they needed to take every precaution not to be caught alone. Most of Lord Artegal's warriors were honorable enough to take no for an answer. The rest just *took*.

Dún Beithe's three female slaves had the worst of it. One was only a child, the little girl I'd glimpsed several times since my first day in the great house. She was spared the humiliation the other two suffered whenever a man wanted conquest without challenge. Still, she was old enough to see what was happening and to understand that this was the fate awaiting her someday. That winter killed her smile.

I couldn't stand to see how dejected she looked, or the grim mouths and lifeless eyes of her fellow slaves.

I'm glad we never had slaves at Cruachan, though it was only by chance, I thought. *But we never had our warriors pass the winter with nothing to do but look for trouble either. Father didn't allow that.* I felt a trace of the admiration I'd once had for him. *Why doesn't Lord Artegal do something about this? Does he care? Does he even notice, or are slaves and servants invisible to him until he has work for them to do?*

They weren't invisible to me. If they were afraid to speak, I decided to become their voice before Lord Artegal. Realistically I didn't expect the same success I'd had at home when my tactics brought freedom to the enslaved, abused brother and sister owned by one of my "suitors." All I hoped for was to make him *listen,* not only with his ears but with his heart.

I wish I knew him better, I thought. It would help me choose the best way to approach him about this. *If Lady Íde were here, she could tell me if I should speak bluntly to her cousin or coax him along. Maybe Lady Lassaire would help. He* is *her husband; she must know how to sway him.*

I discarded that idea at once. I'd been under Lady Lassaire's care long enough to know that Dún Beithe's mistress didn't like facing problems. The only thing she liked less was someone who forced her to admit that a problem existed. She was like a little child who made monsters vanish by closing her eyes.

There was still one person who could help me.

The unexpected gift of a sunny winter day sent all of Dún Beithe out into the crisp fresh air. Lady Lassaire stayed in her sleeping chamber with a bellyache, setting us fosterlings free. I pounced on the opportunity and went hunting for Kian.

I found him and his best friend, Connla, sharpening their swords and spearheads around the side of the great house where the sun shone strongest. Greeting them briefly, I plunged straight to my question: "Kian, if I wanted to ask your father something, how should I talk to him?"

"How?" My friend looked up from his task and exchanged a mystified glance with Connla. "Just . . . *talk* to him, that's all."

"You don't understand. This is important. He has to take me seriously."

"What's it about?"

Before I could reply, Connla stood up and said, "If I give this blade one more stroke of the whetstone, it'll shatter. See you later, Kian." He gathered up his gear and left us.

"I didn't know Connla was so tactful," I said. "I should thank him later for letting me talk to you privately."

"He did it for me, not you," Kian told me, setting aside his own blade-sharpening equipment. "He thinks we're more than friends."

"You never told him the way things actually are?"

"I don't want him feeling sorry for me. He's got a sweetheart of his own, though the two of them are keeping it a secret. Now tell me, what do you want to tell my father that's so important it must be planned out like a cattle raid?"

He listened patiently to my concerns about the slaves, but when I was done he said, "There's no way you can accomplish that, Maeve. Father needs to pacify his men more than he wants to worry about the welfare of his slaves. Approach him any way you like; the results will be the same."

Is your father a chief or not? I thought. *Why is he so scared of his own warriors?* I kept such sharp questions to myself. Kian wasn't responsible for his father's failings. He might dislike them as much as I did, but he'd feel bound by family loyalty to defend Lord Artegal. I didn't want to risk losing a friend.

That was why I smiled at him and said, "At least now I'm free to ask him about this any way I please."

"I wish I could be more help, Maeve. I don't enjoy letting you down. I guess . . ." He hesitated. "I guess you could try charming him."

"You're suggesting I *flirt* with Lord Artegal?"

"Gods, no! Not like that. I mean, he's never had a daughter, so you could try whatever worked when you wanted *your* father to do things your way."

My mouth turned down. "My father never gave me what I wanted unless he wanted it too. His way was the only way."

"Is that so?" Kian didn't sound ready to believe me. "But whenever we had news here about the High King's household, they said you were Lord Eochu's favorite daughter, the one he loved the most, and that there wasn't anything he could refuse you."

Nothing but my freedom, I thought. *Even if it turned out to be the freedom to fall. Nothing must harm the High King's property!*

"My father is a cunning man, Kian," I said. "He knows how to wear two faces when it suits him. The one he loves the most is himself!"

A trickling brook fed by all the little streams along its course will swell into a river rushing wildly on, drowning everything in its path. As I spoke about the man who'd once been my hero—strong, noble, perfect—my words were fed by thoughts of how he had deceived me. I couldn't stop myself. I poured out all the pain of how I'd seen my shining image of him chipped away by broken promises, falsehoods, and finally by a betrayal that cost an innocent man his life. I told Lord Artegal's son the full story of my lost friend, Kelan. I spoke of his sweet nature, good humor, and courage, of how he saved me from a wolf, of how he taught me to use a warrior's weapons, and of how those lessons let me repay my life-debt by defending his beloved Bláithín from a ferocious wolfhound. I left out nothing, not even how Father contrived to keep his own hands clean of that kind young man's death.

When I was done, Kian could only stare. It took him a while before he could speak, and then all he could do was shake his head slowly and say, "Oh, Maeve . . ."

"You think I'm terrible for speaking about my own father like this, don't you?"

He didn't answer that, but only said, "Do you know you're crying?"

I laid one palm to my cheek. It was drenched with tears. I swallowed a sob, aware that we were out in the open. One of the ringfort's other residents could happen upon us at any moment.

"I love him, Kian." I kept my voice pitched low. "He's my father; he'd give his life for me. Once when I was younger, he came home so badly wounded that his life was in danger. If he'd died, it would have been the end of the world for me. He's been a wall to hold me up and a shield to keep me safe, but he never understood that I have to be my own wall and shield. Even after all the wrongs he's done, I still love him. If anything makes me a terrible person, it's that."

Kian stood, sheathed his sword, stowed the whetstone in his belt pouch, and gathered up the three spearheads he'd been sharpening. "A terrible person wouldn't care about servants and slaves. We'll make my father see things your way together."

"Some people don't know how to mind their own business," Dairine muttered as we sat braiding our hair before going to sleep that night. "They're *slaves*, Maeve! They expect to be treated differently."

"Yes, they can hardly wait to be used for worse than animals," I said with a twist of my lips. "They look forward to it. Honestly, Dairine, why does it matter to you if Lord Artegal told his men to leave those poor women alone?"

"I wonder that myself," Ula said in her superior way. "You should thank Maeve for her meddling. It means you'll find more fish waiting when you cast your line."

"Says the girl who never got a single nibble," Dairine responded.

Ula maintained her eternal poise. "We'll see who marries first."

"Don't be so sure of yourself, Ula," Dairine said. "Your oh-so-high birth might get you a husband, but he'll be some greedy, ambitious creature who'd marry a badger if it came to him with enough gold. You'll mean nothing to him but a shrewd bargain."

"Bargains go both ways," Ula said, unfazed by Dairine's spite. "I know I'm worth more than one night's diversion. My husband won't come to me just because he can't find something better to do."

Dairine threw a shoe at her. "At least I *like* men," she snapped. "I care about their feelings. Our warriors serve Lord Artegal faithfully. He shouldn't take away their pleasure like this. It's made some of them unhappy."

"Oh the poor, suffering things," I said with no emotion in my words or face. "How will they ever survive the winter without women who haven't got the power to tell them no?"

"It isn't funny, Maeve." Dairine turned on me. "They're not happy and they know that you and Kian are responsible. You're making enemies."

"So, these 'faithful' warriors would attack their lord's son over *this*?"

"They don't blame *him*. They say he only interfered because you charmed him into it. Maeve, I'm really worried about you; you're my friend!"

"Me too," said Gormlaith, and Ula murmured her agreement.

Their support made me feel warm and secure, even if I thought they were dressing a mouse in a wolf's skin. "Then none of us needs to worry," I said affectionately. "As long as I have my friends, I can face my enemies."

CHAPTER TEN

Travelers on a Winter Road

ON A DAY made remarkable by snowfall, two travelers appeared on the road to Dún Beithe. My friends and I saw them coming at almost the same time as the sentry atop the ringfort wall. We were at the foot of the stronghold's mound, tasting the falling flakes and flinging handfuls of sparkling whiteness at each other, shrieking whenever a wet, icy lump slid up our sleeves, down our necks, or into our shoes.

We'd been at these games since the earliest, darkest part of the morning. We wrapped ourselves in our thick wool cloaks and ran out of the great house the instant we overheard the servants remarking about the weather. If they were telling the truth, we had to see the miracle before it melted. We girls couldn't treat such a rare event like any ordinary day, so we drowned out the rumbling of our bellies with cries of delight as we romped through the whiteness.

Gormlaith was the first to spy the travelers. "Someone's coming!" she cried, pointing down the road an instant before

Dairine pitched a fistful of snow into her mouth. While she coughed and spit it out, we turned our eyes in the direction she'd indicated and saw two dark shapes approaching. Like us, they were swathed in heavy cloaks. The taller of the two walked with a short wooden staff and looked oddly misshapen. The other came a few steps behind.

By now, the watchman on the ramparts was sounding the alert. A band of young men came pounding down the slope, Kian and Connla in the lead. They raced past us, though Connla dropped back. With every other eye on the travelers, I was the only one who noticed that he paused long enough to ask a still-coughing Gormlaith if she was all right. The smile she gave him wasn't the shy, humble one I knew. She beamed at him with gratitude, but also with something more. He patted her on the back and sped off to rejoin his companions. The incident I'd just witnessed was over in less than three breaths, but it told me a tale worthy of the most eloquent bard.

So she's *Connla's mysterious sweetheart!* I was happy for her.

She looked my way, saw the expression on my face, and realized I'd spied out her secret. The poor girl turned whiter than the snow. Her eyes begged me not to speak.

I shook my head and laid a finger to my lips, smiling. I would not betray her, even if she never gave me any sign to let her secret stay untold. The thought of how Dairine and Ula would tease her about it was enough to tie my tongue forever.

By this time Kian and our warriors had reached the travelers and surrounded them. We girls went after them, eager to discover who the wanderers might be. Why would anyone journey at this time of year, and on foot? We held our dresses high as we ran. Long-legged Ula outdistanced the rest of us easily and was soon shouldering her way between the men to catch a glimpse of the strangers.

Her cry of surprise and joy rang through the frosty air: "Bryg! Oh, Bryg, is it you?" I reached the crowd in time to see her throw her arms around the smaller figure, a sallow, thin-faced girl, and envelop her in a hug. Our proud, self-possessed Ula was a wild muddle of laughter, tears, squeals, and gasps of amazement.

"Bryg! Bryg!" Dairine shoved aside everyone in her path until she, too, was embracing the girl. Gormlaith hung back, pleased but hesitant, and I kept my distance, not wanting to interrupt such a festive reunion.

Meanwhile, Kian was speaking to the other traveler, a man whose dark-brown hair was shot through with streaks of white and gray. His blue eyes were deeply set in nests of wrinkles, like an old man's, and they held a great weariness. Nothing else about him spoke of age. There was a strange, irregular lump on his back, under the woolen cloak. If it was some deformity, it didn't prevent him from standing straight and tall.

He noticed me staring at him and smiled. "I don't remember this pretty face, Kian," he said. "What other changes have come to Dún Beithe since our departure?" His voice lilted beautifully, like Devnet's. Even if I hadn't known that Bryg was the daughter of a bard, I would have guessed his calling.

"Master Fintan, it's my pleasure to introduce Lady Maeve of Connacht, daughter of Lord Eochu Feidlech, the son of Finn and High King of Èriu." Kian spoke formally, which meant he behaved as though he'd been carved of stone and given a mouth that could only utter words like blocks of wood. His fellow warriors hooted at him mercilessly for that until he blushed crimson with embarrassment and knocked down the ones standing closest. When they got up they struck back, until it looked as if the travelers' welcome was going to turn into a brawl.

Fintan's laugh held even more music than his speech. "I see that the spell condemning all of you lads to perpetual childhood hasn't been lifted yet! At least that's still the same. When you die, I'll see to it that you're buried with your favorite toys and a scrap of your mother's skirts to clutch for comfort." He spoke with good humor, but that didn't change the bard's sharp gift for satire. Kian's comrades looked abashed and my friend apologized for his show of temper.

"Please, there's no need for that." Fintan raised the hand not holding his walking staff and smiled with such benevolence that you'd never know a barbed tongue lurked behind those lips. "My darling Bryg and I have come a long way. We'd rather have something hot in our stomachs than ten thousand apologies in our ears."

He didn't have to wait long to receive the hospitality he desired. By the time we all trooped back through the ringfort gate, Lord Artegal was on the threshold of the great house, poised to greet his guests. From behind him came Lady Lassaire's imperious voice, loudly giving commands to the cook and the rest of the servants. Our simple everyday breakfast fare was magically transformed into a miniature feast, which she offered to the bard as soon as he entered her home.

Fintan cast his cloak aside and took the place of honor beside Lord Artegal. The odd shape I'd seen bulging on his back turned out to be a fine harp. I felt silly for not having guessed that as soon as I learned Fintan's identity. The bard placed his cherished instrument tenderly at his feet, glowering at any servant who ventured too close and risked bumping it.

Meanwhile, Bryg seated herself at Kian's right. Ula and Dairine both lunged to claim the place at her other side, with Ula ending up the winner. Dairine tried to act as though it didn't matter, but the dark looks she continually jabbed at Ula told a different tale. Gormlaith wasn't as keen to be near Bryg. She showed not a moment's regret as she sat down with me, all the way across the central hearth from the three of them.

"What a nice surprise," I remarked as we ate. "Did you ever expect to see your friend again?"

Gormlaith kept eating.

"I guess you weren't as close to her as Ula and Dairine," I went on. "Do you think she's back to stay? I heard that she was . . . that she fell ill and had to go to Avallach for healing. She looks rather frail and thin, but she's got a healthy laugh."

"She always looked that way," Gormlaith muttered. "No matter how much she ate, it all burned away. She hated that. Stupid bag of bones."

Was this Gormlaith, meek Gormlaith saying such a nasty thing about a girl who'd suffered so badly? I blinked in case I'd stumbled into a dream. I wanted to ask her why she felt that way about Bryg, but just then the girl herself was standing before us.

"Hello, Maeve," the bard's daughter said, holding out both hands to clasp mine. "I had to come over and meet you. Ula and Dairine haven't stopped telling me how happy they are to have you as a new friend. I wish I'd been here to welcome you when you first came to Dún Beithe, but I hope we can make up for lost time now that I'm back." She turned to Gormlaith and added: "I've missed you, dear one. I always loved our conversations. When it's time for dinner, I want both of you to sit with me. The others have had their turn." She laughed. "Oh no, just listen to me, speaking as if it's some sort of honor to keep me company! Maeve, please don't think ill of me. Once we get to know each other better, you'll see that I'm really not *that* conceited."

She was completely charming. I warmed to her at once. "I'd never think that," I told her. "Everything I've heard about you has been praise."

"If it came from these three"—she dropped my hands to indicate Gormlaith, Dairine, and Ula—"don't believe it without a *few* questions. Haven't you been here long enough to know that we fosterlings stick together?"

"They're not the only ones who've mentioned you. Lord Kian is in your debt for how you helped him save the wounded bird he found."

A faint tinge of color fleetingly rose and faded from Bryg's pinched cheeks. "He told you about that?"

I nodded. "The kestrel is alive and well, thanks to you. Kian knows it, and he'll never forget what you did for her."

"Her?" she repeated. "When we took care of the creature, I said we should name it together, but he insisted we should wait until we found out if it was male or female. How did he discover the truth?"

"I told him. I learned how to tell the difference from a good friend of mine when I still lived at home. He had your gift for healing animals." When I spoke of Odran, my voice became tender and fond in spite of myself.

Bryg noticed. A knowing look showed in her gray eyes. "It sounds as if your 'good friend' had a gift for more than that. I envy you, Maeve, though you must miss him dreadfully now."

"He and I weren't—" My false protest was cut off by a stir from the other side of the hearth.

Master Fintan was on his feet, harp in hand, about to sing. The entire household stilled, eagerly waiting. He struck the strings and gave us the tale of how King Nuada lost his arm in combat only to have Dian Cecht, god of healing, replace it with a miraculous limb made of silver. His words were so eloquent and persuasive that I could almost smell the bloodshed of battle and see the sparkle of sunlight on the king's new arm.

Fintan ended his song to roaring approval and set his harp down once more. Lord Artegal took off both of his gold bracelets and offered them to the bard, but was refused with a smile.

"If I take your generous gift, it means I've given you no gift of my own," he told the lord of Dún Beithe. "A wise king knows how to accept tribute as graciously as he gives it."

"Then take this as part of my welcome," Lord Artegal said, seizing the bard's hand and forcing one of the rich ornaments onto his wrist. "Come here, Bryg, my dear child!" he called out, waving the second bracelet overhead. "This one is yours."

"What a clever man you are, my lord," Fintan said lightly as Bryg hurried forward to claim her prize. "You make it impossible for me to turn down your gift without making my daughter give back hers as well. I'm too fond of peaceful living to get between a young woman and her pretty adornments." He heaved such an exaggerated sigh that no one could take it seriously. "Now we are so beholden to you that we must leave

Dún Beithe without telling you the reason we've come. Bryg, my treasure, fetch my cloak, put on your own, and pick up your belongings again. We'll be gone before noon."

Everyone present joined in the bard's jest, raising a storm of protest against his departure. Some of the ladies pretended to weep, others howled as if the sky were falling. Kian declared that he'd guard the great house doorway with sword and spear to prevent Fintan from leaving. A pair of young men lifted Bryg off her feet and seated her on their shoulders, shouting that she was their captive, not to be released until her father swore he'd stay at Dún Beithe after all. I never heard so much boisterous laughter in my life, and I took part in it willingly.

"Peace, peace!" Fintan's trained voice was enough to recapture our attention. He raised his hands in surrender. "My friends, how can I do anything but bow to your wishes? Bryg and I will stay"—he let a wave of loud cheers rise and subside— "with Lord Artegal's consent."

"I don't consent; I insist!" Kian's father boomed. "This is your home for as long as you can tolerate us. In fact, nothing would make me happier than to have you stay here always."

Fintan looked wistful. "It wounds my heart to hear what I can't accept. You know I've already bound myself to serve Lord Rus of Laigin. That is my home, though I've been gone from it for so long. When I return, they'll say I was kept prisoner by the People of the Mounds." One corner of his mouth lifted in a roguish smile. "I'd better weave a song about that."

"You must stay with us until spring comes, at least," Lady Lassaire said in her soft, wheedling way. "See how happy my girls are to have your daughter with them again!" She gestured to where Ula and Dairine were clinging to Bryg's feet, trying to get her two bearers to set her down again. "If you leave any sooner, I'm afraid they'll weep themselves sick."

"If that's your only fear, you can help me rid you of it, my lady," Fintan replied.

"Help you?" Lady Lassaire's blue eyes grew enormous. "How?"

"Hear me patiently, please: we bards are masters of a thousand magics, but we sometimes don't know how to end a story. The hero may triumph or die or marry or any combination of the three, but what happens when his tale refuses to stop so neatly? Why don't we bards ever share the secrets of what comes after the feasting or the funeral or the first morning when man and woman wake up together, gaze into each other's eyes, and wonder, *How in the name of all the gods did I get myself into* this *situation?*"

More laughter and one solitary cry of "She said her brother would break my head if I didn't marry her!" answered *that* question.

"My lady, you must help me weave the end of this tale," the bard went on. "It began when you opened your home to my daughter. You took responsibility for her education and upbringing, even though she wasn't nobly born. The child of a mere bard, raised alongside the children of kings! Can I ever repay you for that?"

"You mustn't say such things, I beg you! It was my greatest pleasure." Lady Lassaire was under Fintan's spell. She looked ready to give him a slice of the moon, if that was what it took to hold his notice. "Bryg never gave me a moment of trouble. You see how much the girls missed her!"

"I do." Fintan gazed benevolently at his daughter, rescued

from her perch and jealously guarded by Dairine and Ula once again. "And I mourn the—the ill-fated circumstances that forced me to take her away from them. I acted for her health's sake, but it broke the bond of fosterage. Now that she is well again, I long to know the ending of her story, but I am not the one who has the right to create it." He gazed at Lady Lassaire as if they were the only two people left in the world. "That power belongs to you."

"Master Fintan, what do you mean?" Lady Lassaire chirped.

"He means, my dear wife, that he would like Bryg to come back into our care," Lord Artegal said, chuckling. "He knows that I can't say no to a bard—no prudent man would—but he has to *woo* your consent."

Her husband's reply sent her into a flutter. She blushed, dimpled, giggled, and made Kian squirm to see it. Finally she said, "You didn't need to waste your lovely words on a useless creature like me, Master Fintan. As far as I'm concerned, the bond was never broken. Bryg never left my care."

The bard responded with a renewed outpouring of gratitude and flattery for his hosts. Dairine and Ula shrieked with glee, grabbed Bryg's hands, and whirled in a circle until the bard's daughter broke away from them to haul Gormlaith and me into their frenzied dance. Lady Lassaire began shouting commands to the servants, ordering a fifth bed for our sleeping chamber.

The day sped away with the swiftness of our mad dance. Rumor flew through the ringfort that the welcoming meal Dún Beithe's chief cook improvised for breakfast would be nothing next to the true banquet we'd see served up for dinner. No extravagance was to be spared, even though the dark part of the year was a time for measuring out our stores of meat and grain so they would last until the light came back again. Lord Artegal himself led a hunting party that would scour the woodland for deer and other game.

Lady Lassaire was so busy overseeing the preparations that we fosterlings were left to follow our own desires. I wanted to visit Ea, but Bryg insisted that all of us stay together. She led us to the top of the ramparts and took turns linking arms with each of us as we paced around the wall.

"I want each of you to tell me everything that happened since I went away," she declared as she and Ula made the first circuit.

"That leaves me out," I joked. "There are logs in the wood-pile that've been at Dún Beithe longer than I."

"The woodpile?" Dairine repeated. "Isn't that where Lord Conchobar carried you?"

My face blazed. *How did she find out?*

"Maeve, you're *scarlet*. Did I say something wrong? I didn't mean that the two of you did anything shameful. I'm sure it was totally innocent." Though Dairine spoke false words of comfort, she was visibly enjoying my embarrassment. "Bran's the one who told me."

"Who is he and how does he know *my* business?" I asked, a cold note in my voice.

She tried brushing off my anger. "Oh, *Maeve,* you know him: he's one of Lord Kian's friends, a sweet man who's been taking an interest in me."

"That narrows it down to half of Dún Beithe," Ula remarked.

Bryg snickered and whispered something to the tall

red-haired girl that made both of them laugh until they doubled over.

Dairine gave them a dirty look. Her expression was so poisonous that for a moment it seemed she was contemplating shoving them over the edge of the ramparts. I thought it would be a good idea to distract her.

"Your admirer must be one of the People of the Mounds, Dairine," I said. "Does he own a magic cloak that turns him invisible? I saw no one near when Lord Conchobar and I were talking." I thought I heard Ula's sarcastic whisper, "Oh, *talking*?" but disregarded her petty jab.

"You're so funny, Maeve," Dairine replied. "Bran was standing watch up here that day; that's how he saw you without you seeing him. He was afraid I was attracted to Lord Conchobar so he told me about what he'd seen to discourage me. He wants me all to himself, the darling!"

Ula looked ready to say something malicious, but Bryg prevented it by breaking away from her and rushing to hug Dairine. "So you're going to be the first of us to marry! Isn't this exciting? I must meet your husband-to-be and congratulate him. Where can I find him? What does he look like? He has to know what a perfect bride he'll have."

Dairine hesitated. "That can wait," she said. "We haven't made any formal pledges yet."

"But that's wonderful! You can do it now, today, or tomorrow at the latest," Bryg enthused. "I'm so glad I won't miss seeing you promise yourselves to each other. Take us to him this very instant!"

"I—I'm not sure where he is right now."

"Then it will have to happen at dinner, even if I *die* from waiting." Bryg pressed her pale cheek to Dairine's flaming face. "Meanwhile, tell me everything about him. I'm so sorry I never paid attention to the names of Kian's friends. Who is this Bran? Is he a fosterling or was he born to one of Dún Beithe's subject lords? Who are his parents? Does he have any brothers or sisters?"

I listened to Bryg chatter on, showering Dairine with questions that sounded innocent enough until you understood what the bard's daughter was really doing. It didn't suit her to let Dairine cling to the lie that Bran cared about her enough for marriage. She was nothing special to him, and Bryg was a relentless huntress, intent on pursuing that harsh truth and forcing it into the open. Her every word made Dairine cringe and shrink into herself. It was frightening to watch.

I glanced at Gormlaith and Ula. They looked on calmly, not a trace of surprise or pity on their faces. *They've seen this before,* I thought. *Why don't they put a stop to it? Dairine's sometimes difficult to like, but she's our friend! If they won't say something, I will.*

I scowled as fiercely as I knew how and stormed my way between them so that my back was turned to the bard's daughter. "Never mind reciting every single boring detail about your *precious* Bran, Dairine," I said. "I just want to tell him to his face that if he doesn't learn to mind his own business, I'll pull every last hair off his empty head and weave them into a gag to shut his mouth!"

Dairine's jaw dropped. Ula and Gormlaith were equally stunned. I could only guess at Bryg's expression, but judging from the absolute silence behind me, she must have been dumbstruck as well. I pressed my advantage.

"How *dare* he spy on Lord Conchobar and me?" I seized her hand. "We're going to find him and settle this right now." I spun around in a false fury and glared at the other three girls. "And we're going *alone*," I declared with such violence that none of them stirred so much as a finger when I dragged Dairine away.

I towed her after me into the shelter of the great house where I made her sit beside me at the hearthside. She was short of breath and thoroughly bewildered by what I'd just done.

"Maeve, if you want to talk to Bran, he's probably out hunting with the others now, not in here."

"All I *really* wanted was to get you away from Bryg and her endless questions. You looked ready to wriggle out of your skin."

She stared at her feet. "You didn't have to bother. She'll just wait until she sees me again and pick up where she left off. She doesn't give up when there's something she wants."

"Something like humiliating you?" It was hard for me to accept that the girl compassionate enough to save my Ea was also capable of such meanness. *This sounds bad, but I mustn't judge her too soon. I hardly know her.*

Dairine shrugged. "It was my fault. I never should have claimed that Bran and I were closer than we are. I should have remembered how much Bryg hates lies."

So do I, I thought. *But this one was small and harmless. Bryg was the one who turned Bran from Dairine's special sweetheart into her promised husband. Why couldn't she have let it go?*

A notion came to me. "Dairine, I know a way we can fix this."

Hope lit up her eyes. "How?"

"Keep yourself out of Bryg's way until dinner and you'll see."

That evening the feast awaiting us was even more lavish than the rumors suggested. When Master Fintan left Dún Beithe, he'd have no choice but to praise the generosity of his hosts and glorify Lord Artegal's reputation as an openhanded king. The air was filled with a dozen mouthwatering aromas. Fat sizzled as it dripped from a roasting goose, one of several the men had brought down. The savory scent of venison blended with it, for the hunting party had also been lucky enough to take four deer. All this was besides the preserved beef we had from thinning the herds at Samhain. No one would go to sleep hungry.

Dairine appeared at the hearth when the meal was well under way. She cast an uncertain look my way. I smiled and waved at her, which attracted Bryg's notice.

"Where have you been since this morning, Dairine? You must sit here now so we can talk," she called out, patting the bench beside her. When the black-haired girl hung back, the bard's daughter frowned. "Are you snubbing me? Why are you being so unkind? I thought you were my friend!"

Lady Lassaire heard. How could she help it? Bryg knew the bard's trick of pitching her voice so softly that it seemed like she was whispering, yet her voice still reached every part of the hall.

"Dairine, this is *not* how one of my girls acts toward another, especially not when we're all so glad to have Bryg back again. Sit down beside her right—"

"There you are, beloved!" A broad-shouldered young man with spiked hair like Kian's marched up to Dairine, flung his arms around her, and kissed her so heartily that when their lips finally parted, they both gasped for air. "What do you mean, hiding yourself away from me all day? If I find out you were with some other man, I'll feed his eyes to the Morrígan's raven! Now tell me you love me and do it quickly; I want my dinner!"

"I—I—I—" Dairine regained control of her speech and said: "I love you, Bran."

"Good. Now let's share some of that fine venison." He slid his arm around her waist and steered her to the far side of the hearth.

That night we fosterlings slept five in a room that had been a little snug when there were only four of us. We were as tightly squeezed as kernels in a pinecone, and the whole situation was made worse when I discovered that skinny little Bryg snored twice as loudly as Gormlaith.

As I was struggling to fall asleep, I felt a hand touch mine. "Maeve? It's me." Dairine crouched by my bed, a ball of shadow.

"What is it, Dairine? Is anything wrong?" I suspected she had an upset stomach. There were bound to be many of those after the huge meal we'd enjoyed, and for some folk the banquet was still going on. The shouts and laughter and singing of the most dedicated revelers' celebration reached my ears from beyond the bull-hide door curtain.

"I just wanted to thank you," she whispered. "Bryg's not going to question me about Bran anymore, not after seeing how he treated me in front of everyone. Here, take this." She pressed something cold and smooth into my palm. "It's my brooch. I wish it were made of gold, not bronze, but I hope you'll like it."

I pushed the large pin back into her hand. "I'll like it if you keep it. If not, how will you keep your cloak fastened? Anyway, Bran's the one you should thank, and you can do that by picking a quarrel with him as soon as possible."

She giggled very softly. "I'll do it in three days' time. The whole household will know that it's over between us, I promise. But tell me, how did you get him to agree to play my sweetheart?"

"Easy. I dared him to do it."

"That was all it took?"

"He's a warrior of Èriu, isn't he?" I yawned, turned onto my side, and fell asleep.

CHAPTER ELEVEN

Departures and Returns

FINTAN THE BARD was back on the road two days after he arrived, heading south to serve his king, Rus of Laigin, once more. Everyone missed his voice, for no other bard lived at Dún Beithe, but I think Lord Artegal and Lady Lassaire were relieved to see him go. It meant they could put an end to offering rich feasts every night and go back to our more modest and sensible winter fare.

The moon's face changed as the dark part of the year slowly retreated and the light advanced. The festival of Imbolc came, which meant spring would soon be with us. My friends and I fell back into the old cycle of instructions with Lady Lassaire, though now that Bryg was a part of all that, our lessons and chores weren't as tedious. She loved to sing as she worked and she always persuaded Ula to join her. If I'd known that the tall, reserved girl had such a wondrous musical gift, I would have begged her to sing for us long before Bryg's return. Ula's pure, sweet voice was as refreshing as a drink of cool water for a weary traveler.

I liked Bryg. She made things lively. Where did she get such a talent? The People of the Mounds must have given her an enchanted bag always brimful of fresh ideas for keeping us entertained. I enjoyed the way she taught us games and songs. I *loved* the way she told us long, dramatic tales about the gods' conquest of Èriu. My skin prickled deliciously when she spoke of how even they, the powerful Fair Folk, were in turn driven from the daylit lands, taking refuge underground or in the enchanted islands of the western sea. I was happy to call her my friend.

The other girls also seemed delighted to have her back. From the moment she awoke in the morning to the time she closed her eyes in sleep, they clustered around her, eager to hear what she had to say, eager to do whatever small task she set for them. If she forgot her embroidery, Gormlaith ran to fetch it. If she frowned over the portion of meat she was served at dinner, Ula insisted they trade dishes. I never heard Dairine laugh so loudly as when Bryg made a joke or agree so swiftly as when Bryg voiced an opinion.

I can understand why they're acting this way, I thought one morning as we all prepared for the new day. *They're so happy to have their friend back that they can't do enough for her. If the gods ever let me see Odran again, it would be the same. I'd become his shadow, his other self, clinging to every word he said, trying to guess his wishes, doing whatever would please him, giving him—*

I caught myself and chuckled. *No, I wouldn't do any of that. He'd hate it and so would I.* I looked to where Gormlaith was meticulously braiding Bryg's thin, dull blond hair, though her own still hung loose and unkempt. *But Bryg doesn't seem to mind it at all.*

There was only one thing that troubled me about my new friend: she never seemed able to rejoice wholeheartedly whenever something special touched anyone else's life. When a messenger brought Ula a new gown from her family, Bryg found a way to compliment it in such a way that we never saw Ula wear it. When Gormlaith discovered a gift of carefully wrapped honeycomb awaiting her on her bed and refused to give even a hint about who might have left it there, Bryg leaped to shield her from our lighthearted teasing. "Leave her alone, you three. Didn't you ever want to pretend you had a sweetheart?"

Gormlaith opened her mouth, then closed it again. If she stayed mute, she'd look like a pathetic creature making believe she had an admirer who gave her gifts. If she revealed the truth—

What would they say if they learned it's a gift from Connla? I thought, looking at my friends. *Bold, handsome Connla, Kian's closest friend, one of Lord Artegal's foremost young warriors.*

I could only imagine how they'd taunt her for having drawn Connla's attention. And what would Bryg add to that spite-filled stew? It would all be a joke—that's what they always said whenever they picked on someone—but Gormlaith wouldn't be able to bear it. She'd reject Connla to save herself and end up breaking her heart.

There never seemed to be a compliment small enough for Bryg not to riddle with pinpricks. When Lady Lassaire praised Dairine for creating an especially elaborate embroidery design, Bryg said, "Isn't that pretty! You should stitch that onto the wrists of a tunic. Donnchadh will be the envy of every man when he wears your gift."

She spoke as amiably as if she'd somehow remained ignorant of what every inhabitant of Dún Beithe knew: that Dairine's short-lived romance with Donnchadh had ended when he publicly declared he'd taken another girl for his wife.

I saw tears drop from Dairine's eyes onto the cloth in her lap. The next time we all gathered to do our needlework, she had a blank piece of fabric and we never saw her beautiful design again.

Oddly enough, I was the only one who escaped Bryg's nettling tongue. She always spoke to me with simple sweetness. If I'd been a different sort of person, I'd have told myself, *It's a shame the way she sometimes jabs at the others, but if it really bothered them, wouldn't they fight back? I'm just happy it's never me.*

Maybe I was too foolish to stay comfortable while others suffered. The day after Dairine abandoned her fine needlework pattern, I sought a moment alone with Bryg.

I found her just outside the storehouse where Ea perched. She was talking intently to Kian, who had a small piece of raw meat in one hand. I hailed them both.

"Maeve! You've come at the best possible time." Kian grinned and brandished the bloody scrap. "I'm just going to feed the kestrel. Do you want to do it?"

Bryg gave him a searching look. "You let her?"

"Why not? She's marvelous with the bird. Come on, Maeve." He led us into the little building and picked up our leather armguards from their place atop a heap of ash wood poles that would someday be spears. "Here you go," he said, tossing my sleeve to me. "Let's show Bryg how we handle this pretty bird. Do you want to take her out and practice bringing her back with the lure? I haven't forgotten about teaching you to use it; I've just been busy since that time we were interrupted by *Lord* Conchobar."

Was that sarcasm? I couldn't tell because I was immediately distracted by what I saw on Bryg's face. Her expression danced back and forth from amazement to disbelief to annoyance to curiosity, before it finally settled on a smile so wide and dazzling it was my turn to be surprised.

"I would love to see that, Lord Kian," she said. "I'm so glad you found someone to help you care for this dear bird of ours while I was away."

"Didn't you think I could do it myself, Bryg?" he asked with a wink.

Two bright-red spots bloomed on her sallow cheeks, and in a strangely husky voice she said: "I only meant—"

I stepped in to set her at ease. "Kian understands. He's just being a mean little boy, teasing you because he's in your debt and knows it. He told me you're the only reason this bird is alive today." I clasped her hands. "I owe you thanks as well. She's an amazing creature. I'm never happier than when I watch her fly."

"Oh?" Bryg's gaze shifted to Kian. "How often is that?" she asked him.

"Not as often as I'd like," he replied casually. "She manages the bird almost as well as I do, and without a moment's fear. I've never met a girl that bold. Remember when you were healing this little kestrel, Bryg? How you squeaked and jumped back when she tried to nip you? You wouldn't go near her after that. I had to salve and bandage her while you told me how to do it from three arm lengths away." He laughed.

Bryg and I didn't share his amusement. "Lord Kian—" she began, but I was so irritated with him that I cut her off.

"Very funny," I said crisply. "Did you ever think of what would've happened if Bryg had been bitten? Lord Artegal would have destroyed the bird! If you don't know the right way to thank her for saving Ea, at least be grateful she had the sense to protect her."

Kian was shamefaced and said he was sorry, but Bryg only half-heard his apology. Her attention was focused on me. "Ea?" she repeated.

How had my beloved kestrel's name slipped out, after I'd spent so long concealing it? It may have been a silly impulse to keep it secret, but her name was like Odran, a special part of me. I couldn't speak of either one of them without opening my heart. Though I thought Kian and Bryg were my friends, the bond between us didn't run deep enough for that. Not yet.

"You named her!" Kian exclaimed. "Good idea. We name our hounds and our horses and Father's always chosen fine names for our best bulls. Ea!" The kestrel turned her hooded head in his direction. "What do you know? She likes it." He was delighted.

"If that's all it takes to make you happy, Lord Kian, why did you wait?" Bryg said drily. "I suggested naming the bird long ago."

"Yes, but I couldn't name her *properly* then." Kian was oblivious to Bryg's deepening frown. "I had to wait for Maeve to tell me Ea's a female. Not even you knew that."

"I apologize for my stupidity." The bard's daughter looked ready to bite someone.

"Ea—Ea's a name that would serve if she were male too," I

said, trying to head off the storm. I needed Bryg to be in good humor if I were going to succeed in persuading her to soften her ways. "What would *you* name the bird?" I asked her.

"Nothing that Lord Kian would like, I'm sure. It wouldn't be *bold* enough to suit him." She strode out of the storehouse.

"What's gotten under *her* skin?" Kian was honestly baffled.

I wanted to go after her, but when I tried to leave, he caught me by the hand. "Don't you want to feed Ea?" he asked. When he said her name, it sounded wrong to my ears.

"I should follow Bryg. You hurt her feelings."

"Me? What did I say?" He wasn't trying to excuse himself by faking ignorance. He had no clue that he'd done anything wrong.

I sighed inwardly. It would take too long to help him understand his mistake and still catch up with Bryg. "Never mind. I'll find her and try to make things right between you again."

"You make it sound like she's my sweetheart." There was that guileless grin again. "She's a nice girl, and she did heal the kes—Ea—but she's just another of Mother's fosterlings to me, so don't worry."

"Worry? Kian, I don't care what she is to you, but she's my friend, she's upset, and I have to do something about that."

"Too late now, Maeve," he said. "You won't be able to find her. She's like a little gray mouse, able to hide anywhere. You remember how I told you she went grief-mad over her brother's death? Well, when Master Fintan was about to take her to Avallach for healing, she hid herself so well that everyone thought she'd run away. We searched the woods, the fields, the bogland—"

"The way you looked for Aifric," I murmured.

"Yes." The lost girl's name cast a spell that robbed Kian of his smile. "Thank the gods this search had a better ending."

"Where did you find her?"

"We didn't. She appeared after four days, of her own will. She'd been within the ringfort's walls the whole time, though we never did discover where. Don't bother seeking that one unless she wants to be found."

"I still have to try."

I left Kian and made a search of Dún Beithe, high and low, but I didn't find Bryg. Frustrated, I trailed back to the storehouse just in time to see Kian giving Ea the last bit of meat.

He saw failure on my face. "What did I tell you?"

I joined him by the perch and stroked Ea's feathers. "I'll speak to her at dinner," I said. But I couldn't help thinking, *If she's there.*

She was. I'd gone early, hoping to greet her, only to find she was already waiting. "Maeve, keep me company!" she called across the round hearth with its simmering cauldron. I was relieved to hear her speak so cheerfully. She gave me a hug before seating me at her side.

"I'm sorry I bolted, but I was going to pick up a spear shaft and knock Lord Kian's head off if I stayed." She cocked her head, mischief in her eyes. "Do you want to scold me for leaving you alone with him . . . or thank me?"

"Has Dairine been teaching you how to fish for gossip?" I joked.

"Silly Maeve, who do you think taught Dairine that skill in the first place?" The other girls arrived to find us giggling together. When they wanted to know the reason, we could only laugh harder until we collapsed breathless against each other and almost slid off the bench.

This turned out well, I thought as I ate my dinner. *Bryg's not mad at me. I'll be able to talk to her about treating Gorm-laith, Ula, and Dairine more kindly. Tomorrow, then!* I looked forward to making life more pleasant for all of us here at Dún Beithe.

"Lord Artegal! My lord, come to the gate!"

Every warrior present leaped to his feet as young Bran, Dairine's onetime "suitor," charged into the great house, spear in hand. The raindrops clinging to the points of his hair and the fibers of his cloak showed he'd been standing sentry duty while the rest of us ate. Now he came into our midst, sounding an alert that might easily turn into an alarm.

"A rider's on the way," Bran declared. "He's coming fast and he's almost to the foot of the ringfort mound. He must be bringing vital news or why would he be daring the road after dark?"

Lord Artegal wasted no time on questions. He strode past Bran, motioning for his men to follow. They poured out into the night to greet whatever fortune, good or bad, had come to Dún Beithe. Lady Lassaire rose, her face strained with anxiety. Her women closed in around her, some reassuring her that the rider might bring *good* news, others nervously mumbling their own fearful guesses as to just how bad the news would be.

"What do you think has happened?" Ula whispered.

"I'll bet someone died," Dairine said.

"Shhh! Don't say that, you witless thing." Ula gave her a

hard nudge and nodded to where Bryg sat turned to stone. "She *remembers*."

I put my arms around the bard's daughter and spoke firmly: "A man who's carrying that kind of news wouldn't ride through the dark to deliver it."

"Why?" Bryg's face was gaunt. "Because once you're dead, there's no rush—you don't matter?"

I tried to hug some emotion back into her hollow eyes. "I know that you didn't find out about your brother's death until years after it happened. I'm sorry for all that you suffered, but this isn't—"

A festive uproar rolled through the doorway of the great house. Lord Artegal scattered the women surrounding his wife and swung her around before setting her down and kissing her. The men at his back cheered so loudly that when their chief tried to speak, Lady Lassaire could only smile, shake her head, and spread her hands helplessly.

"I *said* have the cook bring out more meat at once!" Lord Artegal bawled. "We've got good cause to celebrate. Look who's among us again!" His arm swept toward the doorway.

Rain-soaked and smiling, Conchobar of the Ulaidh was back.

CHAPTER TWELVE

Two Dogs, One Bone

"They're at it again," Ula said. The sounds of a ferocious argument taking place somewhere beyond the great house walls made her announcement unnecessary.

Bryg and I looked up from the game of *fidchell* we were playing. We'd set up the wooden board and painted discs on a bench outdoors to take advantage of the sunlight and mild weather. The other three fosterlings stood by, waiting their turn to play the winner.

"What was your first clue?" Dairine remarked.

"I wish they'd stop," Gormlaith said with a sigh. "Lord Conchobar's a guest. Lord Kian shouldn't keep picking fights with him; it's wrong and it only gets him into trouble with his father. Does anyone even know *why* he does it?"

"You know how boys can be." Ula spoke with her usual disdain. "They fight for the sake of fighting, and if you ask them what set it off, half of them don't know. If you ask me, those two are probably squabbling over something ridiculous."

"Ula!" Bryg crossed her hands over her chest in feigned shock. "What a nasty thing to say about Maeve!"

I made a face. "Just for that, I'm not going to let you win this match." I moved one of my gaming pieces on the board, cornering hers and turning my jest into a done deed.

Bryg scowled at her loss. "This is all their fault," she decreed, clearing the *fidchell* board with one swipe of her hand. Gormlaith scrambled to gather the scattered pieces. "I can't concentrate with all that noise."

"Do you want a rematch?" I offered.

"I *want* you to go tell your lovers to take their clash elsewhere or kill each other now, whichever one brings us some peace!"

I flung myself to my knees before her and struck a begging pose. "Oh please, gracious Bryg, don't say they both must die! Think of how wasteful that would be. Let me keep just one."

She laughed and prodded me gently with one foot. "All right, but only if you make them stop barking *now*."

"At once, my lady!" I sprang to my feet and dashed around the curved side of the great house.

I found Conchobar and Kian standing nose to nose while one of Lord Artegal's hunting hounds sat on its haunches between them. Their hot words centered on the beast, Kian claiming it could outhunt any dog Conchobar owned and Conchobar defending the reputation of the Emain Macha pack. They were so involved in their shouting match that they didn't notice my presence until the hound trotted over to greet me.

"Now you're wrangling over *dogs*?" I asked while the hound licked my hand.

"Dogs are important," Kian said staunchly, but he looked self-conscious.

"We couldn't bring down the best game without them." Conchobar clearly hated having to agree with Kian: it showed on his face.

"Dogs are important," I repeated. "And *cattle* are important. And *swords* are important. They're all *so* important that they set the two of you at each other's throats every day. Do you know what else is important? Treating your guest with courtesy and your host with respect! It doesn't matter if the women of Dún Beithe brew better mead than the women of Emain Macha as long as we can all drink a cup of it in peace."

"They say that beautiful girls brew the best mead," Kian said, taking a step closer to me. "Which means we'd win that contest easily."

"For the time being." Conchobar drew even nearer and let me have his most fetching smile.

"Enough!" I pushed them away to arm's length and lowered my head like a bull about to charge. "Is this why you risked the winter road to come here?" I demanded of Conchobar. "To bicker with Kian?"

"He's not what pulled me here, my lady." Conchobar moved toward me again. "Not while you—"

"Enough." Kian barred his way. "Maeve's too smart to be tricked by pretty words that cover the truth."

The lord of the Ulaidh no longer smiled. "Do you call me a liar?" he asked in a deceptively mild tone.

"I would never say such a thing about any guest my father chose to welcome," Kian retorted, putting just enough emphasis on *my father* to send a pointed message. "Besides, you can't tell her the whole reason for your visit."

"Telling me what I can and can't do?" Conchobar showed his teeth. "Let me return the favor." Conchobar whistled shrilly to seize the hound's attention, stooped swiftly to pick up a rock, and flung it over the roof of the great house. The beast took off after it, barking wildly, while Kian gaped after it. "Now *you* can catch your dog."

Kian had no choice: the dog was huge, part wolfhound, and clearly a valuable animal. If it came to any harm while chasing Conchobar's stone, Kian would face the consequences. The moment he gave chase, the young lord of the Ulaidh grabbed my wrist and ran in the opposite direction.

I dug in my heels before we'd gone twenty paces. He tried to drag me along, but I dropped to the ground and made myself deadweight. "If you want me to go somewhere, you *ask*," I told him. "I'm not going to let you carry me to some isolated spot again, not without a fight you won't forget."

"Don't you trust me, Maeve?" His endearing smile made my heart beat a little faster despite my good sense. I suspected he'd wreaked havoc on many girls' affections with that look.

I won't be another one of them, I thought sternly. *Even if I'd never loved Odran, I will* not *let Conchobar have the satisfaction of winning me over.*

"Don't play that oh-I-am-*so*-wounded game with me," I told him bluntly. "You want to make me feel cruel so that I'll be forced to prove I'm kind by letting you have your way. It won't work. Kian's right: I'm not fool enough to fall for your tricks."

Conchobar looked as if he'd bitten into a wormy apple. "All right then, my lady, *will* you come with me?"

"No, I will not. When you carried me off before, we were seen by a sentry. I had to stay here and stamp out the gossip he started before it ran through the whole ringfort."

"Indeed?" Conchobar's thoughtful expression was galling. "What did he say about us? Tell me everything."

I snorted. "You could have the decency to look embarrassed."

"A guard saw me alone with the most beautiful girl in Èriu and ran to tell everyone in Dún Beithe that I'm the luckiest man alive. What's embarrassing about that? Point him out to me and I'll give him these gold earrings and a kiss!"

"Find him later and kiss him all you like," I snapped. "First you're going to explain why you came back."

"Why Maeve, you know it's because you hold my heart in those delicate hands of—"

I showed him my back and began walking away. He was in front of me, barring my passage, by the time I took my third step.

"I'll tell you," he said. His eyes told me he was done joking. "I will, though some might say I'm breaking the guest-bond. When I delivered my news to Lord Artegal, he decreed we'd keep it hidden from everyone except his son and ten of his most trusted warriors. No one else knows, but I think you should: it concerns your family."

My mouth went dry. Many terrible possibilities flashed through my mind. "Whatever you tell me now will stay hidden; I swear it by my heart and my hand and my head."

"That's an oath worthy of a warrior." Conchobar nodded, satisfied. "Maeve, this touches your father, Eochu Feidlech.

His life and his lordship are in danger. Do you recall Lord Morann?"

How could I forget the treacherous chieftain who'd schemed to dominate and destroy my family? He plotted to force me into marriage by holding our bard, Devnet, hostage. It didn't matter that the birth of my three brothers meant I would no longer have all of Connacht someday. The *findemna*—the beloved, longed-for, fair-haired triplets—were babies, and as Lord Morann so coldly observed, many sad fates could befall them. He'd see to that. With them gone, I'd be the High King's prize again and Lord Morann would have me, but that wasn't all he desired. He conspired to bring down Father and set up a new High King in his place, one that *he'd* control, a lad with good cause to hate my father and rejoice in any plot that put an end to him—

Conchobar.

"What harm can Morann do now?" I asked. "He's dead."

"So he is, and from what I'm told, he shares a place of honor with my father. Eochu displays both of their severed heads on the lintel above his doorway." Conchobar wore a wry smile, but his eyes were filled with sorrow. "But his notion of using dishonorable means to topple the High King still lives. It's found a new home in the heart of a chieftain named Lord Cairill."

"What does this Cairill plan to do against my father?" I asked.

Conchobar spread his hands. "That's the trouble: I don't know any more than that. I heard the bare bones of this from one of my men. That fellow lost his heart to a girl who serves in Cairill's household. One night she told him, 'Your chief will be happy soon. They're saying that the one who took Lord

Fachtna's head won't live to see another Samhain. Maybe then Lord Conchobar can take his place as High King.'"

"Why would she blab such a thing?" I felt a nauseating fear slither its way over my body. It took every bit of self-control to stand still, seem calm, and keep from shivering.

"She wanted him to tell me. She thought I'd be so overjoyed at the news that I'd reward him richly and they could marry." Conchobar shook his head. "I did fill his hands with treasure, not because I welcomed his words but for the chance to prevent a great wrong. I must warn your father."

"By coming *here*?" I knit my brows. "If you want Father to hear about this, why are you lingering at Dún Beithe instead of riding on to Cruachan?"

"The warning can't come to him from me, Maeve. Don't you see? He'd never believe it. He knows me as Fachtna Fáthach's son. He thinks of me as someone more likely to want his death than his welfare."

Conchobar's words made sense, especially when I recalled Father's own artful way of manipulating things. *He schemed to destroy my friend Kelan while keeping his own hands clean,* I thought. *He made me believe I was special to him when I was only a prize he used to buy men's loyalty. He hoarded Derbriu's messages to keep me tame at home. I see your wisdom, Conchobar: a deceiver* would *see deception everywhere.*

"How did Lord Artegal take your news?" I asked. "Did *he* believe you? Has he agreed to carry your message to my father?"

"He agreed that Eochu is a willful man who likes to think of himself as too high to fall," Conchobar replied. "If Lord Artegal contacted him directly, he might dismiss the whole matter because Cairill rules such a small realm. Does a bull panic when a fly bites him? But if he's caught by a swarm—"

I grasped his meaning at once. "Cairill isn't acting alone."

"Neither was Morann." Conchobar's mouth set hard. "When he came to me, he hinted at other conspirators. They're still alive."

"Who else is with Cairill?"

"I'm trying to find out. I've sent as many trusted men as I can spare to look into this, but unless luck favors us, we'll still be groping in the dark when your father's enemies strike. That's why I've asked Lord Artegal to send word to his cousin, Lady Íde, not to Eochu himself."

"Conchobar, that's brilliant!" I exclaimed. "Lady Íde is Mother's closest friend. She'll listen to her and take the news to Father. He'll *have* to accept it if it comes from her!"

"That's how I hope it will be." A hint of Conchobar's lost smile crept back. "Now you know the real reason I came to Dún Beithe. How disappointed you must be to learn that it's not because you've ensnared my heart in these gleaming bonds." He ran a strand of my hair through his fingers. "Nor because I couldn't sleep without dreaming of this intoxicating face." He lifted my chin gently. "Nor because of all the other nights I lay awake wondering what it would be like to taste these tempting—"

I jerked my head aside before his fingertip could caress my lips. "Why, Conchobar?" I said, desperately wanting to distract him, terribly afraid I would succeed. "Why are you doing this for the man who killed your father? Why not stand back and let Cairill's plan play out to your advantage?"

The young lord of the Ulaidh seized my shoulders and

pulled me so close to him that I could look nowhere but into his blazing green eyes. "When I become High King of Èriu, it won't be thanks to the sly dealings of men like Morann and Cairill. They don't deserve the title of lord or the glorious life of a warrior. I hate Eochu for taking my father from me, but there was nothing ignoble in the way he did it, man to man and bravely, in front of the lords of Èriu. I'll win my father's title honorably or not at all."

His lips were on mine. I had no way to escape the power of his kiss. I don't think I would have wanted to, but he acted so quickly I never had the chance to think about where my desires ended and his began. All I knew was that the taste of his mouth was hot and sweet, and that his kiss turned my bones to fire.

A weak thought struggled free of the flames: *This is wrong, wrong! How can you let anyone but Odran kindle such a feeling in you? Have you forgotten him so easily? Are you foolish enough to believe you mean as much to Conchobar as you did to him? Run away, Maeve! Save yourself before you fall into deep water and drown, before these strong arms carry you past the point where you can break away. Run!*

I wedged my hands between us and pushed against his chest. Our mouths parted and cold air rushed into my body with the force of a blacksmith's hammer. I gulped it desperately.

He cupped my face with one sword-callused hand. "Maeve?" His plaintive gaze made me ache to soothe away the hurt I saw there. "I'm sorry. I shouldn't have—"

"That's right: you shouldn't have done that." Kian stood glowering at us, the errant hound at his side, one fist clutching the scruff of its neck so tightly that the huge creature whimpered like a puppy.

I drew scarcely two shallow breaths before he wheeled around in wordless, white-hot rage and barged away, hauling the terrified dog with him. I, too, fled, never looking back, abandoning the too-bold lord of the Ulaidh.

Lady Lassaire's glare was worse than her son's. "What did you think you were doing, behaving like that with Lord Conchobar?" she demanded of me. The two of us were alone in her sleeping chamber. She'd ordered me there almost as soon as I set one foot across the great house's threshold. Kian must have flown to her with the tale of what he'd seen. "Your shamelessness will be on every tongue!"

I took a deep breath. "One kiss," I said. "That was all there was."

Her eyes narrowed. "You are very young. You don't know where one kiss can lead."

I could always ask Dairine, I thought wickedly. *And why haven't you ever questioned any of* her *doings? There's a reason you're picking on me.*

"There's no love lost between the High King and Lord Conchobar," Lady Lassaire went on. "You don't realize what a disaster it would be if your father learned about what you've done."

"It was a mistake, my lady," I said. "My father doesn't need to be concerned. I don't love Lord Conchobar. I'm not even sure how it happened, but I promise you, it won't happen again."

Lady Lassaire's frown faded into her familiar smile, as bland as watered milk. "Poor Maeve, I do know how it happened: our guest has a reputation for taking what he wants when it comes to pretty girls. You deserve better. I'm happy to say Lord Conchobar will be going home in a few days. If we're fortunate, he'll stay there. Until then, you mustn't let yourself be caught alone with him. I'll speak to the other fosterlings and have them look after you in the meantime."

Look after me? Was I an infant who needed nursemaids? I bristled at the thought.

"My lady, I can take care of myself," I said as mildly as I could.

"If that were true, we wouldn't be having this little talk." Her smile became absolutely infuriating. "You *will* be guarded against any further 'mistakes' with Lord Conchobar, but if you'd rather not involve your friends, I have an idea: when you're not with us, you *must* be in my son's company. I'll arrange it."

"Please, Lady Lassaire, you needn't do that," I protested. "I don't want to keep him from his other duties."

She laughed. "You don't have to pretend for me, Maeve. I know how you two use that hawk of his as an excuse to be together. Oh, don't give me *that* look, dear: I'm not going to scold either of you for it. My dearest wish is for my son's happiness—and yours too. That's why I'm going to watch over you from now on, to protect you from any more wrong choices." She tucked back one of my stray curls affectionately. "I understand young hearts."

I returned her smile as best I could, but all I could think was, *You don't understand anything at all.*

Lady Lassaire made good on her threat. I was never allowed another moment alone with Conchobar until his departure three days later, not that I'd wanted one. From the cold looks and colder speech they exchanged at his leave-taking, I gathered that she'd tried to send him on his way even sooner, and not by any subtle means.

The frost between them was like a Beltane bonfire compared to what I now felt for Kian. At my first opportunity, I had him come with me to Ea's refuge and raked him raw for talebearing.

"Are you a man or a toddling child, running to your mother over every scratch?" I demanded. "She spoke as if I were some wild, brazen girl who'd go running after any man! She decided I had to have *you* for my keeper because I'd throw myself at Conchobar if he even glanced at me! How do you think that made me feel?"

"How do you think *I* felt when I saw you kissing him?" he countered.

"Why should you care who I kiss?" I was too caught up in my own anger to realize the answer.

He groaned. "You're impossible."

"And *you* might have lingered long enough to let me explain how it happened."

"I'd rather listen to Master Fintan. At least when *he* dreams up a fantasy, I can believe it!"

My hand rose to slap the insult from his lips, but I caught myself in time. I heard Ea's piercing cry at my back as I walked out in silence.

CHAPTER THIRTEEN

Shut Out and Shut In

"Maeve, *talk* to him." Dairine perched on the side of my bed in the dark and leaned on me.

"Go to sleep, pest," I grumbled, trying to get her off me. She seemed to have the magical ability to gain the bulk of a cow carcass at will.

"No." She shifted just enough to weigh as much as *two* cows, with a calf thrown in for good measure. "Not until you say you'll talk to Lord Kian again."

"I'll talk to Lord Kian again. There. I said it."

"Saying isn't promising. Swear!"

I made a mighty effort and flipped over, dumping my relentless friend onto the floor. Dairine yelped and pelted me with all the nasty names she knew.

"Shush, Dairine," Ula commanded from her spot in the darkened room. "Too much noise and someone will tell Lady Lightning."

"You think she'll leave her nice warm bed and punish us?" the black-haired girl sneered. "If she did, Maeve's the only one who'd suffer."

"Just what she deserves," Bryg put in. "Breaking poor Lord Kian's heart so *cruuuuuuuuuelly.*" She uttered the last word as a melancholy tune and drew it out, up, down, and into a musical knot. Everyone giggled except Gormlaith. The girl could sleep through anything.

"The least you could do is let him know you're sorry," Ula said primly.

"For *what*?" I was tired from the day's work, perishing for lack of sleep, and testy. "I told you what I told Kian: I did *not* kiss Conchobar. He kissed *me*."

"There's a difference?" Dairine spoke playfully, but I was in no mood for games.

"Yes, but it takes brains to see it, not a lump of mud between your ears. Why do any of you care if I speak to him or not?" I cried, sitting up in bed. "It's been four days and there's always one of you nagging me about it. Let it go."

"We feel bad for him," Ula explained.

"We feel bad for you too," Bryg said in her most appealing voice. "You're angry, so you're shunning him, but don't you miss visiting that hawk—"

"Falcon." I corrected her automatically.

"Hawk, falcon, *bird*, you know what I mean." Bryg's sweetness vanished the instant I put her in the wrong. "You're only spiting yourself, you stupid girl!"

"How do you know I don't visit Ea when he's not with her?" I challenged, though it wasn't so.

"Because she isn't *there* anymore," Bryg said triumphantly. "He's moved her from the arms storehouse to a different out-building. I helped carry some of her things."

"Where is she?"

"Ask him."

"You helped him move her; you know where she is too."

"I do. But if you want to see her again, you'll still have to ask *him*." I couldn't see her face in the dark, but I knew the wretched little beast was grinning.

"I'm surprised, Bryg," I said, holding back my temper. "You're encouraging me to make up with Kian, but if you left things as they are, you could have him all to yourself. That's what you really want."

I didn't know if I was right, but it was a good guess. I remembered how sullen Bryg became when Kian accidentally belittled her and praised me when he spoke about Ea. Even if I hadn't witnessed that, which of the fosterlings *wouldn't* want to marry the young man who'd command Dún Beithe someday?

Bryg didn't reply immediately. At last she said, "What's the use of being alone with him when all he talks about is you?"

I held on to my silence for a few more days. Ula and Dairine continued their attempts to soften my heart, though Bryg never said another word about the situation. Kian himself subjected me to long, mournful looks at mealtimes. Then there was Lady Lassaire. Since I refused to speak to her son, the only words she had for me were biting scorn, chill mockery, and harsh criticism of everything I did.

Does she know how unreasonable she's being? I wondered as I set to ripping out a perfectly straight seam that she declared sloppy. *She's making a drop of water into a flood. Can't she* see *herself acting like—like—?*

I blinked. *Like me.*

I wanted to leap up that very instant, find Kian, and mend things between us. Unfortunately, Lady Lassaire decided I could use my time better helping the servants prepare dinner.

"I'm giving you this job as a special privilege, dear Maeve," she said in cloying tones. "You'll be supervising your own household one day, if you ever find the husband you deserve, so you must know everything that goes into the making of a meal."

"Everything" turned out to be nothing: nothing but hard labor. The chief cook never let me watch the preparation of a single dish. Instead she gave me a series of burdensome chores, though she looked more and more guilt-ridden with each new assignment she piled on me.

"It's all right," I said, wanting to set her at ease. "Someone's got to do this." I knew who'd really given the order condemning me to trudge to the woodpile and the garbage pit, carrying one heavy load after another. I was worn out and starving by dinnertime, but when I went to get my portion, Lady Lassaire intervened.

"My sweet child, look at how filthy your dress is. I can't let you humiliate yourself, looking like that in front of everyone. Go change your clothes."

Weary beyond belief, I slumped my way to the fosterlings' sleeping chamber. By the time I removed my work-stained gown, the sight of my bed had become so irresistible that I forgot my hunger, told myself I'd lie down for just a moment, and didn't open my eyes for the rest of the night.

I woke up the next day with a fierce hunger and a fiercer determination to speak to Kian. *Lady Lackwit will think it's all her doing,* I thought bitterly. *She'll congratulate herself so much that she'll probably sprain her arm from patting herself on the back.*

I also awoke to an empty room. My chores had tired me so much that I'd slept late, and none of my friends had bothered to rouse me. *I've missed breakfast!* The thought was alarming, especially when I was hiding a growling, gnawing wolf in my belly.

Fortunately for me, I found the chief cook at the hearth-side, supervising a cleaning crew of servants. She babbled a torrent of apologies for the previous day while she heaped a platter with the best portions of bread, meat, and cheese she could find.

"Enough, enough!" I exclaimed, smiling with gratitude. "This is all much too good for me."

"No, it'd be too good for *some* people," she muttered. "When I've got a grudge against anyone, I have it out with them honestly, face to face. I don't force others to do it for me. It's not right. It's not worthy of anyone, highborn or low." She cast a meaningful look at the household cauldron. "It's not *wise.*"

I hadn't learned much the previous day about making a meal, but at least I picked up one important lesson: *never* rile the cook.

Lady Lackwit, you'd better chew your food very carefully from now on, unless you don't mind finding a nutshell or two in your porridge.

I ran from the great house to search for Kian and had the

good luck to spy his friend Connla manning the ringfort gate-way. "You *want* to talk to him again?" he exclaimed when I told him my mission.

I nodded. "He's my friend, Connla, and I've let a single ill-chosen word stand between us long enough."

"I can guess which one of you said it." Gormlaith's sweet-heart grinned. "He's as dear to me as if we were brothers, but only one of us got the brains. There's a ramshackle hut behind the blacksmith's forge. He told me he'd be there this morning, looking after that bird of his."

"Thank you, Connla. You're as gallant as Gormlaith says."

I left him beaming and headed for the forge. The hut behind it was quite small and part of the roof was missing, but Ea had stayed safe and comfortable in such rundown quarters before, when Odran and I kept her at the crannog.

"Kian?" I called softly as I pushed aside the bull hide cover-ing the doorway.

"Maeve!" He stood in the center of the hut with Ea unhooded on his wrist. "Come in, come in, we were just talk-ing about you!"

"Yes, we were," said Bryg. She'd kept so still, leaning against a wall in the shadows, that I hadn't noticed her until she spoke. Her face was cold and unwelcoming.

"Is that so?" I said, as if there were nothing amiss. I needed to let her know that I wasn't her rival for Lord Artegal's son, but first I had other matters to set right. "I'm afraid to ask what you've been saying, Kian. I've treated you badly these past few days, sulking when we should have been clearing the air. Bryg and the other girls tried to make me see how childish that was, but I can be stubborn. I'm sorry."

Kian laughed. "My mother's been treating you worse. I should apologize for her as well as myself. I get hotheaded, especially over someone I care about so very—"

I hastily cut off his unwelcome declaration by turning to Bryg and exclaiming, "So he hasn't been calling me a monster?"

"Not at all." Bryg lowered her eyelids and wouldn't meet my gaze. "He began by saying how much he missed talking to you, and his memories led him from there to all the times you two enjoyed together with our—with *that* bird." She gave the slightest of nods to indicate Ea.

"Uh, sorry if I bored you, going on like that, Bryg." Kian looked embarrassed.

"Oh no, Kian, not at all! If you hadn't shared all the stories dear Maeve told you from her past"—her glance darted his way for an instant, then down again—"I never would have known the *true* Maeve at all."

"You do know me, Bryg," I protested. "We're fosterlings together, friends—"

"Mmm. And yet, until Kian told me, I had no idea of how *unique* you are, a princess who's a would-be warrior with a bard's persuasive tongue. What a feat, convincing a man to risk teaching the High King's daughter weaponry! And not just once. Why didn't you tell any of *us* about your adventures? Did you think we'd make fun of you for learning how to use a sword?"

"There's nothing to tell," I said uneasily. "I'm done with that now."

"A pity. So it was all for nothing."

"Bryg, you're speaking so strangely. What's the matter?" I tried to take her hand, but she backed away from me.

"Let it be, Maeve."

"I can't. You're unhappy."

Bryg lifted her head and stared. "Does that bother you?"

"Of course it does. You're my friend. I want to help you."

"Well, then—" Her stony expression suddenly glowed with the warm, lively smile I knew. "Promise that you'll confide in *me* from now on. You've had an extraordinary life filled with so many things that I wish I'd known sooner. Why did I have to hear about them from Lord Kian?" She linked arms with me and leaned her head against my shoulder. "Do you know that awful boy sometimes treats me like a child? He keeps secrets from me because he's decided I'm too much of a weakling to deal with any sort of bad news."

"I only did that once since your return, Bryg," Kian protested. "There was a wolfhound pup you liked—"

"Yes, and one of the grown dogs killed it, but *you* told me Lord Artegal gave it to a farmer who'd done him good service. I learned the truth elsewhere." Bryg looked smug. "I always do."

"Sorry, Bryg," Kian said. "I didn't mean to offend you, just protect you. I keep forgetting that you're well again."

"You could do with a trip to Avallach yourself, Lord Kian," she teased. "The druids there would cure your faulty memory. If you travel east to Lord Diarmaid's holding on the coast, you might find a trader willing to ferry you over. From there, any man you meet will know how to guide you to the druids' settlement *if*"—she raised a warning finger—"you haven't already forgotten what I've just said."

It was a great relief to hear Bryg's lighthearted teasing. "I'll try to remember not to forget," Kian replied, getting into the spirit of the joke. "So have you forgiven me?"

"I have no choice." She made a helpless gesture. "I don't dare snub you. If Lady Lassaire's willing to chastise the High King's favorite daughter for making her adored boy unhappy, what do you think she'd do to me?"

"Nothing, if she values her husband's rank," I said. "Your father's a bard. His gift for satire makes him more feared than a dozen High Kings. He could bring down Lord Artegal with a single mocking song."

"He could *not*," Kian said loyally, but he looked uneasy and changed the subject. "The weather's mild today. Let's all go watch Ea fly."

I agreed enthusiastically, but Bryg waved away the invitation. "I have some small chores to do," she said. "Go have fun. And Maeve, look after Lord Kian. Make sure he remembers how to find his way home." The pleasant echo of her laughter lingered in the hut as she ducked through the curtain and was gone.

Kian and I flew Ea over a field close to the ringfort instead of carrying her through the woodland. It gave us more time to let her enjoy the freedom of open skies. It felt good knowing that there was no need to conceal our meetings. That secrecy ended when I decided not to seek his help in learning weaponry any further. As long as I could find solitary times to continue practicing with my sling, I was happy.

I shaded my eyes with one hand, greedily drinking in the sight of Ea hovering in the blue. *Let them all see me here with him,* I thought. *Let them spread as many rumors as they like, saying Kian and I are more than friends. If that's the price for more moments like this, I'll pay it gladly.*

I whirled the lure above my head and drew Ea to my hand.

Kian praised my success as he coaxed her onto his wrist and hooded her. "I'll settle her for the night," he said. And then, shyly: "Will you sit by me at dinner?"

"Bryg and the others will tease me about it," I said. "On the other hand, your mother will be overjoyed."

I underestimated Lady Lassaire's reaction when she saw me choose a place at Kian's side. That woman smiled so victoriously you'd think she was a chieftain bringing home the severed heads of his enemies. My friends made provoking faces at me through the whole meal, and even Ula set aside her poise to lavish kisses on an invisible lover. I expected to endure worse once the four of us went to our room for the night, but it would all be in fun and harmless.

It began as soon as the last of us came through the bull-hide curtain. Gormlaith hurried to her bed in the far corner of the room, made her nightly preparations quickly, and lay down. With her back turned to the rest of us, she began taking long, deep breaths, as though she'd fallen asleep the moment she ducked under the cover.

She doesn't want to join in the teasing, I thought. *Does she think it would be disloyal to her Connla, since he's so close to Kian? That's sweet, but it wouldn't make any difference to me. I'll tell her in the morning.* I started to braid my hair for the night, waiting for the first gibe.

"Let me do that for you, Maeve," Dairine said, dropping onto my bed so clumsily that she almost knocked me over onto the floor. She grabbed a fistful of my hair as I toppled.

"Ow! Be careful," I cried.

"Tsk, I'm *so* sorry. I'm obviously not highborn enough to touch Lady Maeve's gorgeous curls."

"I didn't say—"

She was back in her own bed without waiting to hear me. "*Someone* thinks she's too good for the rest of us," Dairine announced.

"*Someone* always did," Ula chimed in. "Too good, too pretty, too *clever*." She put extra bite behind the last word.

"Clever enough to use one fish to catch another." Dairine giggled.

"Oh, I don't think she was using *fish* for bait, do you?" They snickered.

"What are you talking about?" I pleaded, thoroughly confused. "I wouldn't have sat with Kian tonight, but he asked me, and I didn't think it would be so important."

"Oh, he *asked* her," Dairine said in a nasal drawl. "Lord Kian *asked* her."

Ula snorted. "I'm surprised she's not claiming that he *begged* her."

"Dairine, Ula, shame on you, picking on Maeve this way." Was Bryg coming to my rescue? "She's going to think you envy her for capturing Lord Kian." There was a pause, and then: "She already thinks you're jealous of her for everything else, from the tip of her crooked little nose to the bottoms of her sprawling feet. Isn't that right, Princess Goosefoot?" This time they all laughed.

I felt the blood rise to my cheeks. I'd never thought my feet were particularly wide until now. And if they were, what was wrong with that? But somehow, hearing my friends treat it as a flaw made it seem like one to me. Why were they doing this? I didn't know what to say, and I lay there hoping that if I remained silent, they'd leave me alone.

"Maeve?" Bryg called softly. "Maeve, dear, aren't you talking to me? Did I hurt your feelings?"

"I think she's asleep," Ula whispered.

"*I* think she's trying the same trick on Bryg that worked on Lord Kian," Dairine declared. "The longer she keeps her tongue tied in a knot, the closer she draws her prey until the miserable creature is hopelessly in love with her. Poor Lord Kian, she's tired of him already, so she's moving on to her next victim."

"Me?" Bryg shrilled. "But how—? Oh my, doesn't she know we're both *girls*?"

"Does she care?" Dairine asked archly.

"She thinks she's a man, that's what," Ula said. "I heard that she used to dress like one too. Nothing she'd do would surprise me. You'd better not close your eyes tonight, Bryg, now that you've had the bad luck to catch her eye."

"No, I can't stand it, save me!" Bryg cried. "You're my *friends;* you can't let this happen. I don't want her to have me. I don't want her to touch me. I don't even want to breathe the same air and that—that—"

"You don't have to!" I sprang out of my bed, holding the blanket tight around my body, and bolted for the door.

Three pairs of hands grabbed me before I could slip past the bull-hide curtain. For someone who claimed she didn't want me to touch her, Bryg had no qualms about digging her fingers into my arm and squeezing to the bone. I thrashed in their grip, but three against one was a fight I couldn't win.

"How stupid are you, Maeve?" Bryg hissed. "Do you want to make a spectacle of yourself, running out of here like *that*?" She tore away my blanket, leaving me shivering in a thin, ragged dress no longer good for anything but night wear.

"She just wants to do it to get us in trouble," Ula said. "Now that she's lured Lord Kian back, she'll be Lady Lightning's darling again, Maeve do-no-wrong, Maeve pure-and-perfect." She accented the end of her sentence with a vicious pinch on my shoulder. I yelped.

"There she goes," Dairine said. "Making noise over nothing, fussing like an old woman."

"Like a *baby*," Bryg amended. "Hush, everyone! The High King's infant daughter is full of her mother's milk and sleeping. If we disturb her, we'll pay for it with our lives. Some kings rule by wisdom, but Lord Eochu never had much of that. He's such a fool that he fed his tongue to the Morrígan's ravens and now he can only speak with his sword."

"Shut up! Don't you dare say such things about my father!" I shouted, flailing my arms to drive them away from me. My three tormentors simply danced out of reach and surged in again, shoving me against a wall. I squirmed and pushed back, but they kept me pinned until I screamed in frustration, "Let me *go*!"

My yell brought the sound of running feet to our doorway and a man's voice asking, "Is everything all right in there, girls?"

Silence froze all of us for a breath. Then two hands clamped themselves over my mouth and Dairine replied, "Nothing's wrong. Lady Maeve was having a nightmare."

"Oh. Sorry to hear that. Rest well."

We heard his footsteps retreating. Once he was gone, the hands covering my mouth dropped and everyone but me giggled.

"What's the matter, Maeve?" Bryg asked amiably. "Wasn't that funny enough for you?"

"What you were doing to me wasn't funny at all," I retorted. "Let's do the same to you and see how you like it!"

Dairine guffawed. "What did I tell you, Bryg? Our friend Maeve likes to think she can take a joke as well as any of us, but she wouldn't recognize one if it bit her!" She threw her arms around me. "We had to have a bit of fun with you tonight, Princess Goosefoot. It's our way of reminding you that you're still one of us, and not the lady of Dún Beithe just yet."

"I never said I wanted to be—"

Bryg yawned loudly. "Can we talk about this in the morning? I'm *so* tired." The others followed her lead immediately, and I found myself standing with my back to the wall, shivering in the dark.

CHAPTER FOURTEEN

The Wolfhound's Ghost

IT WAS A joke. They told me so the next morning. All of them said they were sorry and begged me to forgive them, even Gormlaith, who had slept through the whole thing.

I thought that was odd, but I didn't dwell on it. I was still shaken by what had happened. They gave me the opportunity to rush back to the way things were before last night's attack, and I grabbed it.

"I'd never want you to be angry with me, Maeve," Bryg said when I forgave her and the others. All four of us were seated on a long bench outdoors, sewing new dresses for the warm weather to come. It wasn't a task that needed Lady Lassaire's instruction, so we worked unsupervised.

"I was," I admitted. "But we're past that now."

"Good. I was afraid you'd run crying to Lady Lassaire over a ridiculous jest that got out of hand. I'm so glad you're not such a weakling." She leaned her head on my shoulder in an affectionate way. "You're my *friend,* Maeve. Do you know how important that is to me? I've been without anyone like you or the other girls for such a long time! The healers of Avallach were kind to me, but it wasn't the same as having friends."

As soon as she said *healers,* I thought of Odran, and my breath caught in my throat. Had she seen him? His father was determined to make a druid out of him, though Odran told me the only aspect of that arduous training that appealed to him was the chance to learn more ways to help the sick and wounded, animals as well as people.

I had seen too many days pass without any news about him. Sometimes it broke my heart. If the sky matched the exact shade of his eyes, if the flash of a crow's wing in flight reminded me of his shining black hair, I lost myself in tears. Sometimes it terrified me. I'd take refuge in dreams of our sweet, gentle kisses, only to have them jolted aside by memories of the intense, fiery sensation of Conchobar's lips on mine.

Sometimes I felt resigned to it. I told myself, *Our paths have parted forever. His training will take years and years to finish. If I wait for him, how will he know? And even then, would he wait for me? No, I have to believe it's over. If I keep looking backward, I can't see the way ahead.*

What sensible thoughts! Then Bryg mentioned Avallach and they blew away like bits of straw. Avallach . . . Odran . . . the smallest wisp of a chance she'd met him and could tell me how he was—I had to grasp it.

"What was it like on Avallach?" I asked, doing my best to sound only mildly interested. "Is it like Èriu?"

"Oh no, it's *much* smaller. You can walk from one end to the other in a day. The druids have their settlement in the south, not too far inland from Lord Diarmaid's stronghold on the coast."

"It's hard to picture a whole community of nothing but druids," I said. "How do they feed themselves?"

Bryg chuckled. "The same way your exalted father, the High King, feeds himself, silly! They make other people fear them enough to give them all they want—everything from cloth to cattle. Who needs to plow and sow and harvest when bread appears by magic? Who needs to step in piles of cow manure when milk and meat are simply *there* for you?"

It pained me to hear her. I didn't see Father as my perfect hero anymore, but all the ways he'd hurt me didn't change the fact that he was no parasite. He worked hard for the good of our people. And how could she speak so against the druids? It would have been malicious coming from anyone's lips, but it sounded like the worst ingratitude when it came from a girl who owed her renewed sanity to the people she defamed.

"You know they do more than make demands," I said. "Their healing lore alone is worth—!"

"You're defending them so *passionately,* Maeve." The bard's daughter showed her teeth. "Are you hoping to claim Master Cairpre for your next lover?" Dairine and Ula burst into belly-clutching glee, imagining me paired with Dún Beithe's elderly druid.

"I never saw them demand gifts, but you'd have to be stu-pid not to know it's true," Bryg replied indifferently. "I spent my time there far from the heart of things. Their settlement's spread out, a hodgepodge of huts scattered in a clearing, with a few of them tucked among the trees. There's a great house, of course, and a sacred space nearby for the seasonal rites, but—you won't believe this, Maeve—there's no wall! Nothing sur-rounds them but the forest."

"No wall?" I repeated. "How do they protect themselves?"

"What do they have to protect?" She shrugged. "If any raiding party did swoop down on them, what would they find worth taking? They don't keep their own herds. They have no treasures. The best a marauder could do would be to round up all the lads who study there and sell them for slaves."

I took shallow breaths, creeping gradually closer to my quarry. "Ah, so it's a place of healing *and* learning. All the boys at Cruachan were going to be warriors. I never met one who wanted to be a druid or a bard." That was no lie, since Odran had no desire of his own to follow his father's path. "Tell me more about—"

Bryg sat up straight and put space between us. "I'm not surprised. Lord Eochu wouldn't encourage any lad to share my father's art. That would mean he'd have one less sword to serve him. He might fear the bards—as he should!—but respect them?" Her laugh was as sarcastic as her face.

"That's not true," I said hotly. "When Lord Morann took our bard, Devnet, hostage, Father was willing to do anything to save him."

"I know." Her eyes narrowed. "Lord Kian told me." She turned to the other fosterlings, who were all seated close enough to hear our every word. "It was such a wonderful story, especially the part where *you* saved the day. I had to share it with my friends, just to see if any of them believed it."

Ula and Dairine tittered. Gormlaith kept her eyes on her needle. Bryg noticed that the plump girl wasn't joining in.

"You remember how you reacted, don't you, Gormlaith?" she crooned. "Let Maeve hear what you said when I told you how Lord Kian praised her bravery and cleverness."

"I—I don't remember." Gormlaith's thread tangled.

"But you must! Maeve is waiting. You can't disappoint the High King's daughter."

"Bryg, leave her alone," I said. It was a warning.

"Why are you using *that* tone with me? You sound ready to pick up a sword and cut me down. All I did was ask Gormlaith an innocent question. She doesn't *have* to answer." So Bryg said, but a block of wood could tell what she really meant.

Gormlaith knew she had no choice. "I said—I said it sounded like another of those tales that made you shine like a goddess, someone much too good to mix with ordinary girls like us. I—I—I said it wasn't enough for you to be prettier than Ula and able to attract men more easily than Dairine and—and do *everything* better than me. Now you had to fill Lord Kian's head with impossible stories."

"You mean lies," I said, forcing myself to stay calm.

"At least they're entertaining," Ula said. "You have a talent for weaving tales, Maeve. Bryg, did your father ever meet a *female* bard? Princess Goosefoot could have a fine future doing that."

"She'll have to change her name," Dairine said. "Farewell, Princess Goosefoot, and all hail Maeve Two-Tongues!"

I surged to my feet, poised to slap the hateful name from her mouth. The dress I'd been sewing tumbled to my feet, forgotten in the dirt. Bryg snatched it up and looped it over my raised arm, dragging it down with her full weight so that I lost my balance and fell. I felt someone drop hard onto my back. Another person sat on my legs, but I couldn't tell who it was because I'd sprawled facedown.

"Let me up!" I shouted, struggling to kick free of them. It was useless and I knew it, but I refused to lie there without putting up some kind of a fight. "Get off me!"

"Ask nicely, Maeve Two-Tongues." Bryg spoke as if I were a cranky child. "And swear you won't try to hurt poor, innocent Dairine if we do release you."

"Are all the girls of Connacht such awful brawlers?" Ula asked in her lofty way. "Or is it just Maeve?"

I braced my hands under my shoulders and made one huge, concentrated effort to roll sideways. I was beyond delighted when it worked. No bard's song was sweeter than hearing Ula and Dairine squeal while Bryg yelled, "You worthless idiots, can't you do *anything* right?" I didn't linger to hear the next line of that tune. I was on my feet again, my skirt held high as I ran away.

I didn't know where I was going, only that I couldn't remain where I'd been. *If this is another joke, I'm not getting it,* I thought. I must have looked a sight, my dress filthy, my hair in tangles, my face smeared with grime and twisted into a grimace of misery.

Why did Bryg do that? One moment we were talking pleasantly about Avallach, the next she had her teeth in my throat and was driving the other girls to join her in the kill. Did the druids fail to heal her completely when she lost her mind over her brother's death? Is this some remnant of that madness? I ran on, my chest aching, my goal unknown. I began to sob, not from grief but from anger. *Bryg might have an excuse, but the others? Even Gormlaith? What did I ever do to them? I thought they were my friends!*

I paid no attention to where I was going until a strong arm barred my way. "Lady Maeve?" Connla's brows knit in concern as he looked me over. "What happened to you?" I collapsed against his chest, weeping. He stood there, awkwardly patting me on the back while a group of his fellow warriors drifted in around us.

I heard them murmuring guesses about what had turned me into the crumpled, tear-streaked, pitiable creature huddled in Connla's arms. Some were offensive, some were absurd, and all were the new-laid eggs containing rumors with the power to make my future even worse than my present. I had to crush them in the shell.

I pulled away from Connla. He was visibly grateful to have me at arm's length again. "Thank you, friend," I said calmly, wiping my tears with the cuff of my gown. "Thank you for being so patient with me. Have you ever taken such a bad fall that you just lie there, afraid you've broken your bones? And even when you're on your feet again, you can't shake off the fear that you've done something to your insides that you can't detect now, but that might shatter you later?"

"I know what she means," one of the gathered men announced. "I had a cousin who fell out of a tree onto his head. He said he was fine and walked away steady as you please, but he was dead the next morning."

"So that's why you're in such a state." Now that the awful mystery of my wild sobbing was solved, Connla's mind was at ease. He could take control of the situation. "Let's take you to see Master Cairpre. He'll say if that tumble you took did any lasting harm."

I bowed my head demurely and let him lead me in search of

Dún Beithe's druid. I felt a passing pang of guilt for bothering that wise man over nothing. *I never said that I fell,* I thought. *I only asked "Have you ever . . . ?" Should I have told him what the girls did to me, even his beloved Gormlaith?* I mulled it over, then put aside the notion. *Not yet. Not until I learn why they've changed toward me so cruelly. If Bryg's sickness is back, she'll need healing, not punishment. I'm going to find out, and I'm going to stay strong until I do.*

As expected, my visit with Master Cairpre was brief. The druid pronounced me in good health, if a little bruised, and cleaned a scratch on my cheek before sending me on my way. I went straight to Ea's shelter, whisked off her hood, and found comfort in the blazing gold of her eyes.

"Come with me, beautiful lady," I murmured, stoking her feathers with my fingertips. "Both of us need to breathe different air for a while."

I picked up my armguard from the foot of her perch, and soon the two of us were through Dún Beithe's gate and free. The guard on duty was one of the men who'd seen me weeping in Connla's arms. He didn't question my escape, merely saying, "Glad to see you looking better, milady."

I raced down the ringfort slope and cast Ea into the sky as I ran. She flew high, carrying my spirit with her. I shared her wings, sailing far above the muck and confusion that was holding me down. There was no backbiting or insults or attacks in the kestrel's boundless realm of sun and cloud and cleansing wind. No one could catch me, no one could hurt me, no one could make me doubt myself. I shouted Ea's name as though hailing a victorious chief, a king whose enemies lay conquered at his feet, a—

No. Not a chief, not a king—a queen. A queen who stood in no man's shadow, who ruled her land with the same skill, grace, and independence as Ea ruled the skies.

A queen who would be envied and derided, the target of edged words from those who failed to rise, so spent their lives pulling others down. A queen with the strength to strike their grasping claws aside, and if they did draw blood, with the courage to never let them see her cry.

I stopped running and rubbed my eyes, still weary from weeping. "You make it look easy, Ea," I said, glancing up to where the kestrel hovered just above a nearby line of trees. "I wish you could tell me your secret." I blew my breath out sharply and shook dust from my dress. "Well, I'll work on that, but now we should go home."

That was when I realized I hadn't brought the lure.

She did return to my hand . . . eventually. The light was fading when Ea had had enough of flight and finally deigned to notice the frantic earthbound girl calling her name.

"I suppose I should be flattered," I told her as I secured her hood. "You only come back to Kian for food. I must be special to you." She let me know just how special I was by leaving a white stain on my armguard. "Don't tell me you're on Bryg's side too," I said wryly.

Kian was waiting for us in the little hut. "Where have you been?" He sounded more worried than angry. I explained what had happened and showed him my stained armguard, hoping he'd smile. He took it from me and set to cleaning it, but he still looked grim.

"Everyone is talking about you," he said as he rubbed Ea's droppings from the leather. "You and Connla this time. Doesn't it bother you that your friend likes him?"

"Does no one in this place do anything *but* gossip?" I exclaimed. "Your father really ought to try finding a bard to serve him permanently. That way the folk of Dún Beithe wouldn't have to provide their entertainment at my expense."

"It isn't funny, Maeve."

"No, it isn't. I don't take friendship *or* love lightly, and I hate having a crowd of idle gossipmongers making me look like someone I'm not. That includes you, Kian."

"Me? I didn't carry tales about you."

"But when you heard these newest rumors, did you object? Did you challenge them? Did you speak out and say they weren't true?"

"How would I know if they're true or false?"

"Because you know *me*," I said fiercely. "Or I hoped you did."

"Maeve—"

"Did you even bother talking to *Connla* before you threw all of this in my face? You might not trust my word, but you call him your brother. If he defends me, will you accept the truth?"

Kian bent his head over the stained armguard and scrubbed harder. "I'm sorry. I should have done that. It's my own fault for forgetting how Bryg can be."

Bryg?

"Is she the one who told you about Connla and me? She wasn't even there!"

"It's my fault for believing her. I didn't think about how she acts sometimes." He looked up. "What did you do to get on her bad side, Maeve? Whatever it was, apologize and make amends as fast as you can."

"What are you talking about? Make amends for *what*? The only thing I can think of is—is—" I paused. *Should I tell him that she wants him for her own? He's had years to take notice of her as more than just another of his mother's fosterlings. If he hasn't done it by now, he won't do it to spare me her spite. And what if my words make him treat her differently, with pity everyone can see? She'd be humiliated. I won't do that to her. I'll settle our quarrel fairly, or not at all.*

I spread my hands. "I guess I can't tell you any reason for her behavior after all."

"Think harder, then," Kian said. "It may be something small and easily fixed. I don't like the idea that it's the same business with Aifric all over again."

"Gormlaith's closest friend, the one who ran away?" The back of my neck tingled with apprehension. "What did Bryg have to do with that?"

"I shouldn't say. You've made it clear that you loathe talebearers."

I laid one hand on his arm. "Tattlers take joy in spreading rumors. No one has to invite them to open their mouths. If you can tell me anything that will help smooth matters between Bryg and me, please speak."

He looked doubtful, but he did as I asked. "From the day she came here, Bryg ruled the other fosterlings. She was good-natured enough with everyone else, but with them, she always had a sharp tongue and she used it to take over."

I remembered seeing Gormlaith, Ula, and Dairine rushing to serve the bard's daughter. Now I understood it was done out of fear. "If you're not her friend, you're her target," I observed.

Kian nodded. "She was sweet as long as things were going her way. I have to say, I don't know why she started picking on Aifric. That girl was like a blade of grass, bending in any direction the wind blew, always going along with whatever the others wanted. She was especially obedient to Bryg. There were times when she seemed to be testing Aifric, giving her all sorts of tasks, making her jump at every whim, seeing how far she could push her before she fought back." His mouth turned down. "Aifric was no fighter. A lot of people talked about how painful it was to watch."

"Then why didn't any of you *stop* watching and do something about it?" I demanded.

"Uh . . . the one time I asked Aifric if she was all right, she said yes." He caught sight of my disappointed expression and shouted, "Well, what was I *supposed* to do? She said she didn't need any help and she avoided me after that. I couldn't tie her to a post until she admitted what was wrong, could I?"

"Did your mother notice any of this?" I asked gently.

"I don't know." He finished cleaning the armguard and set it aside. "She doesn't like hearing bad news or having to deal with problems."

"So she pretends they aren't there," I said.

He didn't disagree, but he looked embarrassed. "She wants everyone to be as happy and contented as she is. Is that such a terrible thing?" he snapped, on the defensive, his mother's reluctant champion.

"It was terrible enough for Aifric," I replied. "Wasn't that why she ran away?"

"You don't know anything about it. You weren't here."

"But you were, Kian, and you do know the truth of it. If you don't, why are you urging me to beg Bryg's pardon for— for—for *what*? What have I done to her? Aifric was clay in that girl's hands. Did she ever live a single day *without* an apology on her lips? And yet she still suffered so much that she had to flee." I raised my chin. "You don't have to worry on my account. That won't happen to me. I'm going to find her and put an end to this."

"How?"

He looked so nervous that I had to laugh and say, "By cutting her head off. How else? Be a good friend and lend me your sword."

I found Bryg and the other fosterlings in our room, getting ready for the evening meal. I was about to speak to her when I was jolted by the sight of the half-sewn dress I'd abandoned earlier. It lay across my bed, fully stitched, the fabric unwrinkled and spotless. The last time I'd seen it, it was a wad of cloth beside me in the dirt.

"Who did this?" I asked in a hoarse, uncertain voice.

"Do you like it?" Bryg asked, oozing charm. "We felt so terrible about teasing you that we all worked on it together. Try it on. It's the perfect shade for your eyes."

"Here, Maeve, dear." Ula brought me a bowl of water. "Take off that old gown and wash yourself. I'll braid your hair. You'll feel much better."

"You have to sit next to me at dinner," Dairine said. "I'll die if you don't. I'm going to make sure you get the best of everything that's served tonight, no matter what. Please? It's the only way I'll know there aren't any hard feelings between us. You know, if you think about it, the whole thing was actually funny."

"What about you, Gormlaith?" I said in a low, steady voice. "Don't you want to tell me how calling me names and forcing me to eat dust was all one great big hilarious jest? Are you going to make a peace offering that will turn this"—I spread my grubby, bedraggled skirt—"and this"—I pointed at the scratch across my cheek—"into puffs of sunstruck mist?"

The blond girl began to tremble. "I didn't want to do it, Maeve. I don't think you told Lord Kian false tales about yourself. I don't think you're a liar. I—"

"You don't think at all." Bryg silenced Gormlaith with a backhanded slap on the arm. "Why did you tell us all of those wicked things about our friend if you knew they were false? Maybe we should start calling *you* Two-Tongues, you fat sow."

"Maybe you should just *stop*," I said. "I want to talk to you." I turned to the other girls. "If you want to make up for what you did earlier, give me time alone with Bryg now."

"What are you going to do to her?" Ula asked. She sounded more curious than concerned.

"Just what I said: talk. Do you want me to take an oath that I won't hurt her?"

Bryg uttered a short, defiant laugh. "I'm not afraid of anything *this* one can say or do to me. Get out, all of you." The three girls did as she ordered without a backward glance. The bull hide swung back into place after them. Bryg plopped herself down on her bed and cocked her head at me. "Talk."

"Why, Bryg?" I said. "Why have you been making the others treat me like this? It goes beyond the pranks they pulled on me when I first came here. If I've done something against you, you'll have to tell me what it is, but if the only reason you're playing these evil games is to prove you can, I'll—"

"—tell your father?" Bryg cut in. "First you'd better make sure he wants to hear what you have to say. Lord Eochu is a mighty man, but a choosy one too. He has a little wooden box in which he keeps the world exactly the way he wants it to be. If you try to put something in or take something out that doesn't suit him, he washes you away."

I stared at her. What was I hearing—the words of a poet or the ranting of a mind gone mad again? My anger ebbed. I was alarmed for her sake.

Bryg saw and misinterpreted the anxious look on my face. "Scared, Maeve? From what Kian said, I didn't think you *could* be frightened. Where's the highborn lady brave enough to face a vicious wolfhound's jaws?"

"He—he told you about that?"

"That?" Bryg echoed scornfully. "That's only a *crumb* of what I know. You weren't content to be born a girl. You wanted a man's skills. You forced weaponry lessons from one of your father's young fighters. What chance did a good, honest lad stand against a spoiled, artful, conniving princess? He couldn't say no to you.

"Did you have fun playing a warrior's part? You must have loved it when all of Cruachan praised your courage for fending off the beast. As long as you fed your pride with their admiration, did you care if your recklessness enraged the High King? You'd stained his vision of how the world should be, how a daughter should act, and thanks to you, he had to cleanse it—"

"Bryg, hear me, that wasn't—"

"—with my brother's blood!"

CHAPTER FIFTEEN

A Chill in Springtime

THAT NIGHT I ate my dinner without tasting it. I sat with the other fosterlings, but I sat alone. The four of them chattered and giggled and gobbled their food with hearty appetites. I nibbled my portion, but memories of Kelan soon left me gazing numbly at the food.

I kept stealing sidelong glances at Bryg, searching for some sign that her revelation about Kelan had marked her as deeply as it scarred me. All I saw was a happy, smiling girl who sometimes caught me looking at her and responded with a friendly face. Her eyes held no trace of the unforgiving hatred she'd sent blazing over me before she went raging out of our room. She even spoke to me several times, asking if I was enjoying the meal or if she could hand me another piece of bread.

"Bryg, please let me explain what happened," I said, leaning close so as not to be heard by anyone else. "Kelan was my dear friend, almost like a brother to me too. I never wanted him to die. I didn't *seek* a fight with the wolfhound; it was a vicious animal that attacked for no reason. I used the skill Kelan taught me to keep it from harming the girl he loved and the baby she carried. I didn't know my father would—"

"All right, Maeve, I'll bring you some more meat," Bryg chirped and jumped up, leaving me to waste my breath on her empty place. She didn't return, but spent the rest of the meal far from me, fawning over Lady Lassaire.

I tried to talk to her again when we were all back in our sleeping chamber. She yawned in my face. "I'm so tired. Can it wait until morning?" I couldn't say yes or no because she slipped into her bed, covered herself head to toe, and made snoring sounds so loud and crude they let me know better than words that she was done with me. Gormlaith, Ula, and Dairine followed her example. I was alone in the midst of company once more.

They cast me aside. We five were still together at meals, at lessons, and at night, but that changed nothing. Bryg and the others built cobweb walls between us, barriers that were barely visible to the eye, startlingly strong when I tried to get past them. The girls I'd thought of as my friends shut me out at every turn. They never said a word to me, and if I tried talking to them, they suddenly had important things to do elsewhere.

I thought I could get around their tactics by speaking to them when we were having lessons with Lady Lassaire. Kian's mother might own the magic for making problems turn invisible, but she'd *have* to notice if I asked one of the girls a direct question and was frozen out. Even *she* would need to open her eyes to the tension and hostility thrumming among her fosterlings and do something about it.

My plan worked, but only in my head. When I tried it, I

learned just how resourceful some people can be when malice is at stake.

"Bryg, what do you think of this pattern I'm embroidering?" I asked in a clear, loud voice, standing in front of her so she couldn't pretend not to hear me. I was ornamenting the sleeve of the blue gown she and the others had rescued after our last violent set-to. I still didn't understand why they'd done that, but I wasn't going to question their lone kindness too closely.

She looked up from her own needlework and glanced in Lady Lassaire's direction. The mistress of Dún Beithe was watching us with her usual bland smile. Bryg looked back to me and opened her mouth. She was going to break her silence. I'd won!

Her hands flitted under her embroidery. She shrieked and leaped to her feet, a thread of blood already creeping down the needle embedded in her palm.

Ula was at her side even before her first scream faded. "Gormlaith and I will take her to Master Cairpre," she announced, and did so without waiting to be told otherwise. Though Lady Lassaire gasped and fluttered over what had happened, it didn't take long for her to sink back to her jealously guarded serenity. She never paused to question why it should take two girls to escort one.

I knew the answer: *If they're gone, they don't have to talk to me, no matter what I do.* I looked at Dairine, still seated and stitching away. *I should try again. It might work, especially if Dairine remembers how I saved her from being shamed that time with Bran.* I cleared my throat and turned to her.

Dairine met my eyes, held up her needle in one hand, and

deliberately spread the other on her lap, palm up. The threat was clear: *I would rather stab myself than talk to you.* I swallowed my words and bent over my own work, defeated.

It hurt to be shut out. At least Bryg believed she had cause for shunning me, whether or not she was right. What reason did the others have for treating me this way? None except Bryg's command. Kian told me about how she dominated them, but I'd clung to the hope that they cared for me just enough to defy her. When the distance between us continued to grow, I felt like a fool.

Was there ever any bond between us or did I imagine it because I longed for it to be there? I wondered. *Are they betraying a friendship that never existed? Have I been deceiving myself?*

I sat with Lady Moriath at dinner. I'd had enough of the fosterlings' wall of silence. I would have joined Kian, but he was deep in conversation with a group of his fellow warriors. The warming weather meant it would soon be the season for the young men of Dún Beithe to prove themselves by riding out to raid their neighbors' herds or defend their own. They had plans to make, arguments to raise over those plans, and a fight or two to start when they knew the girls were watching.

Lady Moriath looked unwell. I feared she'd lost weight, and she was only pecking at her dinner. When I asked if I could bring her some other dish to tempt her appetite, she declined with a weak smile.

"You shouldn't be fussing over me, Lady Maeve. I always fall slightly ill when the seasons change, but I get better quickly."

"You'd recover even sooner if you ate more," I said more sternly than I intended.

She chuckled. "What has this world come to when the

gosling's telling the goose how to lay eggs? You sound like my mother. Mother, is that you in there?" She cocked her head and peered deep into my eyes. "Have you come back to guide me to Tech Duinn?"

I knew she wasn't serious, but I still felt a chill to hear her name the land of the dead. "Don't say such things, Lady Moriath. You can't leave us yet." I smiled and added, "My embroidery is still hideous. I need you!"

She shook her head. "How sweet of you to say that, even if it's not true. I've heard Lady Lassaire herself praise your needlework. She says you have a wonderful talent."

"I had a wonderful teacher. I wish there were something I could do to repay you for the time you spent on me."

"Hmm." Her mischievous smile let me glimpse the girl she had once been. "You might start by embroidering the cuffs of my new summer gown—"

"Done," I agreed happily.

"—and then by filling these aged hands with gold—" She purposely cupped them together so tightly that a single pair of earrings would do the job.

"Done!" I cried, enjoying our jest.

"—and finally by giving me your promise to keep me as one of your attendants when you become the lady of Dún Beithe. I'm much too old to go seeking—"

"What did you say?" The words came out harsh and angry. The joke was over for me.

Lady Moriath was taken aback by my reaction. "I mean when you wed Lord Kian. That's all Lady Lassaire talks about."

"Not to me." My mouth turned down sharply.

The older woman looked contrite. "My dear, I never

wanted to upset you. It's all just talk. Lady Lassaire loves to weave her son's future even more than his clothes. She has no way of knowing if the High King would choose such a match for you, though she has said that if you told your father how much you love Kian, Lord Eochu might be swayed into giving his consent."

"She's thought of everything, hasn't she," I stated. *Everything but what I've got to say about this. What's the use of leaving home if I'm still confronting people who think they can live my life for me?*

If I let them.

I didn't want to dwell on Lady Lassaire's one-sided decision about my marriage, so I steered the conversation away from it. Perhaps Lady Moriath would have some suggestion for how to deal with Bryg and her hunting pack? Surely at her age she'd seen similar incidents, perhaps even a few that ended more happily than Aifric's story.

I brought up the subject casually, without revealing how much the girls' silence hurt. I wanted advice, but not at the cost of making Lady Moriath fret about me. That was why I described the situation as though pointing out a pesky fly. The unwelcome insect should be swatted, but there was no pressing need to do it.

The older woman frowned. "You should tell Lady Lassaire."

I remembered what Kian had said about his mother: *"She doesn't like hearing bad news or having to deal with problems."*

"I don't think it will do any good."

"You ought to try anyway. Or if it will help, I'll talk to her. There might be less chance of her dismissing it as a girls' silly spat if I speak for you. At least I can make her *listen*." Lady

Moriath smiled. "I'm old, but I'm not toothless. Once I bite, I hold on."

I thanked her, but privately doubted she'd succeed. Another day of chill silence passed for me, and when I looked for Lady Moriath that evening, she wasn't there. Had she offended or annoyed her mistress somehow? Had she insisted too strongly that Lady Lassaire step out of her placid, trouble-free world and actually *help* one of her fosterlings? I hated the thought of my kindly teacher being banished to her sleeping chamber as though she were a naughty child.

I never should have agreed to let her fight my battle, I thought. *I'm going to talk to Lady Lassaire about Bryg and the others right now, and while I'm at it, I'll ask her not to blame Lady Moriath for speaking for me.*

I started across the great hall at once. Lady Lassaire was seated in her usual place at her husband's side, attended by her three favorite companions. They had all received their portions and were eating heartily. I had to thread my way through a crowd to reach them. The space around the central hearth was bustling with people too impatient to wait for servants to fill their platters and too lowborn to be given their food first.

I glanced behind me briefly, just in time to see my former friends settling down on a bench together. Bryg saw where I was headed and gave me a look of pure rage. Then she swallowed her resentment, put on a broad smile, and used her bard's voice to declaim: "Why are you in such a hurry to fill your belly, Lady Maeve? Or do you *need* to gobble two dinners?" She stood up, stuck out her stomach, and used her hands to describe the bulging shape of a pregnant woman's body. The men and women nearest the group of fosterlings laughed.

Ula uttered a shocked gasp so blatant that an infant could tell it was false. When she spoke, it was plain that she'd picked up Bryg's trick of whispering at the top of her lungs. "Oh! How can you say such things? Everyone knows Lady Maeve has never let any man claim her."

"Really?" Dairine feigned surprise even worse than Ula. "Why is that? She told me how much she despises Lord Kian, but she *must* have some other lover!"

"Do you want to know the truth?" Ula asked. She no longer needed to raise her voice. Dairine's lie had silenced every other conversation. All ears perked up, ravenous to hear more. "It's because of the *curse.*"

"The curse?" Dairine wrung her hands. "Poor Lady Maeve! What is it?"

"I'll tell you," Ula said. "But it's so dreadful, I don't think you'll be able to hear it without fainting." She paused dramatically.

The great hall became a beehive, filled with the buzzing of countless muttered speculations. Everyone had a guess to make about my supposed bane. No one thought to question whether it really existed.

Ula decided that she had her audience sufficiently enthralled. She spoke again, as though Dairine were the only person eagerly awaiting her next words: "On second thought, I shouldn't be the one to say anything about it." Several poorly smothered groans of disappointment rose from among Lord Artegal's household. "Gormlaith's the one who revealed it to me. She should tell you."

Now all the attention fell on Gormlaith, who didn't want it. The plump girl remained hunched over her dinner. I swear she looked as if she were trying to turn herself to water, trickle off the bench, and soak out of sight into the floor.

"Don't be difficult, Gormlaith," Bryg said crisply. "Speak up. I want to know too."

"I—I don't know—I never—" Gormlaith was shaking.

"Yes, you *do* know." Bryg was relentless. "Be a good friend and share."

"She, uh, Lady Maeve can never have—have a sweetheart because—because she—she"—Gormlaith took a deep breath—"because she's got a pig's tail growing out of her backside and she's covered in bristles and if any man sees it, the rest of her will turn into a pig too!" She spewed the ugly lie quickly, spitting it out like the mud it was.

I stood by the hearthside and blazed hotter than the cookfire with embarrassment and anger. All around me the great hall rang with the sound of scandalized shrieks and mocking laughter. Even when I closed my eyes, I still saw a swarm of faces contorted by mirth at my expense.

Someone began oinking. I felt the sting of tears.

"Enough!" Lord Artegal was on his feet. "The next man who insults the High King's daughter so rudely will sleep with *my* pigs for five nights!"

Lady Lassaire giggled. "Dear husband, listen to you! What next? Will you insist on sewing a pig's tail to poor Gormlaith's dress to teach her a lesson? All she'll learn is that you have no sense of humor. Maeve, sweet child, come sit by me." She stretched out both arms, beckoning. "You weren't upset by such a trifling joke, were you?"

If I said no, I'd be lying. If I said yes, I'd be admitting that Bryg had the same power over me that she already had over the others. I chose to say nothing and took the seat Lady Lassaire offered.

Lord Artegal ordered a servant to bring me food. "Thank you," I said, accepting the platter. "For this and for putting a stop to that ugliness before. The other girls and I— Things haven't been good between us."

Lady Lassaire overheard and swooped in. "Nonsense! It's only that you're fairly new to fosterage. When I was younger, the same sort of thing happened all the time. You must learn to deal with it. Trust me, it means nothing."

"Aifric didn't feel that way."

The lady's face went from smiling to scowling in a blink. "How would you know anything about that? You weren't here." Her frown melted into a look of self-pity. "It wasn't my fault. Something was wrong with that girl or she wouldn't have run away. I did my best for her, counseling her to ignore all the jokes the others played on her, but she pretended she couldn't do that. Aifric always made a fuss over trifles. She had no mother, so perhaps that was her way of trying to hold my attention. If I'd given in, she never would've learned how to stand up for herself."

She did more than stand up, I thought. *She ran.*

I lowered my voice. "With respect, my lady, how do you know when it's no longer a joke?"

Lady Lassaire patted my cheek and gave me her most benevolent, condescending smile. "Sweet Maeve, you're making this seem like more than it is because you have nothing truly important to fill your days. Don't worry, you'll be married before you know it. Once you're a bride, you'll be too content and *much* too busy to go around seeing problems where there are none. I can tell you that there's at least one young man who'd gladly rescue you from all these imaginary quarrels. I swear by my honor, he is a very worthy warrior and sure to be a king one day. If you agree to accept . . . *him,* whoever he may be"—she was trying to be coy and only succeeded in sounding ridiculous—"we can send a messenger to Cruachan straightaway. You could be a happy wife by Beltane."

It was no use striving to make Lady Lassaire see things as they were when she'd decided how they *must* be. She'd just witnessed an incident bad enough to make Lord Artegal himself intervene, yet she still insisted I faced "imaginary" quarrels? The only way I'd get her help was by marrying Kian, and that was not going to happen.

I set my platter aside. "My lady, I'm flattered to hear that I've got one admirer who's willing to wed me, pig's tail and all," I said with a smile. "But he should know that I'm no longer the prize I used to be. My brothers will rule Connacht, not me. I won't bring much wealth or power to my husband. If this young man, whoever he may be"—I deliberately repeated her words—"is as wonderful as you say, he deserves a better bride."

She pooh-poohed my objections. "Everyone knows how dearly the High King loves you. He won't send you to your husband empty-handed, and he's sure to show favor to the man you love. Let's end these games, dearest Maeve; we both know who I mean. He cherishes you, and though you're too modest to admit your feelings for him, all Dún Beithe's noticed how much time the two of you spend in each other's company. If you'll just say the word, I'll gladly speak to—"

"Where is Lady Moriath?" I broke in, desperate to keep Kian's mother from taking things past the point of no return.

"I don't see her here tonight. My lady, *I* was the one who sent her to tell you about my troubles with the other fosterlings. I should have spoken for myself sooner. I'm the one to blame if you didn't want to hear about such things, not she."

With a quizzical look, Lady Lassaire tilted her head to one side and asked, "What are you talking about? Lady Moriath has been sick in her bed since last night."

"Maeve, you sweet girl, what have I done to deserve such tender care?" Lady Moriath asked. "It can't be fun for you, stuck here day after day, looking after me." She sighed, her hands very white against the earth-colored cover. "You've done more than enough."

"That's not true." I finished folding another blanket and raised her head gently as I tucked it behind her shoulders. Master Cairpre said she'd breathe more easily if she lay propped up. "You're the one doing *me* a favor. Every night I spend here is one less I have to spend crammed into that room with four other girls. And one of them *snores*." I tried to sound cheerful. She was still wheezing badly and her coughing spells showed no sign of going away.

She made a rasping noise when she laughed. "There's *always* one girl in every group who snores. I've heard every one of Dún Beithe's ladies say so when we talk about our time as fosterlings."

"Then you understand why I'm in no rush to go back." I filled a cup with watered-down wine and offered her a drink. She took a single sip and waved it away weakly.

"I understand more than you think. They're still tormenting you."

"I wouldn't call it *torment*," I began, not wanting to upset her with my problems.

"Now you sound like Lady Lassaire." She sighed again, a breath that became a short burst of coughing. "I'm sorry I wasn't able to speak to her for you."

"Never mind that; I spoke to her myself."

And suffered for it afterward, I thought, recalling how Bryg and the rest had leaped on me that night.

"Well, you certainly had a lot to say to Lady Lightning at dinner. What did you tell her?"

"Tsk. What do you think *she told her? Lies and more lies."*

"If you want to get us into trouble, think twice."

"Yes, or learn to sleep with your eyes open."

I tried to explain and they shouted me down. I tried to leave and Bryg ordered Gormlaith to block the doorway. They flung me facedown into my bed so violently that my head hit the edge of the wooden storage chest at its foot. Blue and yellow stars exploded in the darkness. I was too shocked to cry out, and the next instant I couldn't catch a breath at all because one of them was sitting on me. They didn't get up until they heard the sound of my indignant, frustrated tears.

Lady Moriath's cough yanked me out of those painful memories. I gave her a spoonful of honey and some more to drink. "Shall I fetch Master Cairpre?" I asked anxiously.

"No, I'm all right now." She clasped my hand. Her skin felt dry and fragile as a fallen leaf. "You should go."

"I don't want—"

"You should leave Dún Beithe. You can't take refuge here with me forever. I can imagine how bad things must be between you and those girls. If they were your friends, you'd want to spend *some* time with them and leave part of my care to others. Why suffer their cruelties when you have a choice? Go home, Maeve." Her grip tightened. *"Go home."*

I knew she said that out of love. *She must have thought: I couldn't save Aifric, but I can save this girl. If she returns to her family, she'll be safe.*

I thanked Lady Moriath and said I'd think about it. There was no need to tell her that I'd already decided not to leave. Going home would mean renouncing the freedom that I'd fought so hard to gain. It would mean returning to Cruachan and once more becoming no more than my father's daughter. Worst of all, it would mean leaving Ea behind. I'd sooner abandon a piece of my heart.

No matter how viciously Bryg tried to punish me for Kelan's death, I would endure it. If I fled back into Father's shadow, I could live a safe life, but I wouldn't be living a life that was truly mine.

Lady Moriath recovered her health and rejoined the household. I rejoiced to see her well, even though it meant I had to share the fosterlings' sleeping chamber again.

On my first night back, I lay down wondering if I'd have to deal with silence or taunting. Instead I distinctly heard Ula say, "Sleep well, Maeve." Dairine, too, wished me a good rest, and I thought I caught Gormlaith mumbling the same. Bryg didn't say a word; I expected as much.

What I didn't expect was to wake the next morning and find my new blue summer dress tossed across my bed, the backside stained with blood.

Bryg stood over me, her hands on her hips, relishing my

shock as I stared at the ruined garment. "Oh my, Maeve, don't the women of Cruachan teach you how to protect your clothing when the moon touches you? I'm not surprised; piglets always come from a pigsty."

I got up, shouldered past her, and flung open the lid of my storage chest, searching for something to wear. The wooden box was empty. Bryg cackled and flapped my bloodstained dress at me as if to say: *You've got no choice but to wear this in front of everyone!*

I am Maeve. As long as I live, I will *always* have a choice.

I crossed the room and pulled one of Bryg's gowns from the chest beside her bed. I wriggled into it and sailed out of our room with my head held high while she was still gaping at my nerve.

She was shorter and thinner than I, so the dress was a poor fit. Lady Lassaire took notice and questioned me about it at breakfast. Bryg rushed to complain about the theft when she saw Lady Lassaire talking with me, but I interrupted her grievance.

"This is Bryg's gown, as she says, my lady. She wove a spell that made all of my clothes disappear, so I borrowed a bit of her magic, tit for tat, and made one of *her* dresses vanish right before her eyes." I smiled sweetly at the bard's daughter. "Don't glower like that, Bryg. Surely *you* can take a joke."

Lady Lassaire rolled her eyes. "You girls are too much for me. Bryg, give Maeve back her clothing. Maeve, put on your own dress. And don't let me hear about *any* of you meddling with each other's things again!"

We all promised and she was content. Why wouldn't she

be? As long as she didn't have to *hear* about the little war being waged under her roof, she could believe it wasn't there.

I got all of my clothes back and they were never stolen, soiled, or mangled again. I was able to soak and scrub most of the stain out of the blue dress, but so many washings made it fade to the drab shade of an overcast autumn sky. I wish that had been my only loss.

They couldn't steal my garments, so they stole my peace. They hid the half-rotted corpse of a fish under my bed. *Oh! How did* that *get there, Maeve? Were you hungry?* They woke me before dawn by flicking water on my face and gulped down the evidence as soon as I sat up. They begged me to join them in talking about the dreams we'd had the previous night. How *funny* that all of theirs were about me doing crude or stupid or disgusting things. *But it was only a dream, Maeve!* they chirped, and ended the game before it was my turn to play.

Nights were bad, but daylight was no better. They insulted me to my face and spread lies about me behind my back. They became inexplicably clumsy whenever they were carrying anything they could "accidentally" spill on me. If I took my eyes off my platter at mealtimes, even for an instant, I'd choke on a beetle or a long strand of hair with my next mouthful.

If I ever have charge of fosterlings, I won't pretend I'm blind to such ugliness, I thought grimly. *I'm no Lady Lassaire. When I see another person being treated like this, I* will *speak out. I* will *defend her.*

But right now, I have to defend myself.

It was difficult because I'd decided not to fight them on their own dishonorable level. What good would it do to retaliate prank for prank, lie for lie? They wanted to drag me down into the muck. I wouldn't help them by diving in.

I wasn't always able to stick to my resolution. There were times when they nibbled at my nerves so skillfully, I'd snap and give them a taste of their own rotten meat. When Dairine teased me with a midnight sprinkle of water on my face, I countered with a bowlful dumped over her head. When Gormlaith purposely stumbled and dumped stew in my lap, I gave her a double serving of the same thing. And the foul-smelling dead fish under my bed? My Ea's skill at rodent hunting let me "share" her day's catch with Bryg.

Father always said that a king accepts gifts graciously and gives three times as much in return.

I was ashamed of myself after these incidents and didn't repeat them. How could I gloat over using Ea's kill to get back at Bryg when I remembered that I owed the kestrel's life to that unreasonable girl? How could I hate her the way she hated me when I knew how her brother's death had shattered her?

I could ignore what my onetime friends did to me, but I couldn't close my ears to what they said. If you throw filth hard enough, it clings. Cast a net of nasty rumor and you'll always find someone ready and willing to help you haul it ashore.

Even when Bryg and the others were nowhere nearby, I heard my name spoken in whispers as I passed. Men and women put their heads together and murmured, "Did you hear what she——?" and "Isn't it awful? But I can't say I'm surprised." All that saved me from despair was overhearing the occasional "Yes, I heard that, and I thank the gods I'm not enough of an imbecile to believe such tripe about Lady Maeve."

It was harder hearing the girls smear my family. When they

heaped slander on my blood kin within earshot, I wouldn't let it pass unchallenged. I grew a wolf's fangs.

For all the good *that* did. Whenever I confronted the fosterlings in midgossip, I was met by the same reaction.

"We weren't speaking to *you*."

"Mind your own business."

"If your ears get any bigger, I hope you tie them around your throat and choke yourself to death!"

Gormlaith was the only one who never looked like she was enjoying their malicious games. *If I can speak to her without Bryg nearby, maybe I can persuade her to leave their side and join mine,* I thought. *Having even one ally would be a victory.*

I bided my time, kept my eyes open, and found my opportunity when it was the blond girl's turn to bring the midday meal to Dún Beithe's blacksmith. He was an eccentric man, but his mastery of iron gave him special status. If he insisted on having highborn girls and women bring him his food, Lord Artegal indulged his whim.

I trailed Gormlaith to the forge and intercepted her when she left. She reacted to my friendly greeting like a cornered doe, frozen and staring. All my efforts to make her relax failed. I might as well have spoken every one of my carefully prepared words to a wall. In the end, I found myself pleading with her to remember how I'd taken her side in the past, how I wanted us to be friends again, and how my situation was the same as the circumstances that had driven her close friend Aifric to run away.

That was a mistake. Gormlaith's face twisted in a look of agony. She lowered her head and rushed past me, sobbing.

Later that day Connla sought me out. "Lady Maeve, I don't

care if you are the High King's daughter," Kian's friend told me sternly. "You had no right to make my Gormlaith suffer like that. She mourns Aifric to this very day."

His accusation rattled me so badly that I blurted in reply: "Then tell her to stop helping the others plague me the way they tormented her friend!"

"Girls' quarrels," he muttered. "I don't understand them. If I meddle deeper, I could do my sweet lass more harm than good." He looked uneasy, a warrior desperate to protect his beloved from an enemy that laughed at swords.

"Connla—"

He gave me no chance to speak. "I've said what I came to say. We're done, Lady Maeve." His long legs put ten paces between us when he paused, looked back at me, and added, "I thought you were kind."

CHAPTER SIXTEEN

Kestrel's Flight

I HAVE NEVER seen a battle, but I can imagine that even the greatest warrior grows weary of brandishing sword and spear against a host of enemies who never stop their attack. And if he must fight without a single friend by his side, his fight must seem twice as hard, twice as hopeless.

But even with a darkened heart, a warrior fights on.

I continued to deal with Bryg's ongoing attacks with no thought of surrender. Even supposing I did want to name her the victor, what could I do that would make her agree to peace? *Maybe she'd accept my sincere apology . . . if it came accompanied by Father's head,* I thought cynically. *She won't be happy until I'm gone.* I tightened my lips. *Dream on, Bryg. You will never make that happen.*

I was determined, but oh so tired too! There were times when exhaustion brought me to tears after Bryg's latest assault failed to do so. When I felt such an outburst rising in my throat,

I hid myself with Ea, sat on the ground beside her perch, buried my face in my arms, and wept.

There were times when I felt so beaten down that I did consider Lady Moriath's advice about going back to Cruachan. It was only a passing weakness. Something always happened to lift my spirits just enough to give me the strength to stay. Kian's praise for my ever-improving aim with the sling, Ea's breathtaking grace in flight, a visiting bard performing Devnet's old song about my childhood encounter with Dubh the bull, and one time the shyly offered gift of delicate white anemones from the hand of the little slave girl.

While I gathered my small joys and held them close, a far greater happiness was riding toward me at a gallop that spring. Lady Lassaire was just leading us outside after breakfast when we heard the sentry atop the ringfort wall shout a familiar name and: "Open! Open! No one rides that fast unless he brings important news!"

Dún Beithe's gate swung wide and Lord Conchobar charged through.

I ran to meet him without caring how it looked to any of the onlookers. The last time I'd seen him, he'd told me about the fresh threat hovering above my father's head. Was that what brought him here now? Had Lady Íde been able to convince the High King that Lord Cairill needed close watching, or had Father brushed off the message she relayed from Lord Artegal and Conchobar?

Or did Cairill already find his chance to strike? I'd find the courage to bear whatever news Conchobar brought, but waiting to hear him reveal it was terrifying. I startled his horse into a sideways skitter in my haste to know.

Conchobar calmed the beast, dropped nimbly from its back, and clasped my waist. His handsome face was shining like the sun. He tossed me high again and again while a crowd gathered around us.

"A girl, Maeve!" he exulted. "Your sister Derbriu's given her man a healthy, whole, beautiful baby girl!"

"*That's* why he's here again?" Kian gritted. He'd asked me if I wanted to take Ea out for a flight, timing the question so that Conchobar was nowhere nearby to overhear it and invite himself. "Because your sister had a baby? Is there no message that man's willing to entrust to someone else? When does he find the time to look after his own people?"

"He told me he wanted to see my happiness when I got the news," I replied evenly, never taking my eyes from the soaring kestrel. "Don't you take pleasure in sharing a friend's joy?"

"That's not all that oaf wants to share," Kian muttered. I let that sullen remark pass without comment.

"Emain Macha's not that far from Dún Beithe," I went on. "Conchobar's realm won't suffer if he's gone for three or four or even five days."

"He'll be here *five days*?" I could almost see sparks flying around Kian's head.

I folded my arms. "Why don't you tell him to leave? Lord Artegal will be so proud to see how his son treats an honored guest."

"*I* don't honor him," he shot back. "And five days in Conchobar's company is *six* too many, if you ask me."

"Calm down. He told me that another person was accompanying him to Dún Beithe, but that man chose to travel on foot. Conchobar can't leave until his companion catches up."

"May the gods give him swan's wings to bring him here swiftly. And may they give him a slap in the head for walking when he could ride!"

I lost patience with my friend's immature behavior. "Kian, what do you have against Conchobar?"

"I don't like the way he looks at you, as if you were a plump little roasted duck on his plate."

"I sound delicious," I replied with a quirk of my lips.

He let loose a guttural cry of exasperation and struck his thigh with a fist. "I'm sorry, Maeve. I don't know how to use pretty words, and when I think of Conchobar and you, I get so mad that it's hard to speak at all. I just want to knock him over the head, sling him across his horse's back, smack the animal's rump, and see the last of him."

"All that?" I asked impishly, hoping to dilute his anger with laughter. One look at his expression told me I'd failed.

"Why don't you take me seriously? There's so much I want to tell you, ask you, but you always turn it aside with a joke or a question. I see what Bryg is doing to you and I can save you from her if you'll only—"

My hand covered his mouth. "Kian, would you really want me to accept you for my husband only because I had to escape Bryg? You're worth more than that."

He moved my hand away gently and gazed at me with regret. "Not to you."

"You are my dear friend. You're the only friend I have left under your father's roof."

"And that's all I am. It's not good enough for me, Maeve. Can't I change that somehow?"

I shook my head.

"This is his fault," Kian muttered. "If not for him—"

"Conchobar has nothing to do with it," I said firmly. "I give you my word."

He replied, "If you say so," in a way that meant *I don't believe you at all*. With a forced laugh, he raised his eyes to follow Ea's flight. "Do you know who Conchobar's awaiting? Who's important enough to keep the high and mighty king of the Ulaidh hanging around our necks like a noose?"

I ignored his sarcasm. Clearly I'd never succeed in convincing Kian that Conchobar wasn't his rival. "He hasn't told me and I haven't asked. I'll be as surprised as you whenever we find out."

I was wrong. No one in all of Dún Beithe could come close to being as surprised as I when Conchobar's straggling companion arrived the next day. We were having our midday meal when a long shadow fell across the sunlit doorway. A familiar voice made my skin shrink as I heard: "Greetings, Lord Artegal. May your house be favored with health and abundance."

"Master Íobar!" Conchobar cried, hurrying to welcome the man who'd terrified my father, torn Odran from me, and destroyed blameless creatures as easily as snapping a blade of straw. "You're here at last!"

"Idiot girl, aren't you listening? I said *you're* the sole reason he's come here! Am I going to have to come in there and carry you? *Again?*" Conchobar yelled at me through the curtain of Lady

Moriath's sleeping chamber. I'd taken refuge there because I knew if I hid in my own room, the other fosterlings would drag me out and happily throw me to the hated druid.

Lady Moriath faced the inner side of the curtain, her hands on her hips. "I'll say the same thing to you I said to Lord Artegal himself!" she shouted back with remarkable power for a woman of her years. "Don't even *think* of coming in here after Lady Maeve unless you're prepared to draw your sword! The only way I'll let you have her is if you cut off my head first!"

"Don't tempt me, old woman," Conchobar snarled, but the curtain didn't even ripple.

I touched Lady Moriath's shoulder lightly. "I should go."

"Why?" She turned to face me. "Are you afraid of that uncouth boy? Don't be. He may be king of the Ulaidh, but he doesn't rule us."

I had to smile. Me, afraid of Conchobar? Not likely. "I didn't run in here because I fear anyone, Lady Moriath," I said. "I just wanted a little time to think, to clear my mind. That druid, Master Íobar, is someone I hoped I'd never meet again. When I saw him, my first impulse was to pick up something heavy and throw it at his head. Beyond that, I didn't know how to face him." I took a deep breath and let it out slowly. "Now I do."

"You're sure, dear?" The older woman cupped my cheek with one soft hand and gave me a searching look. "I'll stand with you when you speak to him, if you like."

"Thank you, but I ought to do this on my own."

I stepped out of her room and walked past Conchobar as though he were invisible. As I expected, most of the household was massed behind him, gawking at me. Bryg, Ula, and Dairine clustered together, snickering and whispering. Gormlaith stood nearby with the same regretful expression she always seemed to wear whenever our eyes met. Lord Artegal and Master Íobar were the only two missing.

I heard the rustle of Lady Moriath's dress at my back and the older woman's stern, carrying voice: "Don't you layabouts have *work* to do?"

Lady Lassaire rose to her feet, flustered at being rightfully taken to task by one of her own attendants. She turned her embarrassment to impatience and herded all of her women away, as well as my fellow fosterlings, chiding them at every step. The rest of the onlookers drifted away, muttering.

"Well done, old woman!" Conchobar patted Lady Moriath on the back. She wheeled suddenly and slapped his hand away.

"Call me 'old woman' again and you'll find out I still know how to give a rude child's rump some lessons in manners," she snapped.

The young king solemnly removed one of his gold bracelets and slid it onto her wrist, where it dangled loosely. "Please have mercy on me, milady. Here's my pledge that I'll be more polite from now on." He looked at me contritely. "Sorry for what I called you. You know, an idiot?"

I favored him with a warm smile. "You might've been right. After all, look at the friends I choose." Lady Moriath tutted a warning, so I quickly added, "Do you know where I can find Master Íobar?"

The druid was standing in conversation with Lord Artegal outside the great house. I expected a devastating scowl from Master Íobar for my recent bad conduct. Whenever I pictured Odran's father, he always wore a glowering look, and tragic experience taught me to mistrust his smile. Now I saw a strange, sorrowful expression in his eyes, and it shook me badly. This wasn't the Master Íobar I remembered. What had changed him? I dreaded hearing it.

I forced my fears down. Perhaps I was imagining things and he was only weary from travel. "Welcome, Master Íobar," I said calmly. "My apologies for how I—"

"I will not hear them, Lady Maeve." He raised his hand with all his old authority, but spoke in a peaceable voice. "I can understand your reaction to seeing me so unexpectedly, after our last meeting." He turned to Lord Artegal and Conchobar. "My lords, if Lady Maeve agrees, may she and I speak together privately?"

I nodded my consent and they left us, but we were far from alone. As always, the ringfort was filled with people doing chores, running errands, enjoying a rest from their tasks, or simply idling while they pretended to work. Master Íobar observed their presence, dissatisfied.

"I would prefer to speak with you alone, Lady Maeve," he said.

"Come with me, then."

I led him to the top of the stronghold walls and hailed the sentry.

"This is Master Íobar, who serves the king of Munster," I said. "We wish to be undisturbed."

"This is the right place for that, Lady Maeve." The man bowed his head to the druid with respect. "I was on watch when you arrived, Master," he said. "I recognized your rank by that fine six-colored cloak of yours. You may trust me to guard your presence here as long as you like. I'll keep watch over there." He indicated the opposite curve of the circular wall.

Even after the guard was as far from us as possible, Master Íobar remained silent. It fell to me to speak first. "Lord Conchobar says that I'm the reason you've traveled here with him. Was it for this, just to look at me?"

"I wish that were so," he said in a voice so drained of energy and so heavy with sadness that I felt an invisible giant's hand crushing my chest. "Lady Maeve, my son—"

"I knew it!" I cried. "Oh gods, I knew the worst had happened, but I hoped . . . I hoped I was wrong. I told myself that even if I never saw Odran again, I could be content believing that he was alive and happy somewhere. Did I wound your pride so much that you *had* to find me here and take that peace away from me?"

"I, take away—?" My outburst astonished him. "Lady Maeve, you think I came here to tell you that my son, my Odran, is . . . dead?" He spread his hand before his face as if that gesture could repel such a horrible thing.

"He lives, then?" I asked. The druid nodded, and I felt so giddy with relief that I willingly grasped the hands that had taken so many small, blameless lives. "Master Íobar, pardon me for putting words in your mouth. I'm deeply grateful to know I was wrong about Odran, but—" I hesitated. "But I don't understand why a man of your rank traveled so far just to bring me news of my—my dear friend." An old suspicion whispered, *Be on guard. He wants something.*

"You're mistaken, child," he replied, still with that unnerving new mildness. "I came here with another purpose besides telling you about Odran. My lord the king of Munster is a close relative of Lord Conchobar. He had a vital message to send to Emain Macha and chose me to carry it as a mark of respect for his kinsman. I arrived just before your sister, Lady Derbriu, gave birth. I was there when Lord Conchobar declared he'd take that happy news to you himself. Until then, I had no idea you were in fosterage here. I am not blessed with the gift for divining the future, but even I could read such a sign: it was my destiny to travel to Dún Beithe, find you"—he withdrew his fingers from mine—"and implore you to forgive me."

I stood rooted, motionless. All I could do was repeat, "Forgive—?"

"I know you have not forgotten, Lady Maeve." There was no measuring his regret. Everything about him—eyes, voice, body—was laden with it. "I destroyed so much that was dear to you, dear to my son. I killed the wild creatures you two were healing, but also the tame beasts who were my son's joy. In my stupidity, I believed I was doing the right thing, cutting off all ties that would hold him back from following the druid's path." He sighed deeply. "Instead I almost cut off his life. My son was not a healthy child—"

"I know," I said. "He told me about how you nearly lost him after his mother died."

"Did he?" Master Íobar looked surprised, then gave a short, humorless chuckle. "Of course he did. You and he were close. So then you know about how he was saved when my wife's dearest friend lured him out of his life-draining grief by teaching him to care for animals in need. She told me he had a natural ability for that—a gift from Flidais, the lady of wild things." He hung his head. "What I did on that ill-omened day was a crime that enraged the goddess. It was cruel, the work of my pride and stubbornness, but Odran was the one who paid for it."

"You said he was well." I struggled to keep my voice steady.

"I said he lives. Lady Maeve, my son lies desperately ill on Avallach. He was well enough when I left him there, but since that time he's grown weaker, frail enough for the masters of the island to send me word of his condition. They say that he will recover—there are no better healers anywhere than where the art is taught—but I can't believe them. *I can't!*" He cried so loud that the distant sentry turned to stare, then quickly looked away again.

"Have you gone to see him?" I asked. "It might not be as bad as you imagine."

He shook his head. "I'm afraid that I'll find out it's worse. Think of me as a coward if you like, but I tell you that I cannot bear the thought of seeing another of my children dead before me."

"Another?" I repeated softly.

"I had a daughter who held my heart. She was as beautiful and sweet as spring sunlight after a dark winter. I lost her. It happened many years ago, before Odran was born. He never knew he had a sister. He was so fragile: eating poorly, sleeping worse. Why tell him something that would only add to his nightmares? It's enough that she will always haunt mine." Master Íobar's unfathomable black eyes stared into the past. "I was the one keeping watch over her when she vanished. She slipped away from me the way small children can do. She had a wild bird's free spirit, that one." His voice was fainter than the fall of a leaf. "They brought her back to me from the bog where she'd run off to play. I placed her lifeless body in her mother's lap and knew that those small, still lips had given us their final kiss. May you never know such pain. And now Odran—"

I flung my arms around him and hugged him fiercely. The

memories of all his offenses could not stand against the enormity of all his suffering. "Master Íobar, the healers of Avallach *said* he'll be all right."

He pushed away from me gently, refusing to hear any reassurance. "I know better. Flidais will have her vengeance. The gods are clever in their punishments. She could have killed me easily by sending a wolf or a wild boar to cross my path. Instead she'll use my child's death like a spear. Before that happens, I want you to pardon me for what I did. I carry the burden of all those small lives, wrongfully ended. It's too late for me to ask Odran's forgiveness, but I beg for yours. I will not walk in the sun for much longer and I would rather travel to Tech Duinn with one less weight on my shoulders."

I took his hand again and held it firmly. He would not run from me. "Guennola survived," I said. "The little stoat got away, one of Odran's pets. I saw her. Can't you read that as a sign that Flidais will show you mercy?"

"Why should she? It's not as if I spared the beast."

I thought of arguing with him, then realized it would take more than words. "Master Íobar, come with me."

I brought him to Ea's shelter. He stared at the kestrel in confusion until I told him about how she had escaped his attack with her life, how she'd found hands to heal her and restore her free flight. "I thought I'd never see her again," I said. "I had no hope of that, yet here she is."

"What a wonder." Master Íobar spoke with reverence. "Such a small bird, and yet so much strength and life in her! I wish Odran were here. He might take heart, knowing she escaped—escaped my blind stupidity."

"Don't you understand?" I said kindly. "This is a gift from

Flidais herself. The gods are not always harsh. Ea has a second chance to live and soar. I have a second chance to be happy with her. Let her be a sign that you can have a second chance as well." I kissed his cheek. "I forgive you. Now go to your son."

Master Íobar departed the next day. He left Dún Beithe before I was awake, but when I asked Conchobar where he'd gone, I didn't get the answer I wanted.

"He told me he was heading back to Munster, sleepyhead." The young lord of the Ulaidh slid to one side of the bench where he was eating breakfast and patted the plank, inviting me to join him.

I dropped down beside him. "Are you sure? Didn't he mention going to Avallach?"

"Because 'Munster' and 'Avallach' sound *so* much alike." Conchobar was in a jolly mood that morning. I didn't care for it. "Why would he want to go there, anyway? He came to Emain Macha with a message from my kinsman and now he's got to carry the reply. Remember what I told you about Lord Cairill?"

"The traitor," I said grimly. *Did Lady Íde manage to caution Father about him?* "I thought you'd come here this time because you had news of his schemes."

Conchobar took a huge spoonful of porridge and spoke around it. "I have no news to give, but my kinsman did. Says he's worried about me 'cause"—he swallowed—"because Cairill's gone to ground. There's no sign he's up to anything. Eochu got the warning all right, but instead of being grateful, he's seeing it as someone trying to stir up bad feelings between him and his subject kings. Guess who he's ready to blame?"

"You? But that's ridiculous!"

"Tell that to your father. He's not sure I'm involved, but there are enough people ready to throw rocks at me if it keeps their heads safe awhile longer."

"Cairill, for instance?"

Conchobar grinned and gobbled more porridge. "Smart, aren't you, and—mmm, this is good—pretty. Yes." He set down his empty bowl. "Your father's got his eye on me now, instead of where it should be. That's the message my kinsman wanted me to know, along with a hundred different versions of 'Be careful, Conchobar.' No wonder he had to send a druid, what with how they're trained to memorize everything." He looked at me closely. "You seem unhappy. Don't worry about me; I'll stay out of Eochu's way even when we all meet at Tara for the Beltane rites."

"It's not that. I'm just thinking about—" I let the words hang. What use was there in telling Conchobar about my worries over Odran's health and my disappointment that his father had not gone to hearten him with news of Ea's survival?

"About what?" Conchobar prodded. "Tell me." I shook my head. "Come on, you know I'll find out. Speak." He put his arms around me and yanked me against his chest, to the amusement of almost all those present. "Don't make me squeeze it out of you!" he cried, making me laugh even while I tried to break his hold.

"Let her *go*!" Kian appeared in front of us so suddenly, he seemed to burst from the ground. Before Conchobar or I could say anything, he drew back his fist and punched the lord of the Ulaidh hard enough to send him tumbling backward off the bench while I fell onto my hands and knees.

"Kian, stop!" Lord Artegal roared, rushing to seize his son's arm. "Are you insane? By my head, that man is our sacred *guest.*"

Conchobar got back onto his feet, one hand cupping his jaw. "Let him be, my lord," he said. "I won't hold him or you to blame for this if you'll give me one favor in return."

Shame turned Lord Artegal's face crimson. "Anything you name."

I rose from the ground in time to hear Conchobar declare, "I ask that you suspend the bond of hospitality just long enough for Lord Kian and me to settle the one dispute that stands between us." He indicated me.

"There's nothing to settle," I said. "I am not—"

Lady Lassaire didn't give me the chance to finish. She had my wrist in a grip of stone and dragged me out of the great house, followed by her closest attendants and my delighted fellow fosterlings. I could feel rage rising from her like the blaze of iron in the forge. She didn't stop until we were almost to the gateway of Dún Beithe, and then she released me so violently that I staggered into the wall.

"This is all your fault!" she shrieked at me. "Do you *like* making these boys drunk with desire for you? Does it make you feel powerful, you vain, heartless, unnatural girl? Your wicked games will kill my boy! How can you do it? He loves you. Yes, and better than you deserve! Put an end to this. Go back into the great house and say you've made your choice: that you're his. Send Lord Conchobar away before they fight. Do it!"

"She won't," Bryg said, implacable. "She's one of the Morrígan's ravens. She glories in it when men fight. She feeds on their deaths."

"Send her home." Dairine was a hound straining on the leash, eager to please her master. "Be rid of her!"

"Yes, do that," I said, looking at each of my attackers in turn. "Lady Lassaire, you've been blind to everything that's been happening to me here except what you choose to see. If I go, you won't have any problems to sidestep. But *you* will have to be the one to make me return to Cruachan, for I swear by my head that I will not be another Aifric! If I leave Dún Beithe, it won't be because this swarm of horseflies drove me away."

"Quiet!" Lady Lassaire snapped. "What do you know of Aifric? That inconsiderate girl didn't give a second thought to how much trouble she made for us by running off. I curse the day you came here, but I will not expel you. I won't have it said that I failed to discipline any fosterling in my keeping. You will leave Dún Beithe when *I* say, and not a moment before."

"Whether or not I marry your son?" I couldn't resist throwing that in her face after her talk of discipline. Had she ever *tried* to put the reins on Bryg, either for Aifric's sake or mine?

"I told you to hold your tongue!" I got my face slapped for that impertinence. For a small woman, she had a heavy hand. "If you're too dim-witted to know what a prize my son is, I can only pray that he comes to his senses and turns his back on you."

As she spoke, a large crowd came streaming out of the great house, headed for the ringfort gateway. Lord Artegal was in the lead, followed by Kian and Conchobar. The mob swept past us, their voices raised in anticipation. Connla was the only one who paused long enough to call out: "Don't worry, milady, they're going to fight with fists, not weapons!"

Dairine gave a little squeal of glee and joined the throng.

The other girls and women fell in after her, including Lady Lassaire, until I was the only one left standing against the wall.

I was sure that I was guiltless of the fight between Kian and Conchobar, and yet I was still the cause of it. I hated what my life had become thanks to Bryg's unreasoning hatred, and yet I had declared I'd never be another Aifric. I swore that I would never run away, and yet I knew there was only one thing holding me to Dún Beithe.

I raced into the deserted great house, threw on my cloak, made sure I had a knife and my sling, found a waterskin, and scavenged a leather bag and crammed it with as much bread, cheese, and meat as I could find. My feet flew to Ea's shelter where the kestrel drowsed on her perch. I added her lure to the sack of provisions, donned my armguard, set her on my wrist, and dashed outside while she fluttered her wings and complained of such rough treatment. I fed her a scrap of meat to buy her silence as I scanned the battlements for the sentry. When I saw him head toward the side of the wall farthest from the gate, I moved swiftly.

I had a glib tale ready for the man on guard there, but I didn't need to use it. Like everyone else in Dún Beithe, he wanted to see the fight between Kian and Conchobar. He was nowhere in sight. Perhaps he meant to watch just a bit of the brawl and return to his post before anyone knew he was absent. In my heart I gratefully wished him well.

I was not Aifric. I was not running away, but flying to my heart's home, to the one who had always been my shelter without ever being my prison.

I was running to Odran.

CHAPTER SEVENTEEN

Hungers

I KNEW I would be followed. Sooner or later, my disappearance would be discovered and then Lord Artegal would send out search parties. He would probably lead the one headed to Connacht. It wouldn't do to have some less seasoned man present himself to Father saying, "Greetings, Lord Eochu. Is your daughter Maeve here? We seem to have lost her." The master of Dún Beithe himself could excuse his unexpected visit to Cruachan by saying he'd come to see his cousin, Lady Íde.

I felt a passing regret for putting Lord Artegal in such a position, but I had little choice. As far as I knew from Master Íobar, Odran's health was in jeopardy. How could I ignore that? I was not Lady Lassaire. At Dún Beithe, I was useless except as a target for malice and an unwilling cause of strife. If I went to Avallach, I would be needed, a source of help and healing.

No matter what else I felt for Bryg, now I owed her *two*

great debts: she'd saved my Ea's life and she'd provided me with directions for reaching the druids' sacred isle.

A pity she didn't offer more details, I thought, marching through an oak grove. *I know enough to go east and find Lord Diarmaid's stronghold once I reach the seacoast, but how far-famed is he? How soon will I meet anyone who knows his name and can make sure I take the right road? Well, I suppose this is a better situation than if I knew nothing at all about the way to Avallach. Let me worry about asking directions when I meet someone I can ask!*

I was joking with myself to keep my spirits up, but the truth was I couldn't keep my mind from circling the problems I faced. What if some of my pursuers traveled the same east-bound road as I? No doubt they were riding while I was on foot. They could overtake me easily! I pushed away the urge to panic by balancing their advantage against my own: I could go where horses could not follow. I didn't have to stop and search every small farm and petty king's hold between Dún Beithe and the sea.

But just as I found that crumb of reassurance, it blew away on an afterthought: *I won't be delayed in the same way they will, but I'm not free to go as fast as I'd like to either. I have Ea in my care. Even if my arm would never grow tired of carrying her, it isn't healthy for her to be kept blind and unmoving for our entire journey. She must be unhooded, set free to fly, and most important of all, allowed to feed. Whenever I release her, she'll need time to orient herself to new surroundings, to find prey, and to return to my hand.*

I don't know how many days it would have taken me to reach the sea if I hadn't been traveling with Ea. She slowed me, but she repaid me for that by lifting my mood with her whenever she took wing. I'd seen the kestrel conquer the air more times than I could count, yet each flight was as thrilling to watch as the first; each carried me to the heights of beauty and wonder.

But one time Ea spread her wings and came close to sweeping me far from the land of the living into the shadows of Tech Duinn, the realm of death.

We had left the forest behind us and were skirting a broad bog. It was a fine day with flowers blooming everywhere, both on the solid ground I trod and over the expanse of nearby wetland. I took deep breaths, even though they carried mostly the reek of plants rotting in the swampy water. I was convinced that the unfamiliar tang in the air was the scent of the sea.

"What do you say, my pretty one?" I asked Ea. "Would you like to stretch those wings?" I removed her hood and let her look around for a few moments before I threw my hand high and let her soar. I rubbed the stiffness from my arm while I drank in the sight of my lovely bird rising on the breeze. She made several dives after prey. If she remained out of sight, I knew she'd been successful in making a kill and was eating her catch. I confess that at those times, I didn't breathe easily until I saw her rise again.

"All right, Ea, we should move on," I said when I decided she'd had enough. If she ate too much, she'd have no interest in returning to the lure. I baited the long string and twirled it over my head. Ea took notice and turned her flight toward me, but just as she was about to land on my proffered wrist, she veered sharply and flew away.

I didn't know what had possessed her, and I didn't care. All I could do was cry, "Come back! Come back!" as unthinking terror clamped its hands around me. "Oh my Ea, come back to me!" I abandoned my traveler's sack and ran after her.

I never knew my feet had left the safety of the path until I found myself plunged up to my knees in the muck of the bog. A swath of harmless-looking grass had concealed a pit and now it held me. The more I tried to lift my feet free, the lower I sank. It didn't help that my legs were shrouded and snared in the thick material of my cloak and dress. I tried to turn around where I stood trapped, hoping I was within arm's reach of solid ground. It was my plan to throw myself forward, seize two handfuls of well-rooted plants, and pull myself out.

A fine plan, if I could have kept my balance. Instead I became even more tangled in my sodden clothes and fell sideways with a splash. Stinking, filthy water stung my eyes and filled my mouth with foulness. I coughed and spat and snorted, striving to clear it away so that I could breathe. By this time I was in the bog well up to my waist. I craned my neck, praying for sight of something that might save me, but all I could see were the low-growing grass, the sedge, and the taunting beauty of wildflowers. With a last desperate effort, I shouted for help, though I had seen no other wayfarer within earshot when I first set Ea free.

The bog drank me farther down. My mind became crowded with the faces of all the people I had loved, hated, cherished, and lost. I saw my mother's sorrowing face and Father's look of anguish as he stretched out strong arms that could not save me. His phantom lips called to me, *Oh, my spark, my child, my Maeve!*

My Maeve . . . Odran's beloved voice was a dream. I imagined him beside me, the warmth of his body driving back the chill of the slimy water. I reached for him, longing for one last touch of his lips, aching with sadness, mourning the life I'd known that had brought me so much sweetness and that was now slipping away.

"Hey! You, can you hear me? Take this!"

An unknown voice shattered my visions. I wiped my eyes with the hand that wasn't pinned under my sinking body and saw a thick wooden pole looming just above my head. I grabbed it and held on with all my strength.

"Both hands!" the voice came again. "Get it with both hands and I'll pull you out."

"I can't!" I called back. "I fell on my side."

I heard a long string of curses and then: "All right, it'll have to do. Here we go."

The pole began to move. I held on doggedly, though it felt like my arm was being torn from my shoulder. The pain ebbed as soon as I was lifted enough to free my other hand and double my grip. The bog made loud, sucking sounds as my rescuer dragged me out onto grass that hid no deadly secrets.

"Girl, are you all right?"

I looked up into the face of a young man with hair as red as my own. The gold torque around his neck marked him for highborn and the spear he'd used to haul me to safety could only belong to a warrior. He was on one knee beside me, the front of his tunic covered with dirt and grass stains.

"I'm fine." I sat up slowly. The urge to burst into tears rose in my throat, turning my voice husky. *I will* not *cry,* I told myself severely. *A nice time for that, now that I'm out of danger!*

This fellow will think he's encountered a wandering madwoman. I regained my self-control and smiled. "Yes, I'm fine. Thank you for saving me."

He stood and helped me to my feet. I looked at my ruined clothes and had to laugh. "Does this smell as bad to you as it does to me? I wouldn't want to offend my rescuer."

"You're a strange one, worrying about something like that," he replied. "Most girls would be howling their heads off after coming so close to death. I was on the bog walkway over there"—he gestured with his free hand—"when I saw you go running straight into the bog. What made you do that?"

"Look there," I said, pointing to where Ea hovered in the western sky. "That's my kestrel. I was trying to bring her back to my hand when something startled her and she fled. I was so afraid of losing her, I gave chase without paying attention to where I was going." I looked sheepish as I added: "I wish I'd known about the walkway, though I probably would have fallen into the mire anyhow. I couldn't think of anything but her."

"Where are you bound?"

"For the coast."

"Where from?"

"I was born in Connacht." He might encounter Lord Arte-gal's men after we parted, so I didn't want to give him any information that would put them on the right trail.

"Connacht!" He seemed impressed. "I guessed you weren't from around here, but even so, I never expected to meet a girl brave enough to rove so far from home and kin." With a tentative look, he added: "That is, unless you have relatives hereabout?"

I wondered why he was taking such an interest in whether

or not I had family close by. He saw my preoccupied expression and made haste to say, "I thought if you had any friends or family in the area, they'd be willing to give you a change of clothes."

I spread my hands. "No luck there, I'm afraid, uh—" I paused. "How awkward. You gave me my life but not your name."

"I'm Fergal."

"I'm Maeve." There was no need to provide a false name when mine could belong to more than one girl.

"Pretty name, pretty girl, even soaked with mire as you are." Fergal grinned widely. "I'd give my best armband to know how your parents could foresee you'd grow up to be as intoxicating as your name." His gaze lit on the torque I wore and his expression shifted subtly. "Ah! Would you look there? Now I'm ready to give both armbands and earrings to learn why someone wearing *that* rich gift comes running through these lands chasing a falcon!"

Too late, my hand flew to cover the thick gold circlet around my neck. Even a coating of muck couldn't obscure its beauty. When I'd fled Dún Beithe, I hadn't thought to leave it behind nor to bury it in my sack of provisions. It had been mine for as long as I could remember, as much a part of me as hands or feet or hair. Now I realized that something so obviously precious had a tongue to betray me, marking me for more than just another girl.

I forced a bold smile and a light laugh. "Why should I have to explain? Don't you have tales of the Fair Folk in these lands?"

My response made him snicker. "What do you want me to believe, that they gave it to you?"

"It should be my gift to you," I said, hoping that the promise of gold would distract him from questioning me further. "It may not be enough to repay you for saving me, but I hope you'll accept it."

"I'll take it gladly, my lady. That's your rank, isn't it? Or when you spoke of the Fair Folk, did you mean to say you're one of them?" He took a step closer. "You're beautiful enough." He reached out to stroke my hair, and his fingers swiftly strayed to caress my cheek. "How grateful are you for your life, Lady Maeve?"

And just like that, everything changed: my hero was my peril.

I slapped his hand away. "Don't touch me!"

My indignant reaction only amused him. "Ha! So much for gratitude. Or amn't I worthy enough to lie with one of the Fair Folk? Will you use your magic to weaken me?" His hand clamped around my arm. "Let's see if you can."

I flailed so violently that I broke out of his grasp and stumbled backward. He cast his spear aside and leaped at me, but instead of retreating farther, I ducked under his outstretched arms and came up behind him. I seized his cast-off spear, meaning to defend myself with it, but the weapon was outsized and too cumbersome for me. I tried using it like a staff, striking Fergal hard across the ribs when he pivoted to face me, but my blow lacked force and his cloak took most of it.

He spat out a foul name, dodged my second swing, and wrenched the spear from my hands. Wielding the weapon deftly and as easily as if it were a twig, he swung the blunt end low and crosswise, scything me off my feet. I was flat on my back an instant before he dropped onto me, one hand clutching the torque around my neck and twisting so that the metal bit into my throat.

"What do you know?" he said with an ugly leer. "You aren't protected by magic after all."

His face came closer. I smelled disgusting breath and the stink of sweat and grime. No self-respecting warrior would let himself go so long without washing. I was in the merciless hands of an outcast, one who knew I was far from home with no kin close enough to hunt him down. I felt him tugging my mire-soaked dress aside. His mouth closed on mine.

I bit him as hard as I could, hard enough to draw blood. In the breath between his yell of pain and the moment he recovered enough to raise a fist against me, I dug my fingers into the earth and thrust a handful of dirt into his eyes. My attacker swore, sputtered, and clawed at his face. I used that instant's advantage and jabbed him sharply with my knee. I could never have managed it if he hadn't freed my legs from the water-logged cloth. He grunted and fell off me.

That's the second thanks I owe you, Fergal, I thought fiercely as I clambered to my feet. *Not that I'll give you any, you monster!*

He rose from the ground, roaring. I was ready for him. Sling and slingstone were in my hands. A high, thin whistle cut the air. The small, deadly missile made a sickening sound as it shattered Fergal's teeth and sent him staggering back, too stunned to feel pain.

I had a second shot cradled and spinning over my head as I shouted, "The next one takes your eye!"

Fergal stood staring at me for as long as it took to draw two breaths. His glance darted to where he'd dropped the spear. I could almost read his thoughts as he weighed the odds of killing me before I killed him. He stooped to grab it and I braced myself for what I'd have to do. His words echoed in my head, mocking me: *There's gratitude for you!*

He ran away.

I saw it, but I couldn't accept the evidence of my eyes. I watched him turn tail and sprint off, leaving me safe, soaked, and stunned. I continued to twirl the sling overhead for longer than I needed to, unaware that I was doing it. When I finally let it drop to my side, I felt as if I'd awakened from a dream.

"Ea," I said. The sound of my own voice startled me. I looked at my hands. They were trembling. "I have to find Ea," I said aloud, as though testing my surroundings for other hidden dangers. Did I expect that lurking outlaws would reveal themselves when they heard me speak? I think I did, even though it made no sense. My mind was acting on its own, diverting me from imagining what my fate might have been if I'd never learned how to defend myself.

Scanning the flat terrain, I saw a small, dark shape that I hoped was my abandoned traveler's bag. I minded my steps as I went back to reclaim it, then searched the sky for Ea. My kestrel had grown tired of the hunt and was hovering near. I had her on my wrist and hooded without further trouble and resumed our road to the sea.

"There it is, lass: Avallach." The boatman pointed to a thin line of land on the horizon. He spoke my language with a strange accent. I'd met him while he was bidding farewell to his wife and children on the shore below Lord Diarmaid's ringfort. His wife was the one who noticed how intently I was staring at the shallow-bottomed trading vessel riding at anchor and asked me why.

"Thank you, sir," I replied from my place in the prow of the ship. Ever since that frightening encounter with Fergal, I'd been leery of men. It took every fiber of my determination to see Odran again to force me aboard the boat where I'd be alone with this stranger for who knew how many days.

"Not such a bad crossing. The wind was with us. That bird of yours must be a good-luck token. I could use her help when I sail on to Albion and Gaul. Don't suppose you'd think of trading it to me?" he asked good-naturedly.

"I can't part with her." I tensed, readying myself in case he heard my refusal as an invitation to take what I wouldn't give.

He saw my reaction and shook his head. "All right, all right, no need to fear. I wasn't serious. I don't mean you or the bird any harm. You poor girl, my wife said you must've run into bad times on the road to be so skittish around a broken-down old ox like me. And yet here you are! I've heard that the greatest heroes ain't the ones without fear but those who march on even when they're terrified of what's in store."

"If that's true, I must be the bravest person on earth," I said with a wobbly smile.

He grinned back at me. "Not while I'm alive. Who knew that a Roman brat who marched with the legions would find himself riding the seas between Gaul and Hibernia, married to a terror of a woman, and burdened with a household full of screaming little horrors?"

I laughed, remembering how he'd lavished kisses on his mob of children before wading out to the ship. For the first time since Fergal's assault, I relaxed in a man's company. "Perhaps I should change my mind and trade you this kestrel for one of them," I suggested playfully.

"Oh, I couldn't let you make such a bad bargain," he replied. "You're better off keeping the bird. It can feed itself, it can't jabber your ears numb, and it won't keep you up nights worrying about its future."

"True, but she does leave droppings everywhere."

"I thought you *met* my children." We both chuckled.

The crossing to Avallach ended just as the sun was setting. My fears about spending the night in a strange man's power were baseless—even more so since the boatman had proved to be a friend. I'd kilted up my dress to wade out to his ship when the voyage began, but when we anchored at my destination, I didn't reject his offer to carry me ashore.

"Do you have a safe place to sleep?" he asked as he set me down.

"I'll manage."

He shook his head. "I'd be a bad trader if I didn't look after my cargo. I know a leather maker who lives nearby. His wife and I—well, before the two of us settled down, we were . . . *friends.* I have to sleep aboard to keep an eye on things and sail with first light, but I can take you to their place if you don't mind a bit of stink."

I flourished my skirt, still bearing the mark and smell of the bog. "Do I seem like the sort of person who can't live with that?" I asked.

"Why do you think I didn't mind how much space you put between us on my ship?" he replied.

The tanner and his family lived a healthy distance from the

rest of the settlement. A leather maker treats hides with urine, dung, and animal brains to make them pliable. Unavoidable spills contaminate the ground around a tannery, making it smell putrid. The reek of my ruined clothing was as noticeable to my hosts as the whiff of a burnt hair in the midst of a blazing forest.

The stains were another story. "What happened to you, dear?" the tanner's wife asked solicitously as she gave me some bread and cheese for my dinner.

"I took a misstep into a bog."

"And escaped it alive after sinking in *that* deep?" She indicated the telltale marks. "The gods must love you, saving you that way. Pity they didn't show as much mercy to your dress and cloak. I never saw such good fabric." She gazed at my garb with longing. "You know, I'm told I have a gift for getting dirt and muck out of things. Have to, living with *that* man." She indicated her husband, who had joined their children in a knot surrounding Ea. The kestrel was perched on top of the woman's loom. "If you don't mind staying on with us a day or two, I could see about washing those garments for you."

I thought about it, then said, "I have another idea."

The next morning I left the leather maker's hut wearing his wife's best dress and cloak. They were old, a little shabby, and much too large for me, but they served their purpose. Though she wouldn't be able to use my cast-off garb herself, the tanner's wife was pleased with the trade. Once she scrubbed off the bog residue, her eldest girl would look splendid in my former clothes.

I hid in the shadow of an aged oak, my cheek pressed to the bark, and fixed my eyes on the modest house at the edge of the druids' settlement. A cool breeze brought me the scent of burning wood and roasting meat, though no smoke rose from the dwelling I watched. My hair hung down my back in a mass of curls still damp from the slapdash job I'd done of washing myself in a stream that crossed my path on the way. I knew I should have asked the tanner's wife to help me have a proper scrub when we traded clothes, but I'd been too eager to reach my goal. It was good to feel fresh again, even if it wasn't as thorough a cleansing as I would have liked. The pure, sweet water washed away the ghost of Fergal along with the stubborn stink of the bog. I was ready to find Odran.

It was almost sundown. Ea sat hooded on a branch a little above my head. I'd fed her the last of our meat before lodging her there, to keep her contented. I'd spent the daylight hours moving like a shadow through the trees surrounding the druids' settlement, trying to see Odran without being seen. Careful spying let me observe the comings and goings of Avallach's inhabitants until it became clear that this house was the only possible place he could be.

But what if he's not there? I haven't seen him anywhere in the settlement. Why would he spend the whole day indoors? Doesn't he have lessons to attend? He's been sick. What if he—? A horrible fear poisoned my mind. I shivered and pushed it away. *No, he's there, he* must *be! Maybe his illness left him too weak to go back to his studies just yet. O Flidais, merciful goddess, please let it be so! Sweet lady, if I've earned your blessing by helping heal the wild creatures you cherish, show me that my journey hasn't been in vain, that Odran is—is—*

A shape moved in the doorway of Odran's house. A familiar figure stepped into the dying daylight. I nearly called his name, but my breath caught in my throat and caution hissed in my ear, *Not yet, not yet! You don't know if he shares that dwelling with anyone else. Stay calm. Wait.*

I did. It was painfully hard. The inside of my head thundered with all the words I longed to tell him until my temples ached. I watched him take a path leading to the center of the settlement. He wasn't steady on his feet, but at least he was walking. I squeezed my hands into fists and crossed them over my chest, holding myself back from dashing out of the woods and running after him.

Odran returned as the shadows lengthened. He carried a portion of bread and a bowl that I guessed contained his dinner. My stomach grumbled. As twilight fell, I peered at his doorway and saw a spark flash for a moment, followed by the mellow flicker and glow of an oil lamp. No one else approached the little house.

I placed Ea on my wrist, took a deep breath, and flew to reclaim my heart.

CHAPTER EIGHTEEN

Spark, Flame, Embers

"ODRAN?" I STOOD in the doorway of his house, the sun setting behind me.

He was seated on the bed, a piece of bread halfway to his mouth. He leaned back slowly, his hands falling limp in his lap. "Fever," he muttered, blinking. "Back again? I'll have to brew more of Edana's remedy." He rose, swaying, and steadied himself against the wall. His eyes never left me.

"Odran, it's me," I said quietly. "Really, it is. See?" I crossed the room to where the oil lamp burned on a low table and let its light touch my face and the kestrel's plumage. "I've brought Ea. She's alive. I wanted you to see—"

"*Maeve!*" My name tore from his throat. "Oh gods, this can't be true. My mind's been burned away. I swear that since I came here, I've seen you every time I close my eyes, and when the sickness held me, I saw you when I was awake as well. You, yes, and Ea, and my poor murdered Muirín, and Guennola, and—and—" He dropped to the floor, sobbing without tears.

I was with him at the speed of thought, one arm encircling his misery, the other still supporting Ea. "This is no dream," I told him. "Listen, listen, hush, breathe, hear me. Please, Odran. Please, my dearest one."

He pressed his face against my shoulder. His shining black hair held the clean scent of springtime leaves. I held Ea so that he could see her, and I took joy in watching his expression change from mourning to marvel when he brushed her feathers with his fingertips.

"She *is* alive," he said.

"And Guennola too," I told him. "Though I couldn't catch her when I saw her."

"I always believed that my pets could never return to living wild, but if any beast could, it would be her. Stoats are survivors."

"So are kestrels," I said. I kissed his brow. "So are we."

I told him everything that had brought me to him, though I didn't speak of Conchobar and Kian except as *I was blamed for bringing strife to Dún Beithe.* My near-drowning in the bog and my encounter with Fergal became *Sometimes it wasn't an easy road, but here I am.* I wanted to shield him from further distress.

"All this way." Odran held my hands tenderly, the lamplight dancing in his eyes. "You traveled all this way for me." His words were soft with wonder. I had forgotten how sweet his voice sounded. I wanted to listen to its warm tones and gentle lilt forever.

"I thought you were deathly ill," I said, my reply a hoarse whisper. We knelt facing each other on the beaten earth floor. Ea roosted unhooded on a sturdy piece of kindling that Odran had lashed firmly to one of the upright timbers of the wall. A fire crackled in the small central hearth, making our shadows rise and fall.

"I was. I had a terrible fever and a heaviness in my chest that crushed every breath I tried to take. My teachers thought they'd lose me, but they kept trying different treatments. One worked." His well-beloved smile brought more heat to my cheeks than any flame. "Either that, or I knew I had to live so that I could see you again."

He cradled my face in his hands. I welcomed his touch. Something stirred deep in my body: a delicious shiver that spread through me, stealing my senses. How could I be gazing at him so steadily when my head was spinning? How could I hear him speak my name with so much love when I was deafened by my own racing heartbeat? How could I open my mouth to speak a single word when all I wanted was to taste his lips and lose myself in kisses and all that might follow?

We clung together desperately, as though we expected a sword to fall between us at any moment. We didn't need to say what we both knew: *If I must part from you now, I will die.* I could not draw a breath that he did not share. Holding him, kissing him, loving him, I felt that I was teetering on the brink of a great secret: fearful, amazing, and overwhelming.

I clasped him even closer and leaped to meet it.

From that night on, Odran and I lived in a private realm, a refuge of laughter and joy beyond words and sometimes a place of bittersweet shared memories.

We spent as much time as we could in each other's arms. While I rested my head on his shoulder, he told me about his life among the druids and healers of Avallach. He and the other boys met daily for lessons and meals, though lately he preferred to take his food away to eat alone.

"Ever since my illness, it feels as if they're always watching to see if I'm eating enough. At least they're discreet about it, or I'm afraid they'd follow me here to make sure I'm not burying my meals."

"A good thing for us they don't do that. I'm sure they'll be very happy to see you carrying off *double* portions now," I teased.

"I never thought I'd call myself lucky for being so sick," he said. "Edana had me moved to this house, as far from everyone else as I could be while staying within the bounds of the settlement. After I recovered, no one thought to order me back to the students' shared quarters. I was happy: I never liked living jumbled up with them, like a litter of puppies." His arm tightened around me. "I'm even more thankful now that I have something precious to keep hidden."

"I'm grateful too," I said, laying my hand on his chest. "But I'm also curious: Why did your healer think it was a good idea to isolate you?"

"Edana believes that some ailments can take the form of an invisible fog that lingers over you when you're ill. She didn't want my sickness to touch the others."

"A female healer," I mused, fascinated. "And one that the chief druids here obey?"

"She's proved her abilities to the point that no one dares to question them. Some say that Dian Cecht, god of healing, must be her lover. It's the only way to explain her talent."

"Of course it is," I said drily. "She couldn't possibly have acquired her skills by her own efforts."

"Were you always this sarcastic?" Odran asked, smiling before he kissed me.

In the kingdom that Odran and I created for ourselves, time was not the same as it was in the world beyond the little house. It slipped away, yet still managed to make each individual day drag on from the moment Odran left to receive his lessons until he returned with our evening meal. We were like happy children, making no plans for the future, too caught up in the sweetness of *now*. We agreed that I had to stay hidden. He brought extra food and I made a game of portioning it out for my meals while he was gone.

The game grew boring quickly. One day I changed the rules. I became tense and snappish with having to remain out of sight. Like a trapped animal, I became possessed by the urge to escape. I told myself, *I came to Avallach and found Odran without being detected by anyone. Why can't I make small daylight forays away from the settlement? It's not just for me: Ea is wretched. We fly her only when the rest of this community is busy with the evening meal. She's not a bat or a moth! She wants the sun, and she needs to be free to hunt the way she was born to do.*

Once again I claimed my freedom, asking no one's permission. As soon as Odran left each morning, Ea and I darted from the house to the woods and beyond. Now I was not just hiding from the druids and their students, the healers and their patients, but from Odran as well. He never found out, though he did notice how much happier I was and how much more attentive I became when he reported his day's doings.

I couldn't tell him mine. Secrets breed silence and silence can spread as subtly and surely as moss creeping over a stone. It stole more and more of our time together. Our few true conversations were insignificant chatter about the weather or mundane chores, or reminiscences about the crannog and the days we'd spent there tending wounded creatures. We learned the painful lesson that a memory shared too often no longer shines like the finest silk, but becomes as worn-out and threadbare as a beggar's tunic.

Our embraces suffered a horrible change, becoming distractions from what was growing more and more wrong between us. If we couldn't talk, we could kiss and pretend that was all our hearts desired.

There are lies we tell and lies we live. How could I go on believing I loved Odran so much, when I knew that his presence alone wasn't enough to satisfy me? I was betraying him as well as myself. There were times when I caught him looking at me with a furtive expression in his eyes that as good as said aloud that he felt the same.

I found myself wishing we were back in Connacht, working together at the crannog, sharing the labor of caring for creatures in need. When I took Ea out for her flights, I scanned the ground for any sign of a wounded bird or other animal. I was disappointed to find none, then realized what I was thinking. *Selfish!* I berated myself. *Selfish and cruel!*

I don't know how long Odran and I could have lived as we were. All that seemed to hold us together were our times of sweetness, and these began to lose their overwhelming power over us. Every kiss no longer led to more than that. The gentle touch of his hand on mine was pleasant, but kindled no blaze. We became ill at ease, not knowing how a love that once seemed like the blessed path to Tír na nÓg, land of eternal joy, had withered to . . . this.

I was coming home from one of Ea's outings when I saw a woman in green waiting outside our dwelling. I backtracked as fast and silently as I could, seeking to hide in the woods until she left, but before I could retreat far, I glimpsed Odran emerging from the house. He spoke a few words to her. She nodded, cupped her hands to her mouth, and called my name.

I hesitated, shocked and heartsick. Why had he revealed my presence? Was this his way of cutting loose a tie he regretted ever making?

A third figure appeared, coming from behind the house. Master Íobar shaded his eyes with one hand and scanned the trees that sheltered me. He didn't say a word, but began walking straight toward me. I came close to believing he possessed a touch of magical power until I recalled his skill with the sling. *Good eyes make good hunters,* I thought. *He's seen me. And why am I cowering here, after all? If Odran wants to be rid of me, I'll go.*

I walked out of the woodland smiling as serenely as if I were welcoming honored guests to my father's home.

Edana and I sat on a bench outside her home, close to the druids' great house in the center of the settlement. At the healer's insistence, I'd left Ea hooded on her perch in Odran's dwelling before following her here. We were well placed to watch all the comings and goings of Master Íobar's colleagues, who were bustling through the doorway like ants at the mouth of their hill. My discovery was the cause of it all.

"You don't speak much, do you, Lady Maeve?" Edana regarded me with a benevolent smile, as though we were old friends. She was right: I hadn't said three words since sitting down.

"What would you like me to say, my lady?" I sounded as morose as I felt. "That I feel stupid? That I'm a foolish girl who ran off to chase after some boy?"

"First of all, I am not nobly born, so I have no claim to being called 'lady,'" she said calmly. "I am only Edana."

"That seems unfair. Odran tells me you're the best healer on Avallach. We call the druids 'Master.' You deserve some show of respect."

"Titles are no substitute for true reverence and appreciation. I'm satisfied to know my own worth, and to sometimes receive thanks for my work."

"And I believe that mere thanks will never be enough to repay you for saving Odran's life." One corner of my mouth quirked up slightly. "If we were in Connacht, I could give you half my cattle. Shall I send them to you when I'm sent home?"

"Cattle travel poorly," the healer joked. She tucked a strand of her long blond hair behind one ear. I couldn't stop marveling at how young she was, her face fresh and unmarked by any wrinkles. How had she gained so much wisdom in the ways of herbs and other treatments so young? "Besides, no one is *sending* you anywhere."

"What?" I stared at her. "But isn't that what they're talking about in there?"

She shook her head. "Avallach welcomes all who come here in need. We let each person choose when she is ready to leave us, unless we see that she is too ill to make such a decision rationally."

"My choice has been settled for me," I said. "Odran's made it plain that he's seen enough of me."

"How do you know that?"

"He didn't hesitate to tell you I was hiding here."

Edana laid her hand over mine. "He wasn't the one who revealed your presence. Master Íobar came to visit his son. He wanted to be sure that Odran was well again. When he talked to me, he admitted he'd been too cowardly to return to Avallach until now, in case the news was bad. Some people believe that what they don't see or hear doesn't exist."

"I know at least one person like that," I muttered.

"Odran's father would have gone on being just such a person if not for a young woman who encouraged him to deal with his fears. He spoke quite highly of her bold spirit; her kind, forgiving heart; and—if I'd pardon him for admiring the beauty of a lass young enough to be his daughter—the most glorious red hair he'd ever seen." She squeezed my fingers gently. "Picture my surprise when I spied just such a strand of fiery hair clinging to Odran's shoulder when the lad tried to persuade us *not* to enter his house. When I pointed it out, he claimed he'd been spending time with one of the local girls." She sighed. "He's a poor liar. A few more questions and he knew he was beaten. That's the sole reason he gave me your name."

Hearing this made me feel better, but it didn't resolve my situation. "So I won't be forced to leave Avallach?"

"No, but you won't be permitted to go on living with Odran either. He is a student here and there are certain standards he must meet. Perhaps it's time for him to return to sharing a house with the other boys. You can remain in his old dwelling."

"Isn't there another way? He's so much more comfortable in a place of his own. I swear I won't go near him if you leave him be."

"You care about him very much." She looked me in the eyes. "Do you love him?"

I blushed. "Of course I do!" I exclaimed with more force than necessary.

"Indeed. And he loves you as well, I know, but"—her head tilted to one side, like a bird's—"do you *love* him?"

"You just asked me that," I said uneasily.

"I think not. If the gods are good to us, our lives allow us to love many people before Donn welcomes us to the dark shore of Tech Duinn. Parents, brothers, sisters, kin, friends—"

"Even animals," I said under my breath, thinking of my Ea.

She heard me and nodded approval. "That is so. But for the truly blessed among us, a day comes when we find a person who is our second self, someone with whom we can share words but also silence, one who knows us to the core. That is what I mean when I ask if you *love* Odran."

"As much—as much as he loves me," I said.

Edana studied me closely. "I must ask you this, Lady Maeve: have you been here on Avallach long enough to have your moon time come?"

I knew her meaning. "Yes. Only six days ago."

"You sound disappointed. Is it because you want to bear Odran's child?"

"Yes. No. I mean, I thought I did."

"Why?"

I told her about how Odran and I first grew close when we tended the creatures on the crannog. "It bound us more than— more than anything we've ever shared," I said, heat rising to my cheeks as I faced the truth: I had never felt more a part of him than then, not even once during all our time together on Avallach.

"You imagined you could recapture that bond if the two of you had another small life in your care." Edana spoke simply, without any hint of mockery or condemnation.

I looked at the ground between my feet. "I told you I was foolish."

"I wouldn't say that. You're not the first girl to believe that there are magical ways of binding love."

I raised my head. "I'm glad nothing happened. I love Odran, I *do,* but not if I need to weave spells to hold us together. The thing is . . ." I paused, uncertain if I wanted to reveal my thoughts. "I enjoy—enjoy *being* with him, but when we're not—not—"

I don't know how flustered I would have grown if she hadn't saved me by saying: "That happens, Lady Maeve. Yes, and it may happen to you again more than once before you find the one who'll match you in body, mind, and spirit. Learn and let it pass."

A boy came running from the great house. "Edana, the masters are asking for you," he said.

She rose gracefully from the bench. "What about Lady Maeve? Do they wish to speak with her too?"

The lad looked doubtful. "They didn't say so."

"They didn't say no either," I pointed out. Edana laughed and I accompanied her into the great house.

I don't know what I expected to find inside: piles of ingredients for spells and potions? Cauldrons waiting to be filled with uncanny brews? Stones set out in complex patterns making a maze for the druids to walk in secret? I felt dreadfully let down when I saw nothing of the sort.

Five druids of Avallach were seated beside the central hearth, awaiting Edana. One raised his grizzled eyebrows in surprise when he saw me, but the others accepted my presence impassively. Odran and his father stood to one side. Master Íobar was not happy.

"Is this the girl?" one of the five asked.

I stepped forward before anyone could speak for me but myself. "I am Maeve of Connacht, daughter of Cloithfinn and Eochu Feidlech. Blessings to you, honored masters."

The eldest-looking of the group pursed his lips and frowned. "Do you mean you are the child of *Lord* Eochu Feidlech, High King of all Èriu?"

I spread my hands. "We are not in Èriu now. If I'd come here for healing or learning, would my father's title matter?"

A pair of the gray-haired masters nodded approval, but my questioner was not impressed. "But you have not come here for either reason and *that*"—he indicated the ill-fitting garment I'd gotten from the tanner's wife—"is not what a princess wears. If not for your gold torque, you'd be mistaken for a servant."

"With respect, Master, I dress like this now out of necessity. I'll gladly tell you why I—"

He raised one hand imperiously. "Master Íobar's son has told us all we need to know. We will send a messenger to your father, informing him that you are here and well. Until we hear from him, you will remain on Avallach. Edana, are you willing to have the girl stay with you? If not, we'll put her with the convalescents."

I bristled, hearing how glibly my fate was being arranged. *"The girl,"* am I? I thought, eyes narrowed on the haughty druid. *You might as well call me "the bag of apples" or "the bundle of wool!" I will not be shifted tamely from place to place while I have a mind and a tongue of my own.*

"With respect, Master, don't trouble yourself over me," I said, my head high. "I'm leaving your settlement today and Avallach itself as soon as I can find a boat sailing to Èriu." I spoke rashly, my words forceful but ill-chosen.

"Maeve, no!" Odran cried, reaching for me. His father frowned but said nothing and made no move to restrain him.

Too late I realized what I'd done. In my haste to make that dictatorial man stop treating me like an object, I didn't think of the effect such a public declaration might have on Odran. I thought he'd understand me: the druids would never allow us to remain together here, so why stay? I chose to leave, and hoped he'd hear my unspoken message: *You, too, have a choice to make, dear one. What will it be?*

One look at his face told me he'd only heard my intended departure as abandonment, coldly done in the presence of so many others.

"Odran, I—I'm sorry," I said. "I—I shouldn't have said all this here and now, but—" I took a deep breath. "I've made up my mind," I finished lamely.

"Just like that?" He sounded bitter. "I never thought you were this callous."

His reaction stung. *Doesn't he know me better?* "You misunderstand me. I want to talk to you about it, but not here and now. Your teachers are busy men. Now that I've solved their problem of how to dispose of me, they must have more important things to do." I turned to the druids. "Masters, Odran and I will part, but surely you can be gracious enough to allow us one last conversation?"

My request charmed a smile from one of their number who still had a few streaks of red clinging to his silvery beard. "How can we say no in the presence of so much eloquence? Go, Lady Maeve. Speak with Odran for as long as you like. We can use the time arranging your departure. You'll need an escort—"

"She has one," Odran said. "When she goes, I go."

His announcement sparked a commotion among the druids. They took turns berating him for being so impulsive, urging him to remain and continue his studies, even flattering him when they spoke of the exceptional ability he'd already shown for learning their sacred lore. It was odd to see Master Íobar holding himself aloof from the discussion, and irksome to realize that once again I had been set aside to let the men settle matters.

Edana was also being ignored, and she liked it as little as I did. "Masters, you seem to be deciding many things for those who can make their own decisions. Have you also decided why you summoned me? Apparently I've slipped your minds." She sweetened her barbed words with a humorous tone.

"Forgive us, healer," said the one with the red-streaked beard. "You know how we value your wisdom. This outburst of young Odran's is not the first time he's mentioned leaving us. He says he'd rather follow your path than ours."

"Master, if you're hoping I'll discourage him from that, I must disappoint you. Odran has a talent for repairing hurts and easing pain. If he devotes himself to perfecting his skills, he will save many lives."

The eldest-looking druid made a sour face. "Odran is a *boy*, a creature of whims and urges. Today he wants to be a healer, tomorrow a bard!"

"But he never wanted to be a druid," I said quietly.

"What did you say?" came the indignant demand.

I did not shy away. "It wasn't his choice to come here." I looked at Master Íobar meaningly.

"Yes, I saw to it that my son came here." Odran's father spoke forcefully, unashamed. "Why shouldn't I? Children don't know what they really want any more than they understand what's best for their future."

"Maybe not," I said mildly. "But how will we learn to become as wise as you if you don't give us the chance to think for ourselves, to make mistakes, to *try*?"

Odran and I were asked to leave the great house while the druids and the healer conferred. I tried to apologize for what I'd just done. I needed him to understand that it was an accident born in the heat of the moment, but when I opened my mouth, he cut me off harshly with: "Why did you come here if you're so ready to leave without me?"

"I don't want to leave *you*," I said. "But I do have to go while I can still do it of my own will. Otherwise they'll hold me here like a gift for the High King. I won't be treated like that, Odran!"

"Yes, *that's* what matters to you," he muttered.

Before I could speak again, Edana joined us. "There's been a compromise," she announced. "Odran, the Masters have consented to let you escort Lady Maeve to Connacht. Your father will travel with you. While you're gone, you are to think seriously about which direction you want your life to take. If it's a road that leads you back to Avallach, you need to declare if you'll study with them or with me."

Odran was taken aback. "They were happy with this?"

"No one is ever entirely happy with a compromise," Edana replied, smiling. "But that's the nature of such things."

"In that case, I know my answer now: I want—"

She stilled him with a raised finger. "No, Odran. I gave the Masters my word to reject you if you insist you've already made up your mind. You will use this journey to open your eyes, to listen to what the world tells you before you seize on a path."

"But Edana, what if he *does* know?" I asked. "It doesn't seem fair to put him through needless doubts."

"You can't speak for him, Lady Maeve," she replied. "You don't have the right to say whether his doubts are pointless or vital. Iron goes into the fire many times before it becomes a sword."

I mulled her counsel. *I had no doubts about Odran, I thought. I was certain I loved him and wanted to be with him forever. He felt the same way—he told me so. Loving each other seemed like the easiest choice in the world. Now—neither one of us is so sure. Will this journey back to Cruachan give us the chance to save what we had—what we thought we had—the chance to give it all up, or the chance to make something even stronger and truer than what bound us together before?*

I turned to Odran. "She's right. Even if you end up finding out that your instincts were right, that you were fated to be a healer, something precious might be waiting for you along the road." I took his hand and thought, *I hope it will be me.*

CHAPTER NINETEEN

Roads and Roamers

THE FISHERMAN WHO ferried us to Èriu said it was the worst storm he'd ever seen. Master Íobar said that the man was lying to receive a bigger reward for his services, and frankly, I agreed with the druid. The sly-looking fellow had been eyeing my gold torque from the moment we met and throughout the voyage continued to cast similarly greedy glances at every glittering ornament we wore. I felt blessed that I hadn't had to rely on such a person when I crossed the water to Avallach on my own.

Luck's been with me so far, I thought. *But when we reach Cruachan, I'll have to make my own fortune.* I stole a look at Odran, wondering if what lay before me included him.

Before we left the druids' settlement, I made a bargain with myself: I'd try to recapture how things had been between us when the crannog was our refuge and when I first revealed myself to Odran on Avallach. There wasn't much I could do to accomplish that when we were making our way to the shore, but I hoped I'd have some chance of renewing our closeness once we were aboard a boat. Above all, I wanted him to know that I'd never wanted to hurt him when I chose to go home. If I couldn't make him understand, he'd be lost to me.

My wishes faltered and fell. As soon as we boarded the fisherman's small craft, Odran took a seat in the prow and huddled there with his cloak wrapped tightly around him, acting as though he were alone in the vessel and the world. He didn't say a word to his father or me, and all my attempts at getting a response from him were brushed aside with shrugs and noncommittal grunts. The only time he stirred himself willingly was when I asked him to keep Ea safe. He gave the little kestrel such a tender look that it filled me with envy.

The weather was bad, but not as bad as the fisherman claimed. Rain blew over us and the sea gave the small boat a rough tossing, though I never felt the least bit worried that we'd be upended. Even if my stomach kept crying for mercy, I could tolerate the pitching and rolling enough to hold down the bread and cheese I'd eaten before beginning this voyage. Master Íobar fared even better: The druid turned his face to the sky and drank the rain. He wore such a look of satisfaction that it was almost as if he were taking credit for conjuring up the storm.

If he had that power, he might have held it in check out of pity for his son. Odran was a poor sailor. He struggled to maintain his self-possession, but he was soon leaning over the side of the boat, violently sick. I rushed to take Ea back, afraid he'd be too overwhelmed to look after her.

"Master Íobar? Can't you help him?" I asked softly, not wanting Odran to overhear.

The druid looked surprised, as if he'd been completely

unaware he even *had* a son until I told him so. Then he laughed. "He'll be fine."

I didn't think so. "If you'll hold Ea, I'll see if I can do something for Odran," I said. "Wrap a bit of your cloak around your forearm and—"

He pulled back. "I didn't tell him to come here. Let him *be*."

I had to submit to Master Íobar's command. There was no way I could comfort and take care of Odran while I had Ea in my charge. I felt helpless and resentful. Master Íobar had changed, but not enough for me. He might regret some of his actions, but only because he believed he'd earned Flidais's displeasure and endangered his son's life by killing Odran's creatures. He couldn't see that some things we do are simply wrong whether or not the gods pay enough attention to punish us for it.

Our "host" noticed Odran's distress and pretended to be deeply concerned. "Poor lad, that's Manannán's vengeance on him, sure as the sun rises," he said, invoking the sea-god's name. "I've seen grown men die of it. All turned inside out, they were, and squeezed dry."

"You don't look like a bean sidhe," I said sharply. "Unless you can do something for Odran besides prophesying his death, be quiet!" I heard Master Íobar chuckle.

The fisherman looked sullen. "Who says I can't help him? I've got the knack for getting the god's attention when I have something worthwhile to sacrifice to him." He stared at my torque meaningfully.

"This?" I laid my free hand to the thick gold ring around my neck. "You want me to toss it into the waves?" I made as if to remove it and do so.

"Oh, no, no, no, not that!" The fisherman grew so frantic, he nearly abandoned control of our boat. "A *proper* sacrifice has to take place at Manannán's shrine back on Avallach. But he'll save your friend's life right now if I take an oath to give him that"—he jerked his chin at my torque—"as soon as I'm home again."

I wanted to laugh out loud, but I was afraid that it would turn my own stomach upside down.

Master Íobar didn't view the fisherman's shameless, clumsy boldness so lightheartedly. "You will not go home," he intoned. "The sea will rise up to pull you into the depths. The sky will break over your head and rain down fire to consume your bones. Fish will swarm around you as you drown, and you will remain alive while they devour your eyes with their teeth like tiny needles. All this and worse will come to you for your sacrilege."

The fisherman quailed and shuddered before the druid's onslaught of curses. "Master, I swear I never—"

"Liar! I can smell your rotting heart. I know your corrupt thoughts. You mean to keep the lady's treasure for yourself and offer Manannán a pittance, if anything. Fool! You cannot cheat the gods! *You* should be the sacrifice." He stood up in the boat and raised his staff to the heavens. "O Manannán mac Lir, lord of the sea, hear me! Take this blasphemer even though we all perish with him! Let your retribution fall upon—!"

The shrieks and howls and sobs of the poor panic-stricken fisherman were loud enough to blot out the sound of gusting wind and the grumble of the sea. He tore his beard, pulled at his hair, and tried to strip off his tunic to cast it overboard and placate the angry god. I watched in admiration as Master Íobar calmed him down as readily as he'd horrified him. We sailed on to Èriu with no further incidents.

The fisherman recovered enough of his nerve before we landed to punish us for thwarting his greed. He took us much farther south than we wanted to go, claiming that the weather made any other course out of the question. He also insisted that he could not take us close to shore. We had to wade through chilly water that came up to my chest. By the time I reached the beach, my right arm felt ready to fall off from holding Ea high out of harm's way. Odran and his father had the advantage of being taller, but they were still thoroughly soaked by the time we turned to see the little boat sailing off in precisely the direction the fisherman swore was impossible.

We had no idea where we were, which tribe held the land we traveled, or the name of the king who ruled it. All we knew was that Cruachan lay to the west, though whether it was north or south was a mystery. The downpour persisted, and the road from the coast didn't offer much hope of shelter. We saw woodland in the distance, but no sign of people or even cattle. Herds would mean herdsmen and some hope of being put on the right path.

The foul weather dwindled to a drizzle by the time we reached the trees. Even the drizzle ended by sunset and the clear night air brought stars peeping through the leaves. Their beauty didn't make up for the fact that we had to forego the warmth and light of a fire. Master Íobar had the means for kindling one, but the rain had drenched every twig. Ea was a wet, furious ball of feathers. When I placed her on a low branch, she snapped her beak at me.

I resigned myself to our plight only to catch the faint scent of smoke from a distant hearth. "Do you smell that?" I asked. Soon we were all sniffing like a pack of hunting hounds, trying to gauge where it was coming from until we realized we'd never be able to find the source of that delicious aroma in the dark.

"I think it's venison," Master Íobar said as plaintively as a little boy yearning for a slab of honeycomb. "I love venison."

"At least we have something to eat," I pointed out, digging into one of the provision sacks we'd each carried from Avallach. "Look, the seawater didn't get into the bread, and the cheese and dried beef are safe too. What luck!"

"Luck isn't hot roasted venison," the druid grumbled.

I awoke in the middle of the night to the sound of Odran coughing. He had his head tucked under his cloak, trying to stifle the sound. It didn't work; the racking noise grew louder, spiking between the rolling waves of Master Íobar's snore.

I crept close and put my arm over Odran's shaking body. "What can I do to help?" I whispered.

"N-nothing. My throat's dry, that's—that's all."

"Where's your waterskin? If it's empty, I'll give you a drink from mine."

He tensed in my embrace. "*No.* This will go away on its own. Sleep—sleep is the best cure, but I can't rest comfortably with you hanging on to me." He wriggled out of my arms. "Leave me alone."

I withdrew, not wanting to upset him further. His rejection hurt me deeply. This was the first opportunity we'd had since Avallach to hold each other close. That was all I'd wanted, to feel his remembered warmth again, to recall those lost times when we'd both believed there was only one future for the two of us. I curled up on my side, too sad to cry.

Odran was worse in the morning. He lay shivering in his cloak, unable to rise, the cough stronger than the night before. When I touched his forehead, it was so hot that I thought my hand would catch fire.

Master Íobar and I did all we could for him. We didn't speak at first, but worked in grim, desperate silence. Neither one of us wanted to voice our deepest fear. I insisted on giving up my cloak and Master Íobar did the same. We soon had our patient cocooned like a moth. It was the best we could do. As part of his training to become a druid, Odran's father had been taught some healing skills, but he could do very little without the proper ingredients for a fever-quelling potion.

"Willow bark," he muttered, using the last of his water to cool Odran's brow. "We must find a stream, and if we're fortunate there will be willows growing near it."

"Let me search," I said, picking up all three waterskins, which were now empty.

"You'll get lost."

"I know how to retrace my steps, and the ground is soft, thanks to the rain. I'll leave a clear trail, and I promise I won't be gone long. Don't worry about me; look after him. You can do it better than I."

Master Íobar shook his head. "We have to find shelter. He needs a roof and a fire and something hot to drink. I can carry him."

"Carry him where?" I countered. "We still don't know where we are or where the nearest dwelling lies. If we set off wandering in the wrong direction, you'll waste your strength."

"And why are you so sure you know which is the *right* direction?"

"I'm going to try finding the source of those tasty smells that plagued us last night. Even if no one's roasting meat at this time of day, I might catch a whiff of bread baking."

"Hmph. Clever," Master Íobar conceded. "Fine, go, but come back quickly, don't forget we have to have fresh water, look for willow trees, and if you see any strangers, keep your distance and watch them from a hiding place."

I showed him my sling. "Don't worry."

I walked through the trees alert for any sight, smell, or sound that might lead me to food, shelter, and help. Did I hear the sound of rushing water? I turned my footsteps that way.

The stream was waiting for me when I emerged from the woodland. It ran like a glittering strand of silver through a rich meadow, where several fat cows grazed. Cattle meant people, and I was overjoyed to see a small house not too far away. As I moved nearer, a young woman emerged from the modest dwelling. She had two children with her, an infant cradled in the crook of one arm, and a fourth on the way. I had never seen such a welcome sight.

I started toward the house, rehearsing in my mind how I'd greet the mistress of it. *Perhaps she knows of a healer nearby who can help Odran,* I thought. *He'll be safe and warm soon, thank the gods! Let him get well and I won't care if he never speaks to me again.*

The young mother opened her house and heart to me almost immediately and insisted that her older child fill my waterskins in the stream before allowing me to go back and fetch Master Íobar and Odran. When the druid arrived carrying his son, he had to do everything but threaten her with a curse to dissuade her from giving up her own bed. By the time her husband came home, Odran was resting on a pallet, Ea was perched on a beam just out of the children's reach, and Master Íobar and I were well fed and busy spreading our wet cloaks to dry by the hearth.

Everything would have been perfect if only Odran's fever hadn't risen even more. Our hosts became as concerned for him as we were. "Master Íobar, can't you cure him?" the woman asked anxiously.

"I've done what I can," the druid replied.

The man drew his wife aside to whisper, but in the small house there could be no secrets. I overheard them whether I wanted to or not.

"We've got to do something, wife. If the lad dies, Master Íobar will set a blight on us."

"Oh, I don't think he'd do that."

"Can we be sure? I'm going to go fetch help from our chief's household."

"I've heard that the king's healer is so arrogant and full of himself that he won't tend anyone outside the royal family. He won't come here at your bidding."

"He will if the king commands it."

"Husband, you can't just saunter into our chief's stronghold and declare you want to talk to him! You won't even get past the guards."

"Why not? I'll tell them we're caring for a druid's son, and that the lad's traveling with a nobly born girl."

"They'll never believe you. They'll say you're mad and hold you prisoner!"

I approached the couple discreetly. "No they won't." I removed my gold torque and handed it to the man. "Not when you show them this."

The king's healer did not come to us; the king did, and at the head of a party of servants and warriors. He burst into the humble house and filled it with his presence and a voice that shook dust from the thatch as he boomed, "Maeve? Lady Maeve, is it *you*?"

In their hidden realm, the People of the Mounds dropped to the ground, helpless with laughter, knowing that their wicked tricks had brought me face to face with Conchobar of the Ulaidh once more.

CHAPTER TWENTY

The High King's Folly

WITH MY TORQUE safely back around my neck, I rode to Emain Macha with Conchobar. The farmer helped me mount behind his chief, though he made an awkward job of it. He wasn't used to wearing the heavy gold bracelets the king had given him for a reward. His little family clustered in the doorway of their home to watch us go. Conchobar had promised to send them twenty of his best cows. The young mother shouted thanks and blessings after us.

Emain Macha was a tumult of activity when we arrived. I wondered why so many armed men were dashing here and there, but I couldn't spare the scene more than a passing thought until I knew Odran's care was assured. The healer who served Conchobar was talented, but he was also just as self-important as the farmer's young wife said. As soon as Odran was carried into a sleeping chamber, that conceited man banished everyone from it with the exception of Master Íobar. I don't know if he did so out of compassion, respect, or just because the druid scared the porridge out of him.

I was left out and far from pleased. Conchobar noticed. "If you want to share your sweetheart's room, I'll make it so," he told me as we stood outside the great house together. The words were willing, but the look on his face was much the same as if he'd said, *I'm going to eat a handful of meadow saffron seeds and die.*

"Thank you, no," I replied. "I trust your healer's judgment and I don't want to do anything that will hinder Odran's recovery."

"Oh." Conchobar's broad shoulders seemed to slump without actually doing so. "Then he is your darling."

"You were the one who called him that."

"You were the one who didn't deny it. Why else would the pair of you be traipsing all over Èriu together?"

"Are you forgetting that his father's 'traipsing' with us?" I asked archly. "It's not a very romantic arrangement."

"Master Íobar wasn't there when you ran away from Dún Beithe and flew straight into that boy's arms."

"What do you know of that?"

"More now than when your disappearance was first discovered. I was still there, a welcome guest, even if I did give Kian the thrashing he was begging for." He preened.

"I doubt you were welcome if you won the fight. Lady Lassaire would have something to say about it."

"That she did. She tried to send me on my way, but Lord Artegal reminded her that *he* rules Dún Beithe and I could stay as long as I liked. She wouldn't speak to him for two days. Then they found out you'd gone missing and she had enough to handle besides fussing over her baby boy."

"It took them *two days* to realize I was gone?"

"Yes, and it would've been more if not for what's-her-name, the plump one. Those fosterlings knew right away that you'd scampered—it stands to reason—but they hid it and claimed you were ailing."

"I did not 'scamper,'" I said with a resentful snort.

"Scampered, marched, waddled, it was all the same to Lady Lassaire once she found out. I never saw a woman turn a ringfort inside out with her bare hands before. And the tongue-lashings she gave those girls—! She had them in tears." The corners of his mouth turned down. "So were we all, when Lord Artegal's search parties came back empty-handed. We thought you were dead."

A massive pang of guilt struck me. "You . . . and my family. Oh, Conchobar, I'm a fool! I went to Avallach to help Odran, but how much harm have I done as well?"

"Maybe not so much as you fear. Lord Artegal sealed every pair of lips at Dún Beithe and made me swear an oath to tell no one here about your disappearance. Anything to delay your father finding out about it!"

"But he'd have to, eventually."

"Yes, but Artegal chose to play a gambler's game. Maybe he'd come up with an explanation good enough to justify your absence. Maybe Eochu would die before he called anyone to account for you. Maybe you'd turn up at last." He laughed briefly, under his breath. "You win, Artegal."

"I have to send a messenger to Cruachan," I said anxiously. "And one to Dún Beithe as well. It can't wait until I travel on. My parents and Lord Artegal must know I'm alive and well *now*."

"It'll take more than a couple of messengers to make this right," Conchobar said. "I'll speak to Artegal myself when I see him at Tara. We've both been summoned there, and who knows how many of the other kings?"

"Tara!" I exclaimed. So that's the cause of all the bustle at Emain Macha. Conchobar's men are getting ready to accompany him, a properly impressive escort for the lord of the Ulaidh. I didn't need to ask who'd commanded him to undertake the journey. The only one with the power to command a king's appearance was a higher-ranking king, and that could only be: "Father wants you there? Why?"

"His messenger didn't give me a reason; he just said I should attend the High King within three days. I reckon the fellow would've told me more if he knew it; he was chatty enough otherwise, especially once I filled him to the eyeballs with food and drink. He let me know I'm not the only chief Eochu's ordered to be there."

"Yes, but *Tara*—!" I didn't know what to make of this. Tara was a site of great power and significance: holy ground, a gateway to the Otherworld, the dwelling place of the gods. They had traveled there in a time before time and set up a towering stone that possessed the magic power to recognize the true king of Èriu by roaring at his touch. The lords of our land gathered there at certain sacred seasons of the year—Samhain, Beltane, and the rest—but it was nowhere near time for any of the great and solemn festivals now. "What could be important enough for Father to call you all there?"

Conchobar made a noncommittal gesture. "Feel free to guess. I'll find out when I get there."

"No," I said. "We'll find out together. I'm going with you."

He grinned so broadly I thought his face would split. "Truly? With that skinny boy lying ill under this roof, you'd rather come with me than stay with him? Ha! What do you know? He's not your sweetheart after all."

"Whatever Odran and I are to each other doesn't touch this." I spoke in measured tones, keeping tight reins on my impulse to snap at Conchobar for being so reliably provoking. "Friend, sweetheart, even husband—no matter how he touches my life, I would still go to Tara. Odran is in good hands with your healer. He doesn't need to have me here to get better, but I *do* need to show Father and Lord Artegal that I'm all right. Do you understand?"

Conchobar looked crestfallen. "He's your husband? *That* scrawny thing?"

I groaned and covered my face with my hands until I felt calm enough to deal with him again. "Forget about Odran. In fact, forget about me talking to Father when we reach Tara. You say he doesn't know I'm missing. Let him go on thinking I'm safe at Dún Beithe. It would only stir up pointless trouble if he learned otherwise. Take me to Tara, Conchobar, and help me reach Lord Artegal secretly. No one but he should be aware I'm there. Can you do that for me?"

"That and more, my beautiful lady. Just ask!" He lifted me off my feet and kissed me, but only on the brow. I confess I was a bit disappointed.

We departed for Tara the next day. In spite of my bold words to Conchobar, I had misgivings about leaving Odran behind. The healer reassured me that things were looking better, the fever was down, and the patient was resting comfortably, but I still harried him with countless questions.

"I only want to be certain he won't get worse while I'm gone," I said, trying to justify my pestering.

"Why don't I smother him for you right now?" the healer replied peevishly. "I can guarantee he won't get worse than that!"

I asked Master Íobar to look after Ea. My request took him by surprise. "You'd trust me with her, after what I once did?"

"Think of this as a chance to undo it," I said, meaning every word. I handed him my leather armguard. "Always wear this when you handle her. I hope it will be big enough to fit. I don't want either of you to be hurt." I gave him instructions for her care and for how to use the lure to bring her back when he flew her.

"I'll do my best," he said. "But if she escapes and won't come back—" He looked worried. "Maybe I should keep her safe inside until you return."

"That would be worse than if she got away," I said. "Let her fly."

I slipped into Odran's room just before it was time to go. He lay with his eyes closed, breathing without difficulty. I knelt by his bedside and gazed at him in silence, believing he slept. I remembered how happy I'd been in his arms, and for a moment I wondered if we could find a way to bring back that time. *We can try, can't we?* I thought as I rose and leaned over him to place a light kiss on his forehead.

His eyes opened. "You're going now, aren't you? To Tara. My father told me." His lips were pale and tight. "I should have heard it from you."

"I tried to tell you as soon as it was decided," I replied. "Every time I came in here, you were sleeping."

"And yet somehow, Father managed to catch me waking. You didn't try hard enough. You didn't want to." He turned his face to the wall.

"Odran, why won't you understand?" I cried. "I left Dún Beithe for your sake, but I was wrong not to send them word that I was alive." As I spoke, I realized something: I couldn't have contacted Lord Artegal from Avallach even if I hadn't feared he'd demand my return. I was living there in hiding, a fugitive. Where and how would I have found a willing messenger?

Odran flung himself back to confront me. "Oh, be *honest,* Maeve! You told me how badly your so-called friends treated you at Dún Beithe, and no one did anything about it. Yet here you are, rushing off to ease their worries. You're not going to Tara to help them, you're doing it because you're through with me and this is the easiest way out. Reveal yourself and be swept back to the life you really want, the one that's got no room for me in it." His voice was rough and biting. It made me feel like I'd been slapped.

"I have to, Odran," I said, striving to keep him from hearing how much he'd hurt me.

"Then go."

"If you'll only—"

"*Go.*"

I sat in the darkness of a tent pitched within sight of the great hill of Tara and waited for Conchobar to return. We'd reached the sacred ground after three days on the road, the last of these devoted to the challenge of keeping me hidden from the other kings and warriors who'd arrived before us. Conchobar wanted to wrap me in a cloak, sling me over one shoulder, and carry me into his tent, but I'd see myself halfway to Tech Duinn before I'd let him treat me like a bundle again. I suggested he and the men who'd traveled on horseback go up to Tara first and set up the tents. I'd lag behind with the warriors who'd come from Emain Macha on foot and at sunset simply march into camp with all of them massed around me.

"At twilight, even the keenest eye can't spy the bird hidden in the blackthorn," I argued. Conchobar grudgingly agreed to do things my way.

Now it was a matter of waiting for word that Lord Artegal had arrived. Conchobar was out mingling with his fellow chieftains, trying to learn if they'd heard anything about the master of Dún Beithe. As soon as I found out where he'd camped, I'd go to him and all would be well.

Will it? I wondered, resting my chin on my knees. *I'll return to Dún Beithe and then what? Bryg will still be there, goading the others against me. Kian will want "his" kestrel back, and I'll wager he won't let me near her again. I could try cajoling him, but—No. I refuse. Why must I coax and flirt and use false tears to sway Kian or any other man? If I'd been born a prince of Connacht, I'd speak frankly to him and he wouldn't dare dismiss me unless he wanted to be challenged to a duel. And why can't I do that now? My skill with the sling equals his—I'll stake Ea on that—and in a fair contest—*

My thoughts were interrupted by the sound of voices outside the tent. One was Conchobar's, but the other was unfamiliar. I had no choice but to hear them.

"—sure you want no help with that, Cairill?"

A low laugh responded to Conchobar's question. "You mean help drinking it?"

"Well, a swallow or two would lighten your load." More laughter followed, now from both of them.

"No thank you, friend. I've seen you guzzle. It wouldn't do to present the High King with a cask of mead that's half full of air. You know his temper."

"Not at close range, thank the gods. I stay as far from him as I can and still pay him my respects," Conchobar said. "You know, Cairill"—he went on in a wheedling tone—"Eochu isn't *expecting* to receive a gift of mead from you. The two of us could share it and he'd never know."

"Ha! You're as silver-tongued as your father was. Too bad he couldn't talk his way out of fighting Eochu on that cursed day. He was a good friend, always openhanded to me, willing to hear my counsel, and a better High King than the one we're burdened with now. I long for the day we'll see you in his place. *You* won't stop your ears when wiser men offer you advice; not like Eochu. If only that man weren't such an able fighter—!"

"Are you sure you haven't been sampling that mead yourself?" Conchobar joked, but it sounded forced. "You'd better not babble like that where Eochu can hear you."

"Don't fret over it, lad. Eochu's only one man. Sleep well." I heard Cairill's departing footsteps.

"What was that about?" I asked the instant Conchobar ducked into the tent.

"Hey, easy there! You scared me. Why aren't you asleep?"

"I heard you call that man Cairill," I said, not about to be distracted. "Is he the same Lord Cairill who was plotting against Father?" No answer came, so I added: "You know, Conchobar, it's too dark in here for me to see if you nodded your head or shook it."

"Yes, he's the same one," Conchobar responded.

"And you let him go to my father with a gift of mead?" I said. "A gift he refused to let *you* taste!"

"I doubt it's poisoned. Eochu's a wise old badger. He'd have Cairill take the first sip. Besides, I wasn't the only one who saw Cairill toting that cask. He told every man he met who it was for. There'd be no way he could dodge the blame if the High King died after drinking it."

"What do you think he meant, saying my father's only one man? It's not like Lord Cairill's going to challenge him to single combat. He'd have done it by now if he weren't a sneaking coward. Father doesn't stand alone; he has allies, faithful lords who'll follow him against his enemies!"

"Shhh. Not so fierce, Maeve, and not so loud. My men know I'll skin them alive if they betray your presence, but what if you do it yourself? Eochu's a fortunate man to have a fighter like you on his side."

He spoke in jest, but jests can carry truth within. Was I on Father's side again? Was I ready to forgive him for his past wrongs the way I'd pardoned Master Íobar? Kelan's death would always stand between us, and all of the lesser offenses could not be forgotten, but neither could all the love and kindness and trust my father had showed me. I now saw good deeds and bad like sunbeams shining through wind-tossed willow leaves, the bright flicker of light dancing with the somber touch of shadow. The girl who'd made my life unbearable had also saved the bird who meant the world to me. The man who'd saved me from a hideous death in the bog had tried to rape me. The boy I'd loved first and best and completely now filled me with doubt more than desire.

I couldn't worship my father and I couldn't condemn him, but maybe I could save him. Lord Cairill was up to something, and I was going to discover it.

I yawned loudly. Conchobar snickered. "You sound like a bawling heifer."

"I'm a *sleepy* heifer," I replied. "You want me to be quiet? Get out of here and let me close my eyes. If Lord Artegal arrives tomorrow, I'll need to be refreshed and alert for what's to come."

"I could stay here," he said in a coaxing tone. "It's so cold outside, and there's plenty of room, and—"

"I snore," I said. "And I thrash. And since when is the mighty king of the Ulaidh afraid of a little chill that *doesn't exist*? It's almost summer, Conchobar. Your argument's got more holes than a fishnet."

"Well, you can't blame me for trying," he said. I couldn't see his face, but I had the unshakable feeling he was grinning.

"Or blame *me* for sending you on your way."

I waited for a while after he left, then peeked outside. It was a cloudy night and the quarter moon didn't give much light, but I could see well enough to get by. I picked my way past the sleeping men of the Ulaidh who surrounded the tent. Once I left Conchobar's encampment behind, I did not go stealthily but walked as though I had every right to be there. Not everyone at Tara was asleep, and I observed a good deal of comings and goings as men of one tribe struck up conversations with those of another. In the dark, from a distance, my cloak and long hair could belong to a young warrior as well as to a girl. People see what they expect. No one was expecting to see me.

I didn't know where Father was camped, so I had to explore until I heard familiar voices. After my time away, it was good to hear the accent of Connacht and recognize some of the speakers. My people were settled around a large tent, which I presumed was Father's. Like Conchobar, he didn't need it for shelter, but it was a symbol of his rank and power, suitable for impressing the other chieftains.

Now that I was near those who could recognize me, I had to be furtive again. I kept my distance from the few campfires still burning and slipped around to the back of Father's tent. Two shadows showed against the cloth walls, most likely cast by a small oil lamp. I sank into a crouch, swathing myself entirely in my cloak, and harkened to what was happening inside.

It took me a while to adjust my ears so that I could make sense of the low, garbled voices. I recognized Father's and concluded that the other must be Lord Cairill. They both sounded as if they'd fallen under the mead's spell, but Father's tongue stumbled much more.

"—reconsider. Artegal's a good—a good man, Cairill. If I challenge him f'no reason—"

"He was entrusted with your daughter. Where's she now, eh? Eh? Gone." I heard a resounding blow, which might have been Lord Cairill emphasizing his words by pounding the mead cask. "Gone, gone, *gone*!"

"Uh . . . you—you're sure?"

"I told you what I heard 'bout it. Don't you trust me? But Artegal, he's covering it up."

"Gone. Gone, my spark, my little girl, my Maeve, gone." Father's plaintive voice twisted my heart. "D'you think she's . . . dead?"

"I hope not, my lord, but what difference does that make concerning Lord Artegal? Whether Lady Maeve's alive or dead, it's still his fault for letting her get away—for not taking better care of her, keeping watch, protecting her as you would have done yourself." How strange: suddenly Lord Cairill sounded totally sober. "When I first told you what I knew of your daughter's disappearance, you swore you'd make him pay for it with his head, and his son's too!"

"Did I?" Father sounded weak, confused. "But the boy wasn't responsible—"

"Unless he was the reason your precious child vanished." As soon as the ugly insinuation left his lips, Lord Cairill changed his tactics. Now he addressed Father with honeyed sympathy. "My lord, don't look so unhappy. I might have heard a false rumor and your daughter is safe in Lord Artegal's care."

"You think so?" Father sounded pathetically hopeful. "But why did you advise me to summon him and the other lords here? I could've just"—he hiccuped—"just sent a message to Dún Beithe t'ask about my spark."

"And he could have sent one back saying Lady Maeve is well, even if that's not the case," Lord Cairill returned smoothly.

"My messenger wouldn't carry a lie back to me. Not on his life."

"Messengers can be tricked or bribed, or . . . eliminated,

my lord Eochu. No, your plan is best. Lord Artegal and his son will come here and take an oath at the mouth of the great mound, where the breath of the Otherworld seeps into our own. They will be compelled by the holy power of Tara's ground to reveal the truth about your child's whereabouts, and once you know"—his voice dropped so that I could barely hear him— "you will either circle their necks with gold or cut their throats with steel, for Lady Maeve's sake."

For my *sake, is it?* I thought indignantly. *Cairill, you slithering worm, why do you call this deceitful ploy Father's idea when it's plainly yours? Bringing Lord Artegal and Kian here for questioning's one thing, but I heard him say you're the one who advised him to bring the other lords of Èriu here. Why? How will this advance your plot to tear the High King's name away from—?*

All at once, I knew. "No," I whispered into my cupped hand. "Oh no."

It was no secret that my father loved and favored me. It was likewise well known that Eochu Feidlech was a renowned fighter. Challenging him to a duel was serious business, not for any upstart to try lightly. It would take a great provocation to make any man raise a sword against him.

A great provocation . . .

What if the High King showed himself unworthy to rule? What if he demonstrated willingness to abuse his power, ordering his subject kings to make the trek to Tara solely to witness him cut down two of their own? And for what? For failing to keep me from slipping away.

I could imagine their reactions: *Girls are flighty things. They toss their heart at any lad who takes their fancy. Lady Maeve's no different. She's probably gone off with some boy and will return when she's carrying his child. Is it worth destroying a good man for that, and for sending his son with him to Donn's death-shadowed land? Why couldn't he have all of us scour the realm in search of her, and give Artegal and his boy a chance to make things right? But Eochu's fury stole his sanity, or maybe he was mad to begin with, as blood-hungry as the Morrígan's ravens. Cross him and you're doomed. If he's capable of doing something like this once, he'll do it again. I could be next. I cannot live like that, waiting for the blade to fall. I will not live meekly under such a High King.*

It wouldn't be long before someone found a pretense to face him in combat. If the first man to raise his sword against Father failed, another would take his place, and another after that, and so on until the High King fell, exhausted, defeated, slain. Then it would be just a matter of Cairill using his poisonous skills of persuasion on Conchobar. The lord of the Ulaidh was young, strong, and most likely a capable fighter. A second High King would die, Conchobar would take his place, and Cairill would be at his side, ready to feast on the body of Èriu.

Meanwhile, what would become of my family? What would become of Connacht? My brothers were babies, unable to defend us against raiders eager to despoil a land without a leader. Father's warriors would fight for them, but for how long? And could we trust all of them to keep faith with a dead man's children? The kingship of Connacht was a fine prize. Who knew whether some of our men would fight harder to protect it or to take it?

And throughout the raids and battles, those who would suffer most would be our people.

I had to stop Cairill.

My thoughts darted like swift-winged swallows. *If I go to*

Father now, he'll still hold Lord Artegal to blame for not keeping watch over me. Who knows how he'd react? I can't risk it. What if I go out to meet Lord Artegal on his way here? He could send me back to Dún Beithe with some of his men and be able to swear truly under oath that he does *have me safe in his care!*

It seemed like a good idea, but only for a moment. *I don't know which road he'll take. I can't go seeking him in the dark, and if I travel on my own by daylight, the land around Tara offers clear views and nowhere to hide. I'll be seen. If I ask Conchobar to help me, sending me out to meet Lord Artegal with the Ulaidh warriors shielding me from others' sight, it will draw every eye. "Why are Lord Conchobar's men on the move like that? Let's go after them and see!" No, too dangerous, impossible.*

I buried my face against my updrawn knees, desperately seeking a way out that would save Lord Artgeal and Kian and save my father from himself.

Oh sweet goddess Brigid, lend me your power to see things that are to come! Show me the path that will let Lord Artegal admit that I left Dún Beithe but that he could not have done anything to prevent my flight! Give me a bard's tongue to tell a tale that will leave him as blameless as though he'd seen the earth open beneath my feet and gulp me—gulp me—

I raised my head. The goddess had spoken through my own thoughts. I had my answer.

I huddled in my cloak outside of the High King's tent until I was assured that Lord Cairill had left him. I noted the moment when Father extinguished the light, then waited longer, listening for the faint sounds of deep, regular breathing that would tell me he was asleep. When I felt certain that the mead had sealed him in slumber, I stole to the front of the tent and darted inside.

The darkness within was absolute. I dropped to my hands and knees, feeling my way cautiously, guided only by the sound of Father's breath. I yearned to move faster but had to hold myself in check. Haste would make me reckless, and I could not afford to bump into anything that might make a noise and rouse the sleeper.

I knew what I sought and where it would be: my father's sword, never more than arm's length from him. My questing fingers touched the faithful blade and carefully closed around its hilt. Holding it close, I flitted back into the open air, into the night, and away.

CHAPTER TWENTY-ONE

Oath at Tara

I SLEPT ON sacred ground. I waited within the darkness of the great mound at the heart of Tara for my destiny or my death. It was not the first time I'd taken refuge in such a place. When Lord Morann held Devnet hostage, I'd eluded his men by sheltering in a gateway sacred to the Fair Folk. I asked their pardon reverently and they did not punish me for my presence then. Perhaps they took pity on me, if the People of the Mounds can feel compassion for mortals.

This time they might not be as forgiving. So be it.

I thought of Conchobar, remembering his expression when I'd roused him from sleep, told him my intentions, and showed him Father's sword. He tried to talk me out of it, even threatened to drag me to the High King, but I soon persuaded him to see things my way. (Menacing *him* with how I'd explain my presence in his company was quite convincing.) He vowed to keep my secret and gave me what he could to help me with my plan, but he refused to see me enter the great mound.

"I can't watch you go, knowing you might not come out again," he said. "You're taking a greater risk than any man I know, and that includes myself. If you offend the Fair Folk—" He shivered.

"I'll ask them for pardon and permission. That's all I can do."

"You could stay. You could try to reason with your father."

"Even if he'd listen to me, he'd still have to do something to save face after calling you and the other kings here. For what? An offense that never happened. Can you swear there won't be some among them who'll resent him for taking them from their homes for nothing? Ambitious men will see it as weakness, and you can guess the fate of a weak High King." I kissed his cheek. "I've chosen."

Now I waited, cold stone at my back, the air of the Otherworld sighing through my hair. Daylight glowed at the mouth of the passageway, but it did not penetrate my lair. I heard the sound of kings arriving at Tara with their escorts, the outcry as men scrambled to discover the whereabouts of the High King's sword, the murmur of nervous voices speaking of omens, and the comings and goings of druids who watched over the holy site.

A great host began massing before the stone-framed portal, my father at the fore, Lord Artegal and Kian with him. I rose slowly, taking care not to strike my head on the ceiling of the passageway, and moved silently toward the light.

Father's voice reached my ears: "—swear by this sacred gateway to the Otherworld and by the gods who guard and govern it to speak the truth?"

"*Swear* to that, my lord Eochu?" Lord Artegal replied,

suspicion, resentment, and a trace of anxiety in his tone. "You never thought to question my honesty before."

"My father is no liar!" That was Kian, leaping to the defense. "Why must he take an oath? Will you ask all of these men here to do the same? Do you trust none of us?"

Father laughed dismissively. "My question is not for them, boy, but I have called them to witness your father's answer so that afterward there can be no room to doubt it."

"What do you want from him?" Kian would not back down. "Do you question his loyalty? Has some poison-tongued wretch turned you against him? Will you take that creature at his word, whoever he may be, but refuse to hear my father's denial unless he swears by the holy stones and soil of Tara? How can you—?"

"Hush, my son." Lord Artegal intervened before Father's temper could kindle against Kian. "If the High King of Èriu asks for this, he has his reasons and I will prove my fidelity by giving him what he wants."

I heard footsteps and saw a shadow cast across the grass outside. Lord Artegal must have been standing at the side of the mound, his hand on one of the gateway stones. The master of Dún Beithe raised his voice so that no one could deny his words: "I swear by wind and water; by earth and air; by my hand, my head, and my heart; by my blood and the blood of all my kin; by the sword and spear that sustain me in battle; and above all, by the sacred power of this place that I will speak the truth to any question Lord Eochu asks of me. May my bones burn and my blood boil within me for a hundred years before I win death's release if I break this oath."

A rumble of approval and admiration came from the gathered kings. Even Father must have been impressed, for it took him a while before he could speak again. "I accept your pledge. I wouldn't have asked it of you if this were a small matter. Lord Artegal, some time ago I entrusted you with my greatest treasure, after my sons. I was confident I'd picked the right man to guard something so priceless, but lately I have heard—"

I lost some of what he said in the loud muttering of the crowd. Many of them already knew the rumors of my disappearance, and soon they all would. Their voices ebbed as fast as they had risen. I sensed the chieftains bracing themselves to witness what must follow, and I could hear my father clearly once again as he demanded: "—if you can tell me by your oath that you now have my daughter Maeve safe in your keeping?"

"By this blade and by my life, he cannot!" I stepped back into the land of the living and lifted the High King's sword above my head with both hands.

The roar that greeted me was deafening. It raged through the crowd long enough for my eyes to adjust to the light. Questions slammed against me from every side. The druids of Tara called for silence as they strode forward to surround me, staring as if they were children beholding the terror and marvel of their first lightning storm. I grew weary from keeping Father's sword raised, but it would spoil the spectacle of my appearance if I lowered it too soon.

At last it was Father who provided me with the chance I wanted to ease my aching arms. He edged himself into the druids' ring and held out his hands. I gave him the blade, faced the crowd, and spoke: "What was taken from you is restored." I didn't need to raise my voice. No one wanted to miss a single word I had to say. Every eye was on me, every tongue was silent.

"I have seen wonderful things," I went on. "I have touched the border between life and death. I have traveled to an island none of you may ever know, but now I have come back, my steps bringing me to you from *there*." I pointed to the open portal of the mound.

The men chattered, whispered, and shouted, all of them debating what I might mean. And in the end, what else *could* I mean but that I'd visited the shores of Tech Duinn and survived, that I'd breathed the blessed air of Tír na nÓg's isle, that I'd braved the path from the Otherworld to return to Èriu? Certainly not that I'd nearly drowned in a bog, sailed to Avallach, and emerged from only a spear-cast down the stone-framed passageway!

As I said, people see what they expect to see, and they tell themselves the stories they want to hear.

I approached Lord Artegal, took his hands in mine, and fell to my knees before him, much to his astonishment and dismay. "Forgive me, my lord," I declared. "Forgive me for all the distress you've endured since I left Dún Beithe. You brought me into your home and treated me like a daughter. I'm sorry to think that you must have felt a father's anguish after what happened. I would not have left if I could have stayed, but you must not—you *can*not blame yourself for any of it." I regained my feet and let my gaze pass slowly over the kings, the warriors, and the druids as I told them all, "There are things that not even the most watchful guardian can prevent. Not every challenge can be settled by the sword. Sometimes we must gamble for our fate." I gave them a victor's grin. "Sometimes even the Fair Folk lose a wager."

The lords of Èriu cheered. Father threw his arms around

me and shouted orders for a feast to be assembled at once. Men ran for their hunting gear and their horses. A minor lord whose stronghold lay close to Tara dispatched messengers to fetch additional supplies and the hands to cook and serve them. By the time all the preparations were in order, the scraps of truth I had tossed to the assembled nobles had been stitched into a fantastic tale that every bard would embroider with his own touches. The gist of it was that one of the Fair Folk became so enthralled by my beauty that he carried me away to the Otherworld against my will. He tried to woo me with Tír na nÓg's eternal pleasures and to break my spirit with the threat of Tech Duinn's grim shadow, but I resisted both. In the end I outwitted him by striking a bargain: we'd gamble with my freedom as the stakes. I won and he released me. That was all.

That night my father heaped Lord Artegal with treasure, praising him for keeping my disappearance a secret. "You meant to spare my feelings, old friend; I'm sure of it. You must have torn up all the countryside searching for my girl, striving to find her before I could hear she was gone."

Lord Artegal looked flustered. "I—I felt responsible," he said.

"Nonsense! What could you or any mortal man do against the Fair Folk's magic?"

"That's true, Father," Kian said. "Do you remember that falcon of mine? He vanished at the same time as Lady Maeve! I'll bet he was that Otherworld prince in disguise. He used his spells to learn she was coming to Dún Beithe, turned into a wounded bird, and put himself in my path so he could be waiting there for her when she arrived. He bided his time, and when he saw his opportunity he carried her off in his claws.

Oh, they're a sly bunch, the People of the Mounds!" He hic-cuped loudly, thanks to the same vast quantity of mead that had let him forget Ea was a female. I pictured myself dangling in midair from a little kestrel's talons and nearly choked trying to smother my laughter.

Apparently the story of my abduction to the Otherworld was like a tree that grew more robust with every fact-bearing limb that was lopped off. It flourished so vigorously that before I left Tara, I overheard a couple of Conchobar's men saying what a brave girl I was to stand up to a lord of the Fair Folk and outwit him. They had traveled with me from Emain Macha for three days, yet here they were talking about my adventures as if such things had truly happened.

I wondered what Devnet would make of it. I couldn't wait to hear.

CHAPTER TWENTY-TWO

Wings

THE NEXT MORNING Father again called his subject kings together at the great mound. This gathering was as different from the first as mead is from mud. Spirits were high after the previous night's celebration. I stood at Father's side and scanned the crowd, seeking Kian and Conchobar. I'd wanted to speak to them at the feast, but Father kept me all but chained to his wrist from the moment we were reunited.

"Stay close, my spark," he whispered. "I've missed you so much, and now I fear that if you take one step away from me, the portal to the Otherworld will open and the Fair Folk will claim you once more."

"You can't keep me within arm's reach forever, Father," I said gently but firmly.

"I know, I know." He shook his head. "But just for now"—he gazed at me with pleading eyes—"humor me?"

My heart was touched; I let him have his way, though it meant delaying my business with Kian and Conchobar. I owed thanks to the young king of the Ulaidh, and I needed to talk to Kian about my future at Dún Beithe. He had to know that if I returned to fosterage, I'd want his help as a friend—*only* as a friend—to settle matters between me, Bryg, and the other girls.

I spotted Kian easily that morning. He and Lord Artegal were in the front rank of the assembled men. Conchobar stood farther back, staying a prudent distance from my father. I was silently debating which one of them to approach first when one of Tara's druids called for the crowd's attention to hear what the High King had to say.

"My brothers, from this day we are allied by more than loyalty and honor." Father gave the men his most winning smile. "We are bound to each other by the marvel we witnessed together on Tara's holy ground: my daughter's escape from the Otherworld!" He beamed at the loud cheers that greeted his words. "I have always known her merit, her cleverness, and her courage, but what father *doesn't* think his child is destined for great things?" He chuckled, and his audience answered with a ripple of appreciative laughter. "What we saw here proves that my Maeve is worthy of much more than just a father's fond words. Lord Artegal! Come forward, you and your son!"

Both men found themselves clasped in the High King's arms. He released them only to strip himself of every ring and bracelet he wore, heaping their hands with gold. He refused to hear their thanks.

"You will have more riches as soon as I return to Cruachan, I promise. Forgive me, but all of it won't be enough to make up for the treasure you're about to lose."

"Lord Eochu—?" Lord Artegal struggled to keep his voice steady.

Father smiled. "I mean my daughter."

I tensed. My time at Dún Beithe had not been easy to bear, but it was *my* choice to go there, *my* choice to stay. If Father intended to take me back to Cruachan now, I'd have to fight for my freedom all over again.

I forced a loud laugh. "Dear Lord Artegal, how unhappy you look," I said. "I'd look ten times as sad if I thought my father were serious about tearing me from your care. What an insult that would be! He'd never dishonor you so." I knew I was playing a chancy game, but I had to try.

To my relief, Father put one arm around me and the other around Lord Artegal. "My spark speaks the truth. I'm not *taking* Maeve from your fosterage; I'm *giving* her a realm of her own."

My jaw dropped as my ears filled with the clamor of Èriu's assembled lords. It took the druids of Tara several tries to restore order and let Father continue speaking.

"Friends, there are times when even an ordinary man can read the will of the gods. If my girl has proved she has the courage, strength, and wit to save herself from captivity in the Otherworld, it would be a great shame not to let her use those skills for our people. I'm giving her a share of Connacht to rule as she chooses." He turned his gaze to the assembly. "All of you, witness that I swear this by the holy stones of Tara! If any man wants to dispute my decision or Lady Maeve's merit, let him say so now."

No one spoke. No one wanted to die.

"And what if *I* challenge you?" I asked abruptly.

"You, my spark?" It was Father's turn to be startled. "Don't you want—?"

"Oh, I do! But on this condition: that if I can't bring my people justice and prosperity, I'll return your gift and go back to Lord Artegal's fosterage with no objections from you or any other man."

Kings, warriors, and druids all made the sacred mound of Tara shake with their accolades. They stamped the ground, thundering, "Lady Maeve! Lady Maeve!" And if some chose to hail me as *Queen* Maeve—? They were entitled to that choice.

I was entitled to smile.

I couldn't take possession of my new realm until I had a well-fortified stronghold from which to rule. Father promised to provide this, so while he dispatched men and supplies for the task, I went back to Dún Beithe to pack my possessions and say goodbye. Devnet the bard joined me, vowing that since he'd escorted me to Lord Artegal's stronghold when I entered fosterage, he'd do the same when I left. Who would dare tell a bard no?

I must admit, I didn't go to Dún Beithe just to make my farewells. I had much more than that to say to Ula, Dairine, Gormlaith, and especially Bryg. I wasn't certain exactly *how* I'd confront them, but they all needed to know that what they'd done to me—and before me to poor, lost Aifric—must never happen to anyone ever again.

That's a fine thought, a good intention, I mused. *But how to give it teeth? How to make them do more than smile and nod and claim that they'll change their ways and then, once I'm gone, mock me and change nothing? Kian might be willing to help, but if they* wanted *to outwit him*—I shook my head. *Bryg alone could do that easily. Kian's not the answer.* The problem preoccupied me all the way back to Dún Beithe.

I was met with the warmest of welcomes from Lady Lassaire, of all people. She knew all about what had happened at Tara thanks to swift-riding messengers, and she no longer saw me as the ungrateful brat who'd refused betrothal to her precious Kian. Now I was the valiant girl who'd cheated the Otherworld in time to save his life and her husband's.

"Lady Maeve, dearest one, this house is yours!" she exclaimed when she greeted me at the ringfort gateway. At every third step from there to the great house, she removed another of her gold or silver ornaments to give to me, even her torque. I didn't want to accept, but I had to do so or offend my host.

"Come, you'll sleep here." She led me to a curtained chamber as far as possible from the room I'd shared with Ula, Dairine, Gormlaith, and Bryg. I had it all to myself. I still wasn't sure about how I'd deal with my former tormentors, so I was glad to have a refuge where I could gather my thoughts before seeing them again.

A temporary *haven,* I reminded myself as I put on a fresh dress. *I'm going to see them the moment this household gathers for dinner tonight.*

I was wrong. They weren't at dinner. Lady Lassaire had ordered a feast that lacked nothing except the presence of her fosterlings. I'd be lying if I said that I missed them. It was such a nice reprieve to be able to enjoy the mead and meat and merriment of that celebration without having to look at those girls!

Tomorrow will be time enough for that, I thought happily as I sat in a place of honor between Lord Artegal and Kian.

But tomorrow dawned with no sign of them at breakfast, or at the midday meal, or at a second lavish feast that night, or at any other time. A third day came and went, the same as the ones before, with not even a glimpse of Ula, Dairine, Gormlaith, or Bryg. By that time I was no longer concerned about *how* I'd deal with them but *if* I'd get the chance to confront them at all.

"Are they still here?" I asked Kian when I could stand it no longer.

My question puzzled him. "Where else would they be?"

"I don't know. Banished by your mother? She didn't do enough to control them when they were plaguing me, but now? She might have done too much."

Kian shook his head. "I know she did no such thing. They're still here. After how they treated you, why do you want to see them?"

"I have to," I said. "There are things I need to say to them, but I'm afraid they won't give me the chance. You're the one who told me how skilled Bryg is at hiding, even inside these walls."

"I could ask some of our warriors to track down and fetch them for you," Kian offered. "Just give the word. Or you could just march into their room in the middle of the night and take them by surprise. They couldn't escape you then, and no one in this household would dare object. After all"—he smiled shyly—"you can do what you like now that you're a queen."

"That's not the kind of queen I'm going to be. All I'll ask is that you spread the word that I want to see them."

"Anything for you, my lady." He rubbed the back of his head and looked doubtful. "But I can't promise it will work."

On the last day of our stay, I sat listening to Devnet's newest creation, his version of my adventures among the People of the Mounds. As always, he was brilliant, but I failed to give his fine voice and dancing words their proper attention. Kian's efforts on my behalf seemed to have come to nothing. Bryg and the others still eluded me. The shadow of unfinished business would haunt me when I left Dún Beithe.

"Well, Princess?" my father's bard asked when he finished his song. "What did you think of that?"

"Wonderful," I replied from my place beside the hearth. "I didn't know I slew *three* monstrous hogs with bloodred eyes to win my way out of the Otherworld. I could have sworn I only killed two."

"Ah, details." Devnet dismissed my jest with a wave of his hand. "They ruin all the best tales, the worst lies, and every straying man's reply to 'Where have you *been* all night?' I promise you, what I've sung is among the least outrageous of the bards' contributions to your legend."

"I don't want a legend," I said. "I want a life."

"Well, you're certainly going to have one. I hear that the people who farm there are already blessing the gods for your coming. They remember you from the time you used to ride with your father and he'd ask your opinion in settling disputes. They liked your common sense and good judgment."

I blushed. "I'll do my best for them."

"Your share of Connacht doesn't lie too far from Cruachan," Devnet reminded me. "You can always turn to us there if you need help."

"No," I said firmly. "If it's to be *my* land, I must be able to safeguard it myself."

"Ah." Devnet's silvery eyebrows rose. "Then shall I tell Lord Eochu not to send any of his warriors to serve you?"

I laughed. "If you do, I might reconcile with my prince of the Fair Folk. Who would dare attack a ringfort built and manned by the People of the Mounds?"

The bard feigned horror. "Have mercy on all Èriu, my princess—my queen—and let the beings of the Otherworld stay on *that* side of the veil, I beg you!"

"Oh, very well," I replied, pretending resignation.

Devnet rose from the bench we shared. "I'd better see how the men are getting along with packing your belongings. It shouldn't be taking them this long; you didn't arrive here with much."

I sighed. "When I came here, I didn't have Lady Lassaire heaping fresh presents on me whenever I turned around. I liked her better when she didn't pay attention to me," I said, though that was not exactly true. "Maybe I should stay out of sight. She can't give me any more gifts if she can't find me." I got up and started for the door.

"Just don't choose a portal to the Otherworld as your hiding place," Devnet said as he fell into step beside me.

"Don't worry, I know just the—" I stopped short on the threshold. Dairine, Ula, and Gormlaith stood in a row outside the great house. Their intense, agitated looks made it clear they'd been waiting for me. I caught a glimpse of both Connla and Lady Moriath watching them from a distance, but as soon as they saw me come out of the great house, they left. Kian must have made my wishes known. The fosterlings had been persuaded, not compelled.

With a bard's intuition, Devnet took in the situation at a glance and smoothly excused himself. Now that I was facing them at last, I didn't know how to begin speaking about all the hurt they'd caused, all the harm they'd done—to me, to Aifric, and to themselves as well—by cloaking malice as harmless teasing and cruelty as a joke. They'd outnumbered me, taunted me, and used the power of slander and silence and outright injury against me. Now I was a queen in my own right, far beyond their reach, and all the power was mine.

Mine . . . and not. I couldn't touch it. I didn't dare. I was too afraid that if I tried, I'd stumble into the temptation to abuse it, and then—?

Then I'd be like them, like Bryg, like every mean-souled oppressor who ever tormented someone more vulnerable just because they could.

I couldn't find the words—not yet—and so I waited to hear what my former "friends" had to say. They didn't speak immediately, but continued to fidget and to dodge my gaze. Though I had no reason to like them, I also had no reason to enjoy their suffering.

"Where's Bryg?" I asked crisply, breaking the silence.

"Maeve, we're so sorry!" Dairine ignored my question and threw herself forward to clasp my hands. "We never meant to be so awful to you."

"We couldn't help it," Ula put in. "It was Bryg's doing. You know what she's like. She would have used that nasty tongue of hers to spread ugly gossip about us."

"Not just here," Dairine added, rushing to strengthen Ula's excuse. "Her father's a bard. She'd tell him all sorts of lies and he'd carry them to every noble house he visited. Our names would be smeared so badly it'd ruin our chances for a good marriage anywhere!"

"You don't seem to be so scared of her now," I replied coolly. "Aren't you afraid she'll hear that you've apologized to her enemy and punish you for it?"

"She won't," Gormlaith said in her shy way. "Not if you forgive us. You have the favor of the Fair Folk. If she spoke one bad word against your friends, they'd curse her and she knows it."

I wanted to say, *Do you believe you can become my friends again after all you did to me? Would I want to renew my friendship with any of you, the ones who drove away another, weaker girl to who knows what sad fate?*

I looked at the three of them: Ula, who carried herself so high that she might never find anyone good enough to love her; Dairine, whose desperation to claim a nobly born husband made her a joke among the young men of Dún Beithe; and Gormlaith, who let her fear of Bryg's hunting pack force her to abandon her one true friend. She might marry her beloved Connla and make a happy home with him, but every year at Samhain all her joy would turn to darkest mourning and terror at the thought of one small, sad ghost coming back to ask, *"Why, Gormlaith? Why did you betray me?"*

Pity touched my heart. I couldn't change these girls any

more than I could expect Ea to nest at the bottom of a river. They would have to find their own road to courage.

"I forgive you," I said. "But remember what *you* said about the Fair Folk and know that from this day on, I count every girl who comes here as a fosterling to be my friend." The threat was clear: Bryg's wrath or the Otherworld's curse. I was fairly certain which one they'd fear more. I'd done what I could for the sake of any girls who would come after me here at Dún Beithe.

They bid me farewell guardedly, with stiff, formal smiles and nervous laughter. Suddenly, Dairine's head jerked up. "There's Bryg," she said, pointing to where the bard's daughter came walking toward us in Kian's company. The three chastened fosterlings mumbled a last goodbye and fled.

I centered myself for this meeting. *She can't hurt me,* I thought. *She never could, unless I let her.* "Hello, Bryg," I said.

"You hate me." The words broke from her lips on the harsh edge of a sob. "You hate me and you have every right." She began to weep so wildly that Kian had to gather her into his arms to shield her from the curious glances of passersby. I could almost hear their maliciously amused thoughts: *Is she losing her mind? Again? I wouldn't be surprised!*

I touched her shoulder gently. "You were the one who hated me, Bryg," I said quietly. "And you had no right to do it. I told you, your brother Kelan was my friend and I had nothing to do with his death."

"I know!" she wailed. "Oh, I know it now! If you'd been guilty of shedding his blood, you never could have escaped the borderland between life and death. He was a great warrior and a great hunter. He would have tracked you down and pulled you into the darkness with him."

"Well, he didn't," I said, trying to calm her by keeping our talk matter-of-fact. "You were wrong, very wrong to treat me or anyone the way you did, but it's over. I forgive you for it. There's no more need to cry." I admit that I didn't speak purely out of compassion. I just wanted to shake off this mean-spirited girl's shadow and get on with my life.

"Thank you." I never heard Bryg speak in such a small voice before. She sniffled and eased herself out of Kian's arms. "Thank you, Lady Maeve."

Lord Artegal's son gazed at her with enough sympathy for the two of us. "Ask her, Bryg," he coaxed. "Go on, ask her." The bard's daughter shook her head.

"Ask me what?"

"Did you see him?" Bryg's question was a trembling whisper. "Did you see my brother's spirit? Does he—did he say anything to you? Anything about—about me?"

I took a deep breath and bit my lip. "Your brother spoke to me about you. He told me how much he loved you. I feel that he always will." I didn't add that Kelan had said such things while he was still alive. Devnet wasn't the only one who could wave away details when it suited him, or when it was a necessary kindness.

She poured out her heart's thanks to me and walked away. I turned to Kian. "Take care of her," I said. "She has a talent for healing, but she'll need help to heal herself." He nodded sadly and I kissed him once, as a friend.

We broke our journey to Cruachan at Emain Macha. I felt a dizzying mix of anticipation and worry as soon as Conchobar's stronghold came into view. I was about to see Odran and Ea again, and though I yearned for them both, I didn't know what sort of a welcome Odran would give me.

As our party entered the ringfort, my anxiety vanished at a sight so unexpected, so wonderful, that every other thought flew out of my head and I nearly broke my ankle leaping out of the chariot.

"Derbriu!" I cried, rushing into my beloved sister's embrace. "Oh, Derbriu!" We held each other tight and laughed until tears of happiness streaked our faces. The magic of that moment made everything around us seem to vanish.

Conchobar was finally able to break into our sealed world by barging up to us with a baby in his arms. "You said I'd only have to hold her for a little while," he accused my sister. Derbriu took back her daughter and introduced me to my namesake.

"I only hope she grows up to be as wise as you, dear sister," she said.

"It wouldn't hurt if she turned out to be as pretty too," Conchobar put in, uninvited.

My joy at seeing Derbriu again was dampened by the message she had to give me. "Lord Conchobar summoned me as soon as you sent him word that you'd be coming to Emain Macha. There was a young man staying here, a handsome boy named Odran—"

"Was?" The word terrified me. "What do you mean 'was'?"

"Oh, Maeve, darling, no, he's not dead," my sister reassured me as quickly as she could. "I know how it was between you. He told me."

Was again. I prepared myself to endure whatever else she'd say.

She recounted how Odran asked for her the moment he

heard she was my sister. He begged her not to treat him with contempt for being a coward, but he was deathly afraid to face me and speak the words we both knew would come. I heard his voice behind hers: *I love you, Maeve. I always will, but this isn't the love you want, the love you need and deserve. You know this is the truth. You sensed it even when we were together on Avallach. I love you, but I'm not a part of you. And as much as I wish it were otherwise, you are not a part of me. May all the gods guide you to find what I can't give you. Be free, beloved.*

He was right; I knew it. That didn't stop the tears, or the hope that one day I would see him again. "Where did he go?" I asked, wiping my eyes.

"Back to Avallach. He's made up his mind to resume his studies there, but as a healer. You only missed him by a day. Do you want to go after him? I'm sure that Lord Conchobar would—"

"No." I wanted him to be free too. "Did his father go with him?"

She shook her head. "He's still here. He told me that he couldn't leave until he saw you. You trusted him with a treasure." She smiled. "I've seen it. It's a very pretty bird."

"Seen *her*," I corrected automatically. "And she's not pretty; she's beautiful."

We made an odd group—Conchobar, Ea, Master Íobar, and me—as we climbed to the top of a low hill within sight of Emain Macha. I could see a grove of oaks in the distance, and fields where all manner of small prey might lurk. I wished my sister could have come with us, but little Maeve had turned so fretful all of a sudden that Derbriu feared the baby might be sick and refused to leave her, even for a short time.

We chatted as we made our way to the top. Master Íobar apologized for his son's manner of leaving me. I assured him that it was a choice I understood and accepted. Conchobar asked me if I'd like him to send me Lord Cairill's head to decorate the lintel above my doorway when I had a great house of my own.

"I should do that myself," I said flippantly. "You're not the one who's got a reason to want him dead."

"I'll think of something," he replied. I wasn't sure if he was joking.

When we reached the crest, Conchobar made a sweeping gesture over the landscape. "Is this what you had in mind, milady?"

"Yes, thank you." I removed Ea's hood. The kestrel blinked in the sunlight, stretched her wings, and gave a strange call, different from her usual *kee-kee-kee!* This sounded more like *quirrr-rr, quirrr-rr.* I gave her an inquiring look. "What did you say, Ea?"

"She's made that sound many times in the past few days," Master Íobar said. "I feared it meant she was ill, so I kept her from flying."

"Probably lovesick, poor bird," Conchobar teased, then swallowed his grin and shot me a sheepish look in case I didn't feel this was a joking matter.

"You could be right," I replied softly, but my gaze was on Ea and Ea alone. I saw the bright glint of flame in her eyes, the spark that had first bound me to her, heart to heart. "And if you are, that's all the more reason to do this. Give me your knife; I've neglected sharpening mine and I need a keen edge for what I have to do."

Conchobar drew his blade and offered me the hilt. I slipped the point under the loop of braided hair that still encircled Ea's foot. One flick and it was severed; one toss of my hand and she was flying.

I watched her until she was out of sight. I was unaware of Conchobar's arm around my shoulder and of the tears trickling down my cheeks. From that moment, she would wear nothing binding her to the past, and I would fly with her in spirit, free of all ties I did not choose for myself, with a bold heart. It was a future that was frightening, exciting, challenging, and glorious as any bard's song.

It was the most splendid hero's portion ever known, and I had won it for myself.

Places and Faces, or "How Am I Supposed to Pronounce *That*?"

As a writer, I am sometimes called upon to read aloud from my books. I love seeing my readers' reactions face to face, without the smoke, veils, and anonymity of the Internet. I will know straightaway just by looking at them if they're not enjoying what I've written.

I will also know if they *do* like it.

It's one thing to write a book and another to read from it. I know how to spell words like *yolk* and *espresso* and *Givenchy*, but reading them aloud is something else. For example, the yellow part of an egg is the "yoke." I was pronouncing it "yolk" with an *l.* Sorry about that, folks.

So *now* what have I done? I've written two books filled with characters and places whose spelling often has little to do with how they should be pronounced. Welcome to the Romance of Romanization.

Not all languages use our alphabet. Some languages use a nonalphabetical system, such as the characters of written Chinese or the hieroglyphics of ancient Egypt. Romanization lets us take a word from Chinese, Arabic, Cherokee, Hawaiian, Nahuatl, or the Celtic tongue of Maeve's people and represent the sound of that word in a way that we can read.

I have no idea how the powers that be decide how to

represent the words of a particular language. Sometimes said powers even decide to change the previous Romanization. For example, the first dynasty of China—and the one that gave the country its name—was the 秦. This used to be Romanized as *Ch'in,* but now it's *Qin.* Another example is the capital of China, once written in English as *Peking* but now written as *Beijing.* The change in Romanization happened in China in 1949 and then was slowly adopted by Western countries.

I thought it would be handy to include a pronunciation guide for the Celtic names, places, and so on in *Deception's Princess* and *Deception's Pawn.* In some cases, the pronunciation is so uncomplicated and obvious ("Tara") that you might wonder why I bothered. I say, better too much information than too little.

Remember, I'm doing this for myself as much as for you. I want to get it *right* when I read these books before an audience.

By the way, there may be *alternate* pronunciations for many of the following names and terms, due to variables like dialect and locale. Example: My husband comes from Los Angeles and I come from Brooklyn. When the word in question is *horror,* he pronounces it "HOR-er" and I pronounce it "HAH-rer." Then we argue about who's right.

In other words, po-TAY-to, po-TAH-to.

Special thanks to Mary DeDanan, who helped me with this pronunciation guide. Eagle-eyed readers will notice that it includes the names and terms used in both *Deception's Princess* and *Deception's Pawn.* This is not a mistake; we wanted the second book to have a complete list.

1. Maeve and Her Family

MAEVE: MAYV

CLOITHFINN: KLETH-fin

CLOTHRU: KLAW-rah

DERBRIU: DJER(ah)-broo

ÈILE: AY-lah

EITHNE: EN-ah

EOCHU FEIDLECH (son of FINN): OH-ah FED-lekh

FINDEMNA: FINJ-djehm-nah

> The fair-haired triplets.

> BRES: BRESH

> LOTHAR: LAH-har

> NÁR: NAHR

MUGAIN: MUH-gan

2. Friends, Fosterlings, and Other Residents of Cruachan and Dún Beithe

AIFRIC: AH-frik

ARTEGAL: ar-teh-GIHL

BLÁITHÍN: BLAW-heen

BRAN: BRAHN

BRYG: BR(eh)G

CAÍLTE: KEEL-teh

CAIRPRE: KAHR-preh

CERA: KEHR-ah

COLLA: KAL-la

CONNLA: KON-la

DAIRE: DAW-reh

DAIRINE: DAW-RIH-neh

DEALLA: DAW-lah

DEVNET: DJEV-nit

DONAL: DUN-al

DONNCHADH: DON-uh-huh

FECHIN: FEH-heen

GORMLAITH: GARM-leh(k)

GUENNOLA: GWEN-no-la

ÍDE: EE-djah

ÍOBAR: EE-bvehr

KELAN: KIHL-lin

KIAN: KEY-en

KINNAT: KIHN-nut

LASSAIRE: LAW-seh-reh

MORIATH: MAW-ree-eh

NIALL: NEE-ul

ODRAN: AH-drin

OWAIN: AH-win

RUADAN: ROO-ah-din

SABHA: SAW

ULA: UH-la

3. MISCELLANEOUS PEOPLE AND DEITIES

ÁED: AYD

AENGUS: ENG-gus

ÁINE: AWN-ya

AIRMID: AWR-ah-mid

BRIGID: BRI-ged

CAER IBORMEITH: KER eh-BROOM-mah

CAIRILL: KAWR-il

CINEÁD: kee-NOD

CONCHOBAR: koh-NA-ber

DANÚ: DAN-oo

DIAN CECHT: DJIH(en)-kekt

DIARMAID: DJEER-mahd

DONN: DUN

EDANA: EH-djeh-nah

FACHTNA FÁTHACH: FIR(tih)-na FWAH-ah

FAOLÁN: FEE-LAWN

FERGAL: FAIR(eh)-gil

FINTAN: FIN-chen

FLIDAIS: FLI-dish

GUAIRE OF THE GANGANI: GU(ah)-reh /
     GAN-ga-nee

LUGH: LEW

MANANNÁN MAC LIR: MA-neh-nahn mak LIHR

MORANN: MOH-rin

MORRÍGAN: MOHR-ee-gahn

NUADA: NU-eh-deh

RUS: ROS

4. ANIMALS

DUBH: DOO

EA: AW

GUENNOLA: GWEN-no-la

MUIRÍN: mir-EEN

TREASA: TRA-sa

5. Places

ALBION: AL-bee-en

AVALLACH: AH-va-loh

CONNACHT: kon-NAWKHT

CRUACHAN: KRUA-kihn

DÚN BEITHE: DOON BEH-heh

EMAIN MACHA: EM-en MA-ha

ÈRIU: AY-ru

GAUL: GOL

HIBERNIA: hy-BER-nee-ah

LAIGIN: LAWG-in

MUNSTER: MOONJ-ster

TAILTEANN: TAL-ton

TARA: TAH-reh

TECH DUINN: tjekh DIN

TÍR NA NÓG: TEER na NOHG

6. Miscellaneous Terms

BEAN SIDHE: BAN SHEE

CRANNOG: KRAN-og

FIDCHELL: FIDJ-khel

FIR DOMNANN: FAYR DOM-nen

SLIOTAR: SHLIH-ter

TRIQUETRA: tri-KWEH-tra

ULAIDH: oh-LEE

7. Holidays/Holy Days

SAMHAIN: SOW-in

November 1, festival honoring the dead, start of
winter, and the Celtic new year

IMBOLC: IM-bolk
    February 1, festival of lambing and births
BELTANE: BEL-tane
    May 1, festival of fertility, start of summer
LUGHNASADH: LEW-na-sa
    August 1, harvest festival, time for fairs

About the Author

Nebula Award winner ESTHER FRIESNER is the author of over 40 novels and 150 short stories. Educated at Vassar College and Yale University, she is also a poet, a playwright, and the editor of several anthologies. Her Princesses of Myth books include *Nobody's Princess, Nobody's Prize, Sphinx's Princess, Sphinx's Queen, Spirit's Princess, Spirit's Chosen, Deception's Princess,* and *Deception's Pawn.*

Esther is married and the mother of two. She harbors cats and lives in Connecticut. Visit her at sff.net/people/e.friesner and learn more about the books in her Princesses of Myth series at princessesofmyth.com.